MYSTIQUE

First Edition

Published by The Nazca Plains Corporation
Las Vegas, Nevada
2010

ISBN: 978-1-935509-77-6

Published by

The Nazca Plains Corporation ®
4640 Paradise Rd, Suite 141
Las Vegas NV 89109-8000

PUBLISHER'S NOTE
Mystique is a work of fiction created wholly by *Lew Bull's* imagination. All characters are fictional and any resemblance to any persons living or deceased is purely by accident. No portion of this book reflects any real person or events.

Cover Male Photo,
Vladislav Gansovsky

Art Director,
Blake Stephens

MYSTIQUE

First Edition

Lew Bull

FORWARD

The word *MYSTIQUE* means, among others, an air of mystery or secrecy, charm, magic, inscrutability or charisma, and each of the stories in this collection encompasses some aspect of these qualities. There are moments of rough passion alongside gentle loving; there is humor and sadness; there are moments of fetish pleasure for those who enjoy the tactile feel of leather or soft Lycra and moments for both young and older guys, and for those of color and those not.

Whatever your taste, I hope there is something among these stories for everyone and that each reader gets the same erotic pleasure that I got writing the stories.

Lew Bull

CONTENTS

A ROOM WITH AN AMAZING VIEW

Everyone's version of what constitutes a good view differs. There are some who think the view from the top of a mountain is heavenly, while others will look at a sunset over a tranquil sea as being idyllic. I have known people who have thought the best view in their world was sitting in an open space in a desert, surrounded by nothing other than sand and emptiness. I have spent many nights watching the stars in the sky through my rather limited telescope, while sitting on my patio. However, for me, the best view happens to be from my fourteenth-floor apartment in Silent Heights, a building in the heart of the city. Being so high up in the building allows me to view not only the smaller buildings below my line of sight, but also over to the parks, river and naturally, the busy streets below. There is, however, one place that far exceeds all these views around me and that's on the tenth floor of Temple Towers, the building opposite to mine, and it is this view that brings happy memories to my heart.

Both my lounge and bedroom windows overlook the busy street below and both look onto the smaller Temple Towers across the road from my building. Many an evening, when I had nothing to do, and watching TV was a chore, I would sit on my patio and look at the views. Although the daylight views were stupendous, it was at night that I got most of my pleasure looking out of my windows. At night, the twinkling lights of the city danced in the dark as they were switched on and off, or the neon advertising boards glowed in the dark, lighting up the sky in the process.

It was on a warm summer's evening when I first noticed a new view which I found interesting. I had poured myself a drink, settled on a chair on my patio and sat listening to the hum-drum traffic noises below. Something made me look down towards the street below and that was when I saw it. On the tenth floor of the Temple Towers building, I noticed a softly lit apartment with its curtains open. I saw someone walking around the apartment in nothing but a pair of white briefs. At first I could only see the back view from the waist down and wondered if it was a woman, but eventually, the person came partially into view and I realized my mistake, as it was a guy: I could see the bulge in the front of his briefs! I put down my drink, fetched my telescope and sat watching his every move. Holy shit! What a close-up I got! That bulge resembled Mount Everest – huge! And I would have given anything to climb it!

He had been busying himself in the kitchen, probably preparing dinner when I first noticed him. I wasn't sure whether he was making dinner for one or perhaps he was expecting a guest. Once he had done whatever needed to be done in the kitchen, I saw him go into the bedroom. He seemed to be laying out clothes on his bed, and then I saw the white briefs he'd been wearing, thrown on the bed. I waited anxiously to see his naked body, but my luck was not in.

He had obviously taken a shower, because after about ten minutes, he appeared at his bedroom window with a towel wrapped around his waist. This was the first time that I'd seen his face, and from the view I could estimate that he was in his mid-twenties. His hair was wet and slicked back and from what I could see, he had worked on his physique as his chest was buffed and he had a small waist with tight abs. As he turned to move away from the window, he dropped the towel and I saw two beautiful mounds of flesh, like two ripe melons, waiting to be molded in someone's hands.

I saw him pull on a clean pair of briefs, his jeans and saw him tucking a shirt into his jeans, and then he disappeared. I sat waiting for an hour to see him again, but without luck, so I assumed that he must have gone out.

An hour later, I happened to glance down towards the tenth floor and noticed that there were two people in his bedroom; him and another man. I went into my bedroom and switched off my bedroom light and sat in the dark, watching their movements in his bedroom. I watched with interest as I saw him strip down to his briefs, and then I saw the other man in a similar position, then I saw them both get onto the bed. All this was taking place with the curtains to his room open and a bedside light on in his room.

As their bodies became entwined and their lips met, I found myself becoming more and more aroused by their actions. My hand slid down to my shorts, found my stiff shaft and began stroking it as the young man on the tenth floor made love to his guest. The young man's mouth was working on his guest like a vacuum cleaner, sucking up everything in sight, cock, balls, ass and nipples. I waited until I saw him frantically stroking his guest's hard cock and saw the guest shoot a load onto his stomach and then I fired the first of my salvos.

After both men had come, I saw the visitor get dressed and disappear, probably leaving, and then the tenth floor man came back into his bedroom with a towel around his waist, drop it on the floor and hop back into bed and switch off the light. Entertainment over.

Every chance I had, I would get back home from work, sort out some food for myself and settle down for my evening's entertainment and the magnificent view I had. Soon I began to realize that there was a pattern forming. Every Monday, Wednesday and Friday evening, a different person would be seen in the tenth floor apartment with the young man, and sometimes over a weekend, there might be two or more visitors a day there.

I never knew the apartment number nor did I know the young man's name, so I fantasized and gave him a name. I had thought of people I knew who might resemble him and thought of their names, but somehow they didn't match. However, because of his physique and the way he seemed to control the actions in the bedroom, I gave him the name of Butch. The visitors who went up to Butch's apartment, varied in both age and size, and most of those whom I saw regularly were given names. There were young guys, probably his age, and then there were older men. There were also really good-looking guys and then there were some who shouldn't have been let loose on the streets, but no matter who appeared in his bedroom, he always seemed to give of his best.

I remember one evening, sitting on my patio at about eleven at night, because I couldn't sleep, and I noticed that Butch's bedroom curtains were open and his bedside lamp was on. I grabbed my telescope and began to watch. I saw him kneeling between the widely spread legs of a guy similar in age and build to him. I watched as he trailed his tongue up the young man's thighs, heading towards an erect cock that lay across the young man's stomach. Butch's mouth found its target and as his tongue traveled up the length of the man's thick cock, I saw him lean forward and grab the man's nipples. Instinctively the man thrust upwards, forcing his long cock down Butch's throat. Oh how I wished it was my stiff cock down his throat! I watched with fascination as he slurped up and down the man's length until it glistened in the warm light from the lamp. I ran my hand over my engorged cock and felt the slick pre-cum that had been leaking from the tip. I lubricated my cock with it and began stroking myself, imagining that it was Butch's mouth making my shaft slick and wet.

Butch slid his body up over the young man's until I saw that their cocks were rubbing together, then I saw how Butch moved higher up the young man's body until I could see the erect cock of the young guest sliding between Butch's ass crack. Was Butch going to be fucked by this guy, I wondered. I'd never seen anyone of his guests fuck him before but now things looked different. I watched with anticipation as Butch took hold of the man's thick shaft and guided it to his hole, and then once it was positioned at his entrance, Butch slowly began to sink down on the shaft. I could only hear traffic noises, but I was sure that they were both groaning with pleasure, because I knew that I was.

Butch rose and fell onto the hard muscle that was embedded in his ass and didn't seem to be enduring any pain. The young man who was fucking him was rising to meet Butch's downward thrusts and with each thrust, I groaned with pleasure as my cock became more slick from my pre-cum. Eventually, I couldn't contain myself any longer and I shot my load onto the patio floor while Butch and his friend built up their own climaxes. This was better than watching *Sex in the City* or any other TV show.

Perhaps my best viewing took place over the weekends when Butch seemed to have a busy schedule. Most Saturday and Sunday mornings, Butch spent either sleeping in or going out shopping, but from the afternoon onwards, his visitors seemed to stream through his apartment. I could understand why Butch was busy because he had the body, the equipment and the looks to attract and please any man, including me.

An average Saturday afternoon would have Butch running around his apartment in a jockstrap or a pair of running shorts and a vest while he waited for his first customer. I say customer because, although I had never seen money changing hands, I was certain that Butch was doing a roaring trade in men. Either that or he was just very lucky, unlike me!

Early Saturday afternoon, Butch would get his first regular; a middle-aged man, rather on the heavy side, who I called Slim. They would go into the bedroom and Butch would have to give him a massage. I would watch as Butch's hands slid over the mounds of blubber, but at no time did I see any displeasure on Butch's face. He seemed very professional at what he did. The man would, at some stage, begin to fondle Butch's thighs in search of Butch's cock as Butch massaged the man's back, then he would flip the man onto his back and work on the guy's thick legs until his hands reached the small, but hard, erection that the man had acquired. Butch would massage the small protrusion and then he would lower his mouth over the man's small cock and take that and his balls into his mouth at the same time. I could see that the rotund man was on cloud nine when Butch did this to him. Butch would continue this for a little while, then raise his head and wait for mini-Vesuvius to erupt. Once the man had shot his load, albeit a small load, he would leap from the bed, rapidly dress and leave.

Later on a Saturday, Butch often had a guy much younger than himself who would arrive, strip off and wander around the apartment in a canary yellow Speedo. I decided to call him Swimmer Boy, and Butch would follow him, wearing a white jockstrap and whenever they felt ready for some action, they would lie on the carpeted lounge floor where Swimmer Boy would strip off his Speedo, kneel on all fours in front of Butch who would then ram his super hard cock into the young guy's hot ass until Butch was ready to shoot, then he'd withdraw his throbbing cock from the young man and fire his load onto Swimmer Boy's smooth ass and back. It was like watching two horny dogs on heat. When Butch had exhausted his supply of warm cum, he'd clean the young guy's ass and back with the yellow Speedo, so his guest had a memento of Butch's juices, then the guy would dress and leave.

Saturday nights never often revealed regulars. Instead, Butch had an array of different men each Saturday night. There were young, old, fat, thin, muscular and athletic men, but all seemed to leave satisfied.

Sundays were no different from Saturdays, except, there were odd occasions when I would wake up very early on a Sunday morning and look out of the window to see Butch sprawled across his bed with another man sleeping next to him – this was obviously someone who had stayed the night, for a larger fee perhaps.

One Sunday afternoon I was very surprised to see two young men in Butch's apartment, sitting in the lounge talking to him. One of the men looked around Butch's age and build, while the other was much younger, probably about nineteen-years-old. I wondered whether these were visiting friends of his or if they were customers, but soon I found out.

I watched Butch, along with Tom and Jerry, the names I'd invented for his visitors, go into Butch's bedroom and saw the nineteen-year-old, Jerry, strip off his jeans and shirt and lie on the bed in a jockstrap. His body looked young, firm and toned from where I was watching. Butch and the other man, Tom, knelt on the bed on either side of the young boy. I watched as they ran their fingers across Jerry's young, taut body, caressing his nipples and licking his six-pack stomach. Then I saw Butch stand up and disappear for a moment and return with a burning candle. Tom then tied Jerry's hands to the bed-head and spread his legs, attaching them by rope to the legs of the bed. With Jerry spread-eagled, both Butch and Tom stripped off their clothes and then Butch began to trickle melted candle wax over the young boy's nipples. I could see how he writhed on the bed while his partner continued to lick his stomach. Butch then trickled the dripping wax down Jerry's stomach while Tom began kissing the young man, possibly to stifle the cries from the burning wax. My eyes then caught sight of something glinting in the light and I saw it was a knife. I panicked, thinking they were going to harm this young man, but then I saw Butch slip the point of the knife into the waistband of Jerry's jockstrap. With one quick movement, the jockstrap was sliced open revealing a long, thin, hard cock hidden beneath it. Butch then trickled more wax along the length of Jerry's cock and I saw the way in which the young guy's cock throbbed with each drop of hot wax and his foreskin peeled back to reveal a glistening pink head while he writhed and wriggled to break free.

Tom then left the bed and returned a little later with another shiny object. He knelt over Jerry and I watched as he attached two alligator clamps onto the young man's nipples. I wasn't sure if Jerry was crying from the pain, but his face seemed to be contorted. Throughout all this, I noticed how Butch and Tom both had enormous erections that were bobbing in the air as they worked on the young man.

Tom moved up to Jerry's face and stuffed his engorged cock into the gaping mouth of the young man, who instinctively began gulping his friend's cock, slurping it down his throat. Butch, in the meantime, had taken the knife and was, with the point of the knife, steadily scraping the wax from the young guy's body. I watched, fascinated, with my cock getting harder and harder each time as Butch scraped closer to Jerry's cock and balls. Once he had cleaned him of the wax, Butch sank his warm mouth over the distended uncut cock of the young man and began sliding the long, thin cock down his throat.

After a while, they decided to untie Jerry and once the ropes were removed, Tom leant over to the bedside table and I saw his squeeze some lube from a tube onto his hand, then he ran his hand along Jerry's ass crack and I realized that he was readying him to be fucked. Jerry lay on his back on the bed while Butch held the young man's legs high in the air, allowing Tom access to the young guy's tight ass. I watched as Jerry's pucker twitched when the thick cock neared it and began to sink into the tight hole. As Butch continued holding Jerry's legs in the air, the young man took Butch's cock into his mouth and began sucking long and deep. The kid was plugged from both ends and from the expression on his face, was enjoying every moment.

Butch and Tom took turns in plowing into their young friend's tight ass and just as their cocks slid in and out, so mine slid in and out of my hand. I squeezed some lube onto my cock to slick it up and then my hand slid smoothly along my length, creating an exciting sensation on my cock head.

I then watched as Butch slammed into Jerry's tight ass and Tom positioned himself behind Butch and slowly pushed his solid muscle deep into Butch's ass. All three were now connected and their rhythm began to increase until I could clearly see the expression on Jerry's face. Suddenly a stream of white cum flew through the air, landing on Jerry's stomach. I focused the telescope on Butch, whose face was streaming with sweat, and then watched as his cock slid forcefully into Jerry's throbbing ass. I saw him tense and then drive in deeply, holding his position for a moment as he obviously fired his load into the young, tight ass. Tom in the meantime, having felt Butch coming, pulled out of Butch, ripped off his condom and stroked his length until he too fired his juices, covering Butch's ass and back. By this time, my cock was raw and sore from the friction I had created and was only too pleased to offload my supply onto the floor.

The three men dressed after a few moments of coming off their high, and Tom and Jerry soon disappeared from my sight, leaving Butch to clean up his bedroom. For the rest of the afternoon, I noticed that Butch simply relaxed, which is probably what he needed to do, because that evening Tattoo Tommy would arrive.

Tattoo Tommy, as I had chosen to call him, was a slim, tall man of about mid forties or early fifty, who was covered in tattoos. Without his clothes on I thought he was nothing to look at, except he had one of the longest cocks I had ever seen before. The first time I saw him through my telescope I was shocked to see how long his cock was and, added to its length, he had a ring inserted through the head of his cock a la *Prince Albert*. I had to admit, that the artwork on Tattoo Tommy's body had been beautifully and artistically drawn, but the man himself was not a pretty sight.

For some reason, I always thought that Butch enjoyed his evenings with Tattoo Tommy, because from the expression on his face, there were always signs of pleasure and enjoyment – maybe it was the good length that sank into Butch's tight ass that pleased him. Tattoo Tommy was always the top in their action and Butch seemed to enjoy his passive position with the man, lying with his legs in the air or riding the older man's cock as though he were a rodeo rider. Whenever Tattoo Tommy went to Butch's apartment, I knew what would be in store for my evening's entertainment, and would get myself a beer and my eight-inch dildo ready.

Whatever position Tattoo Tommy got Butch into, I would imitate Butch's position and insert my dildo, imagining that it was Tattoo Tommy's massive dick sliding into me. Sunday nights were heaven for both Butch and me, thanks to Tattoo Tommy. I would watch as Tattoo Tommy's skinny body pounded against Butch's muscular one and see how his massive cock slid as far into Butch as was possible, then slide out until the mushroom-shaped head was about to pop out, then he'd slam it back in. Tattoo Tommy's sex was quick and frenetic. He never spent more than half an hour in Butch's apartment as he would come quickly, fire his load into Butch, pull out his long, thick cock, rip off the condom, tuck his still hard cock into his jeans – he never wore briefs of any kind - and would then leave. I would watch Butch after Tattoo Tommy had left and would see him lying on his bed as if in a dream-like state, fondling his beautiful cock until his body would tense and he would shoot his load high into the air, to land on his chest and stomach, then he'd fall asleep.

After following Butch's patterns for a month, I was standing on my patio one Saturday afternoon when Butch came onto his patio, wearing a jockstrap, possibly in preparation for Swimmer Boy's visit, when he looked up and saw me watching him through my telescope. Immediately I panicked, having been caught spying on him, but I saw him smile and give a slight wave of his hand, then he ran his hand down over his crotch and I focused on the large bulge that was hidden from me by the coarse material. I was about to swing the telescope away from him, when I saw him signal to stay where I was. I saw Butch move inside, then he re-appeared on the patio with a large piece of paper on which was written: APARTMENT 1045. My heart gave a flutter of excitement at being given his address but I wasn't about to rush downstairs and across the street – I wasn't that common! Butch disappeared again and when he re-appeared, I saw that his jockstrap had been removed and between his legs hung his beautifully shaped cock, just waiting to be exercised on someone and when I noticed another piece of paper in his hand, it read, COME DOWN, I'M ALONE.

When I saw the second notice, I decided it was time to become common. I raced down my building, my cock already becoming hard at the thought of what might transpire between Butch and me, crossed the busy street and made my way up to apartment 1045.

Now I've become a regular of Butch's, fitting into his tight schedule and on occasions, his tight ass and I love it!

PASSING THROUGH

To me, traveling is always fun. It's fun to visit different places, fun to meet new people and sometimes, fun as to where you spend the night.

My intention was to drive the 1000 mile journey in one day by leaving early in the morning, probably before sun up to arrive in the evening at my destination. One might always have good intentions, but on this occasion, fate was to have a hand in the journey.

I had been invited to spend a week's holiday with a friend and as I felt I needed a break from city life, I had decided to accept the invitation and head west. I had packed my car, filled up with gas the night before and while it was still dark, had set off. My radio was my only company on this long journey, but that didn't worry me unduly. With the drone of the engine and the melodies coming from the radio, I seemed to be lulled into a relaxed mode of driving, not to say that I was falling asleep or anything like that.

I had stopped at the odd garage to fill up with gas and get something to eat when I was hungry, but other than that, the journey was uneventful. By approximately three in the afternoon, I was in doze mode when I was suddenly brought hastily back to reality with a bang and the car veering to one side.

"Damn it!" I had myself a flat.

I pulled the car over to the side of the road, checked the left front wheel and saw that I was going to have to change it. I went to the trunk and pulled out the spare, only to find if was virtually flat as well. I cursed my stupidity at not having checked it before starting out on my journey, but there was nothing much I could do about it now. I stood cursing and swearing at the side of the road. All around me was silence. There was no sound of other vehicles, no sound of birds twittering, I was in the middle of nowhere. I was also not sure how far it was to the nearest town otherwise I might have tried driving on my almost flat spare. I sat in the driver's seat contemplating my misfortune, when in the distance I heard the sound of a speeding car's wheels on the road. I leapt from my vehicle and looked in the direction from which the sound was coming. ON the horizon, I saw the miniscule shape of a car heading in my direction. I waited until it neared me and then ran to the center of the road, flagging down the driver.

"What's the problem, buddy?"

"I've got a flat and my spare isn't much better. I was wondering how far it was to the nearest town from here?"

"Not far. Probably a twenty minute drive," said my Samaritan. "Can I give you a lift?"

I was very grateful to the driver, who looked to be in his late sixties.

I locked my car and we set off to the nearest town, where I would hopefully find a garage. We passed a notice that said *Welcome to Abbots Town*. We drove a little further and saw a garage, where we pulled in. My driver was courteous enough to wait until I had checked with the garage owner that he could take me back to my car and fix the wheel or make some other arrangement. After confirming this with the garage owner, my drover left to continue his journey.

"How far is your car from here?" asked the garage owner, a man of about fifty who looked closer to forty.

"Probably about fifteen or twenty minutes drive from here," I replied.

"Fred, could you please go with this gentleman," shouted the owner.

Fred appeared.

A tall, well-built young man of about mid twenties, with cropped brown hair and a day's stubble on his face appeared in greasy overalls. I looked at this young man, looking a little rough, and felt a twinge in my groin. I could see from the unbuttoned overalls that he had a fine mat of chest hair that seemed to trail down his stomach and then disappear into the waistband of a pair of white briefs. What was in the briefs was hidden by the remaining buttons of his overalls.

"My son will drive you there, sir," said the owner.

I looked at the two men, father and son, and saw an uncanny resemblance. Both had kept their bodies in shape and both had a rugged look to them, which appealed to me.

The son, Fred, climbed into a two truck, with me alongside of him and we set off.

"By the way, I'm Brad," I said to Fred as we sped off.

"Hi there! I suppose you've already realized that I'm Fred?"

I nodded and smiled. I found it very tempting yet frustrating to sit next to this young hunk and not being able to touch him. Our eyes met occasionally as we spoke to each other and I noticed every now and again how he scratched his crotch. I wasn't sure whether this was his manly habit or whether it was to taunt me in some way, but I knew that my own crotch was growing and desperately needed someone to scratch it for me.

We arrived at my car and both of us went to check the wheel. I showed Fred the spare and he laughed when he saw how flat it was.

"The idea of having a spare is so that when one goes flat you can replace it with the spare!" suggested Fred, smiling as he reprimanded me.

I smiled back as he scolded me, feeling quite elated at being scolded by this young man. We attached my car to the tow truck and headed back to his father's garage.

"How long do you think this should take to fix up?" I asked, wondering whether I'd have to stay the night somewhere or whether I'd have time to continue my journey.

"Shouldn't take long and then you can be back on the road," he replied. "However, if you feel like staying the night in Abbots Town, you're more than welcome."

My mind raced at the idea. Maybe I would be able to see Fred again. Maybe Fred had ideas of wanting to see me again. Maybe I was barking up the wrong tree, so to speak, and Fred wasn't even into guys.

Fred took the spare wheel to test that it didn't have something wrong with it and soon returned to tell me that I would need to have it mended as it had a nail going through it. Fred handed it to one of his juniors and went over to another car to work on that. I watched with interest as he pulled off the top of his overalls so that they hung on his hips, revealing a V-shaped chest with two majestic mounds on which were situated two full nipples just waiting to be nibbled and chewed. His waist was trim and tight and my mind began to imagine what lay hidden in his white briefs as I was able to see the start of a bulge that had my lips going dry. Standing there watching Fred, made me make an instant decision.

"Fred, could you tell me where I might find some accommodation for the night?"

"We can always chat to my Dad, but I'm sure you'd be welcome to spend the night at our place, if that's fine with you?" replied Fred, half hidden under the car he was about to work on.

"Dad! Can Brad stay the night at our place?" shouted Fred.

"Who?" came the reply.

"Me," I answered as Fred's father came out of his office. "I'm Brad and I wondered if I could stay the night somewhere in the town and carry on my journey tomorrow morning."

"I see no reason why you can't stay at our place. We've got a spare room…"

"…I'd be very grateful," I replied.

Fred's father came up close to me and almost in a whisper said, "My name is Frank, and you're more than welcome to stay the night with us, but I must warn you that I have another son. He's not here, but back at the house."

I wondered why I had to be 'warned' about his other son. Was he some kind of delinquent? Was he an embarrassment to his family? I had no idea and wasn't about to question my host about his son.

My car's wheels were repaired and I waited for Fred and Frank to close up for the day and head home. I followed them in my car and arrived at a country home on the outskirts of the town. We all climbed out of our vehicles and both men led me into their cozy home. I could see from the furnishings that they were simple folk but proud. I was offered somewhere to sit in their lounge while Fred rushed off to the kitchen to grab me a beer. Frank made his way to what must have been his bedroom and soon returned having changed out of his work clothes. The man had on a pair of shorts that enhanced his muscular legs and a string vest which showed off his good physique. Fred brought me the beer and was just about to sit down when his father chastised him.

"Don't even think of sitting on the furniture in those greasy overalls. Go and get changed."

Fred willingly obliged his father's instruction and soon returned in similar attire to his father. I looked at the two men and it was like looking at a reflection. They were similar in build and looks and from their shorts I could see that both men carried a hefty package in their crotch.

I don't know who prepared their dinner for them, but a table had been laid and a hot meal awaited them on the dining room table. I saw three places set and wondered where Fred's brother was. I hesitated once we got to the table as I wasn't sure where to sit.

"Sit you down there," said Frank, pointing to a chair at the side of the table.

Frank placed himself at the head of the table and Fred sat next to me. I wasn't sure whether I should ask where Fred's brother was going to sit, but decided to keep quiet about him. We sat and tucked into out meal of meat, potatoes, green beans, pumpkin and a thick gravy, and of course, our beers, but still there was no sign of the missing brother.

The two mechanics asked me where I was from and where I was headed and I asked them about why they had chosen to live out in the country away from any major cities.

"We prefer the country life," retorted Frank.

"Not in the public eye," responded Fred.

"Is your other son not joining us for dinner," I asked politely.

Both Fred and Frank glanced at each other, and then Frank replied.

"Not tonight. Now tell me, what are you doing in this part of the world?"

"I was on my way to visit a friend for a holiday."

"We don't see many passers-by here," said Frank, getting up to grab another beer. "Can I get you another, Brad?"

"Thanks, if you're having one," I answered.

I noticed that there was no woman in the household, but hesitated to ask why.

"Who does your cooking because this meal is delicious," I continued.

"We take it in turns. Paul cooked this," replied Fred.

"Is Paul your brother?"

"Twin brother," responded Fred.

"Here we go," said Frank, handing me another cold beer. "Tell me, are you married?"

I smiled sheepishly at both men.

"No, not at the moment," I added.

"My wife died about three years ago so it's just me and the boys," said Frank

"I'm sorry to hear that," I commiserated.

Dinner continued in a very jovial manner and every now and again I felt Fred's thigh press up against mine. I didn't remove my leg from his whenever this happened and his gentle touch sent shivers through my body and as I sat eating, I could feel my cock getting harder. On one occasion, Fred leant across me to retrieve some salt on the table and his hand brushed mine. Our eyes met and I noticed that Frank saw the interaction between us but said nothing. After this incident, dinner progressed without undue problems and when we had finished our meal, Frank gave Fred instructions that he had to wash up. The plates were removed and we left the dining room to go to the lounge while Fred began washing dishes in the kitchen. Frank suggested that we go out onto the patio and have a nightcap.

Frank and I stood on the patio in the cool evening air. A full moon shone down on us and as we stood together, I felt him put an arm around my shoulder. I felt him pull me closer to him and then he said, "It's really nice to have a visitor here. We don't get to meet many people so it tends to be a bit lonely sometimes."

The hard-on that I had developed at the dining room table suddenly was awakened as I felt Frank's arm around me. Instinct kicked in and I automatically placed my arm around his waist.

"Thanks for letting me stay here tonight," I said.

"You're very welcome," he responded, giving me a squeeze.

As he did this, I looked into his face and saw him smiling back at me. The guy was coming onto me, I was sure, but what the hell; he was good-looking, well-built and I was ready for some fun. In fact I wouldn't have minded either father or son. We stood with our arms around each other for some time, and then Frank suggested he show me around the property.

We walked off the patio and headed around the back of the house. The only light was from the full moon and the occasional light that was on in the house. When we reached the back of the house, we stopped and Frank pointed ahead of us.

"Do you see the moon on the lake there?"

I looked in the direction in which he was pointing and saw the silvery gleam on the still surface of the water.

"Wow, that's beautiful," I responded.

As we stood looking at the lake, I felt Frank's heavy hand land on my ass. I tensed.

"Nice ass you've got there, Brad."

I didn't know how to respond, but my cock in my jeans certainly knew how to. It was getting harder by the minute.

"Nice and firm," continued Frank. "Anything else firm and hard like that?" he asked, grabbing my crotch and feeling my swollen cock.

"Hmm! That feels good too," he said, rubbing his hand along my thick, hard shaft. "If you ask me it feels like it needs a bit of relief."

He was so right. I was longing to have him take my cock into his mouth, suck it then fuck me silly, but who was I kidding! Suddenly the silence was broken.

"Dad! Are you out there?" shouted Fred.

"Maybe later," muttered Frank to me, giving my ass a squeeze.

Fred came walking over to us as we stood looking at the picturesque lake. He came and stood next to me so that I had father and son on either side of me.

"What are you two doing out here?" asked Fred.

"Just showing Brad the lake and how beautiful it gets when the moon shines on it."

The three of us stood side by side and I felt that I wanted to take both men in my arms and hug them.

"How about some coffee, Dad? I've washed the dishes so you make the coffee."

Frank heaved a sigh and turned to return to the kitchen.

Fred and I remained staring at the lake, and then Fred said to me, "Has my Dad been coming onto you?"

I was startled to hear him say this. I wondered if that's what his Dad often did.

"Don't mind him," continued Fred, "it's just that he gets very lonely here."

"I'm sure that he does, but what about you? Don't you also get lonely?"

"Of course, but there are times when I head to the nearest big town to let off steam, but he never goes anywhere because of my brother."

I was tempted to ask more about Fred's brother but decided to avoid bringing up the topic again.

Fred seemed to exude a sexual presence as he stood next to me. I couldn't resist my arm touching his and he chose not to move it when our arms did touch. As for his Dad coming onto me, I chose not to respond.

"You look as though you've got a pretty good body," said Fred, standing even closer to me.

"You're not so bad yourself," I replied. "I thought you had an awesome body when I saw you with your overalls pulled down to your waist."

Fred chuckled.

"Don't talk like that, because you're making me hard," he said.

I felt the urge to grab his package to feel how hard he actually was, but I refrained. Instead, I noticed how Fred began to fondle the swelling bulge in the front of his shorts. To me this was like an invitation to assist him. I stretched my hand across in front of him and reached the long, thick stem that was hidden in the soft material of his shorts.

"Wow that feels big! So you're big all over by the feel of things," I chirped, sliding my hand over his engorged cock and then down to his balls. "Hmm! Even those are big!"

I couldn't contain myself any longer and pulled down his shorts and briefs to let his massive cock throb freely in the night air. I knelt in front of Fred and licked along the underside of his thick shaft up to the broad, flared head. My lips wrapped around the circumcised head and then my mouth began to slide his length down my throat. This was like an after dinner dessert, but more delicious than anything produced in a kitchen. Fred began fucking my face, thrusting his hips and forcing his length deeper down my gaping throat. We were just getting into a rhythm when we heard Frank's voice from the kitchen.

"Coffee's ready!" he shouted.

Fred pulled his cock from my mouth and hoisted his shorts. I quickly rose to my feet.

"Maybe later," said Fred, smiling at me. "You're fucking hot with your mouth."

"Thanks, but you've got a fucking awesome cock. Is it like father like son?"

Fred never responded to that, but again chuckled to himself, as we set off back to the kitchen.

Back in the kitchen, Frank had made a steaming pot of coffee, so we took our cups and the pot into the lounge and sat chatting. I noticed how both men began to flirt with me and thoughts were flashing through my mind – maybe a night with Frank would be fun, but maybe it might be even more fun having Fred; better still what if I had both. I could feel myself becoming hard again, just thinking of the three of us together – father, son and me!

Coffee was finished, dishes washed and packed away and now it was time to go to bed, so that I could get up early the following morning and continue my journey. I made my way up to my room, undressed, drew the curtains to cut out the moon and fell into bed, falling asleep almost instantly.

I don't know what time it was, but the moon was still shining outside, and I awoke to feel a mouth tightly wrapped around my erect cock. The mouth was sliding up and down my length, lubricating it with his saliva. I wasn't sure whether it was Fred or Frank, but to me it didn't matter because I was enjoying the treatment that I was getting. I thrust my hips upwards, impaling my long cock in the welcoming mouth and throat, and then I felt the mouth move to my balls and engulf them one by one. The journey continued until a tongue dug into my ass hole, and I felt the person probing my innards with a thick finger. I lifted my legs high into the air to allow my guest easier access to my pucker and encouraging him to penetrate me.

The mouth and the tongue soon disappeared and were replaced by the thick head of a solid cock, pushing to gain entrance to my hole. I wanted this badly, so never fought against his entry. I felt the flared head push past my sphincter and drive down deep along my chute. I gasped as he sank into me, but the feeling that traversed my body was one of exhilaration. I pushed down onto his hard cock and began thrusting. My guest was grunting with each thrust, plowing his massive cock into my tight ass, massaging my chute with each thrust. As he fucked my tight ass, so he grabbed my cock, which was oozing pre-cum, and began stroking my shaft, like crazy, bringing me closer to shooting my load.

"Ah fuck! That feels so good. Fuck me harder!" I cried out, as the powerful cock gyrated in and out of my throbbing pucker.

My instruction was obeyed and the speed of the thrusts increased, and so did the breathing. We were both nearing our climaxes and I knew that although this was going to be over soon, I felt satisfied.

"Fuuuck! I'm coming," I bellowed, firing a load onto my stomach, to be followed hastily by another that landed on my chest.

I could feel the flared head inside my chute swell and suddenly I felt the warm spurts of cum fire into me. My ass felt raw and sore from the constant pounding that I had received, but I still kept up my thrusts onto his solid cock, as I wanted more.

I felt the gradual subsidence of throbs and the gentle withdrawal begin as the solid muscle started to emerge from its tight confines and soon my body relaxed as the still hard cock left me and I once again felt a warm mouth encompass my cock and suck the remains of my cum from its head. As my cock began to subside, I felt the gentle kiss on the tip of my cock and then my guest left my room, leaving me to fall asleep almost instantly.

At seven in the morning, I was awoken by the gentle knocking on my bedroom door.

"Come in," I sleepily responded.

Fred entered carrying a cup of steaming coffee. He was all smiles as he handed me my cup.

"I hope you slept well?"

"Yes thanks, Fred. And you?"

"Fine thanks," he replied happily. "Breakfast is ready for you whenever you want to get up."

Fred then left my room and I wondered to myself why he had not said anything about the previous evening. Maybe it was Frank who had crept into my room.

At breakfast, Frank was seated at the dining room table when I finally had got dressed.

"Good morning Frank. Thanks for last night," I whispered so that Fred wouldn't hear me in the kitchen.

"Oh it was great having you spend the night with us," he replied. "I hope you slept OK?"

"It was great, thanks," I smiled back at him. "I woke up early, but after a while, I was soon happily asleep," I said, hoping he'd say something apropos the previous evening. "I don't know who to thank for last night's rest, you or Fred, but it was fucking awesome."

Frank smiled at me, but also looked a little perplexed.

After breakfast I packed my things, got into my car, which no longer had a flat and headed off on my journey, after promising Fred and Frank that should I be passing their way again, I would call in and see them.

"Fred, did you visit Brad last night?" asked Frank.

"No Dad. I thought you and he had made some sort of arrangement, so I decided not to butt in and spoil your fun."

"Well the way that Brad spoke, he had a good night with someone," said Frank.

Just then Paul, Fred's twin brother hobbled into the dining room on crutches; his body bent and disfigured, and his face distorted and grossly blemished from the skin grafts, all as a result of having been involved in a fire in his youth.

.

THE BUS SHELTER

The mist-like rain floated softly from the heavens to the tarred road, creating a darkened surface on which reflected the golden glow of the street lamp. The slim, erect, metal pole stood with its golden light, alone on the stretch of road, alongside a bus shelter, under which stood a young man, waiting. The road was devoid of both traffic and humans, yet the young man waited.

Was he waiting for a bus? Was he waiting for a friend? Or, was he just waiting for life to pass?

Although the evening was wet, it wasn't cold, so the young man was dressed casually, as though he might be going out for a drink or some such thing. He had on a cotton T-shirt and blue jeans. Nothing extraordinary about his appearance, yet if one caught a glimpse of his face in the illuminated light of the street lamp, one could see his chiseled features were both attractive and appealing. Like the street lamppost, he too was tall and slim, probably about six–four in height, tapered waist and firm legs encased in his jeans. He stood, leaning up against the side of the bus shelter, a cigarette drooping from his full lips, waiting.

In the distance, the sound of a vehicle's wheels squishing on the wet road surface could be heard. The young man remained stationary while the sound drew nearer. A pair of lights came around the corner and the vehicle headed in his direction, but still he remained leaning against the side of the bus shelter. As the car drove slowly through the illuminated area of the street lamp, one could see it was a dark-colored vehicle. The car went past the bus shelter for approximately fifty yards, and then stopped. The red of the break lights lit up the darkened area along the road, then the car was put into reverse and slowly it glided back towards the bus shelter, its reverse lights now illuminating the road. When it was adjacent to the shelter, it stopped, with its engine still running. The electric window on the driver's side slowly slid down to reveal a face inside the car. The face looked to be about late forties or early fifties, slightly rugged and weather-beaten like that of a sailor or someone used to being outdoors a great deal. Across the upper lip stretched a thin moustache and above that were two piercing blue eyes, staring at the young man under the shelter. Neither spoke. The young man inhaled on his cigarette and then exhaled a cloud of smoke, which was soon dampened by the falling rain.

"Going somewhere?" asked the man in the car, his voice sounding strong, but without any menace.

The young man removed his cigarette from his mouth and looked at the man speaking to him, but never answered.

"Want a lift?" asked the strong voice once more.

Again the young man refrained from answering.

At this point, the man in the car decided not to waste his time in the rain, so the electric window slowly slid back up to close off their worlds, but he didn't drive off. Instead, he sat for a moment looking at the young man through his vehicle's slightly tinted window, as the rain slid effortlessly down the windowpane. The young man dropped his cigarette onto the wet curb and squashed it with his cowboy boots that he was wearing. This movement was the first that the young man had performed since standing at the bus shelter. The driver watched for another short period, then put his foot on the pedal and slowly moved the car forward, but continued to look at the young man until he was out of sight of him. He drove for another mile or so, and then stopped.

There were no other vehicles on the dark road either coming towards or following him. He pulled over to the side of the road and made an about turn to head back to the bus shelter. The rain had begun to fall a little harder by now, but as he drove back, he saw the golden glow of the street lamp ahead. As he reached the bus shelter, he slowed down to a crawl and looked into the shelter. It was empty. There was no young man standing there. He did an about turn and stopped adjacent to the bus shelter and unwound the electric window once more. He looked out and saw an empty bus shelter. He switched off the engine and got out of the car, the rain now wetting his slightly gray hair and his clothes. He strode to the shelter and stood looking around him. There was no one.

The driver was a strapping man. Through his wet, tight-fitting shirt one could see his bulging biceps and broad chest with protruding nipples and from the shape of his thighs, one could deduce that he had spent a life of manual labor. He looked the type to have developed his physique from hard work and not from frequenting a gym. He looked down at the wet ground as he had remembered the young man smoking, but there was no evidence of a cigarette having been stubbed out, on the ground. He dug his hands into his jeans' pockets and stood in the shelter wondering if he'd been dreaming when he's stopped earlier, then he made his way back to his car. He turned the engine on and drove off, but not before having one last look into the bus shelter.

Five miles down the road stood a hotel, so the driver decided to pull in there for a drink. He pulled up to the front of the hotel, climbed out of his vehicle and went into the reception area. A middle-aged woman sat behind the counter reading a book.

"Evening ma'am. Can I get a drink here?"

She put down her book and stood up.

"Sure. Bar's down that way," she said pointing the direction.

"Thanks," replied the driver, who headed in the direction shown.

The bar was relatively empty. Apart from the barman, there was an elderly couple and two men at the counter. The driver sat on one of the bar stools and ordered a beer, which the barman gladly gave him.

"Say, what's your name?" the barman was asked.

"Joe," replied the barman.

"Hi, Joe. I'm Bill. You don't seem too busy tonight."

"It's probably the weather," came the reply. "People don't usually go out much here when it's raining."

"Have you lived in these parts for long?"

"About four years," replied Joe. "I used to live on the East coast, but then decided to move inland. I got tired of city life and all its hassles, so I moved to quieter pastures. What about you? Are you just passing through?"

"I live about thirty miles from here, but I've only recently moved there, so I'm not familiar with this area. There don't seem to be many houses in this area. Where does everyone live?"

"Oh, mainly on farms. I think that's also why this hotel sort of sticks out. There are no other buildings for quite a way around here. This place is like a stop-over for travelers," answered Joe.

"So how do people get around here?" asked Bill.

"You have to have your own transport. There are no trains or buses here."

Bill's mind flashed to the bus shelter and wondered why there was one if there were no buses.

"That must make peoples' live difficult not having trains or buses."

"I think most people have grown used to that, so it's not a serious problem for the locals."

Bill finished his beer and ordered another for himself and one for Joe.

"Thanks for the drink, Bill."

"You're welcome, but there's something worrying me, Joe. You said there were no buses traveling in this area, but why is there a bus shelter a few miles back?" asked Bill.

Joe looked a little puzzled.

"I didn't know there was one," he replied. "I don't remember having seen one in this area."

"I saw one tonight on my way here. In fact I stopped there because a young guy was standing there obviously waiting for a bus. I was going to offer him a lift as it was raining, but I didn't get round to doing so."

"Hey, there might very well be one, but I don't remember having seen one. I could be wrong, though."

Bill finished his beer and decided to head home. The rain had softened to a gentle drizzle as Bill headed back the way he'd come.

Five miles back, Bill saw the bus shelter on the side of the road. He slowed down as he neared it and sure enough, there was the young man standing in the shelter, smoking. This time Bill pulled up to the shelter and stopped his car. He unrolled the electric window and leaned out.

"Would you like a lift?" he asked the young stranger.

Once again the young man merely looked at him without answering.

"I believe there aren't any buses coming along this route, so can I give you a lift somewhere?" enquired Bill.

The young man stubbed out his cigarette and sauntered over to the car window. He leant his elbows on the window ledge and looked in at Bill. A slight glimmer of a smile creased his young face.

"Hop in," said Bill. "It's warmer in here. You look cold." He opened the door for the young man who climbed in alongside Bill.

Bill could feel the coldness as the door opened and the young man got in.

"You're so wet you'll get sick if you don't dry off soon. I'll take you back to my place where you can dry off and then I'll take you wherever you want to go," said Bill, turning on the heater in the car to help dry the young man.

"I'm Bill, and you are?"

"Jeff."

"Well, Jeff, we'll get you back to my place and dry you off. You seem to be shivering. How long have you been waiting for a bus?"

"Quite some time."

They drove along the darkened road, Bill casually chatting to Jeff, but also noticing how the young man seemed to continue to shiver.

"Don't worry, we're nearly there so you can have a hot shower if you like and I'll give you a change of clothes," said Bill, smiling at the young man.

When they arrived at Bill's home, he parked the car and together both men went into the dry, warmness of the house. Bill went into his bedroom and grabbed some dry clothes for Jeff as well as a towel with which to dry himself after his shower. When he returned to the lounge with the items, Jeff was seated on the edge of the couch still shivering.

"Here we go," said a sprightly Bill, as he handed over the goods. "I'll show you where the bathroom is and you can have a shower to warm up.

The two men wandered down the corridor and into the bathroom.

"Make yourself at home," said Bill, pointing to the shower.

Jeff smiled, possibly for the first time that evening and began to pull off his shirt before Bill had left the bathroom. Bill noticed the well-defined torso of the young man and smiled to himself as he exited the bathroom and returned to the lounge. As he sat in the lounge, he heard the water running and splashing on the shower floor and wondered what his visitor would look like naked. He knew the bathroom door wasn't closed completely and wondered if he should take a peek through the crack in the door, but then decided against it in case Jeff spotted him.

The sound of the water stopped and soon Jeff reappeared in the lounge with the towel Bill had given to him wrapped around his waist while he carried both his wet and dry clothes with him. Jeff seated himself in an easy chair, and although he was half naked, Bill noticed that Jeff still had goose flesh on him suggesting he was still cold.

"You still look cold. Why don't you get dressed?" suggested Bill, although he had to admit to himself that seeing Jeff half naked was a wonderful sight to him.

"I'm fine thanks," replied Jeff, still holding the clothes.

Bill rose from his seat and crossed to where Jeff was sitting and took his wet clothes from him.

"Let me put these in the kitchen to dry."

He wandered off to the kitchen, but when he returned he found Jeff still sitting in the same chair, but the towel had been removed and his entire naked body was there to be viewed by Bill. Bill was a little taken-aback, but admired the taut, young body that was displayed to him. His eyes focused on the defined, hairless chest, the trim stomach and then shifted down to the crotch area where a long, thick cock lay, as though sleeping. Bill smiled at Jeff, who returned the smile.

"You have a fine body, Jeff," said Bill, allowing his gaze to wander over the slim body on display.

"Thanks," replied Jeff. "You seem to also have a good body by the looks of it."

Bill blushed a little at the compliment, and instinctively ran a hand across his chest, as though stroking his nipples. Jeff's legs parted slightly allowing his cock to move and in doing so, Bill's focus was attracted by the movement. He saw how there seemed to be some growth in the girth and length of Jeff's appendage. The result was that Bill could feel his own manhood adjusting itself in his briefs. At no stage did Jeff try to hide his arousal, but soon Bill was trying to adjust his own.

"You look awkward," said Jeff, smiling casually at Bill.

"You're right there buddy. Do you mind if I make myself a little more comfortable?"

He wondered why he was asking this stranger for permission to get comfortable in his own house! He stood up and unzipped his jeans, pulling them and his white briefs to the floor, slipping off his shoes and with them his jeans and briefs. Although he still had on his shirt, he felt less constricted and this allowed

Jeff to see his arousal. Both men sat opposite each other with engorged erections, smiling at each other. Neither touched themselves, but both appendages continued to grow until they were slapping up against each one's stomach. Bill watched with fascination as his foreskin slowly peeled back to reveal his pink head, while Jeff's mushroom-shaped cock head throbbed gently. For the first time, Bill took hold of his hard-on and began to stroke it slowly, but still watching Jeff to see what his reaction would be. Jeff watched, smiling, but not touching himself. At length, Bill rose from his seat and crossed to Jeff and sank to his knees between Jeff's legs. He bent forward and extended his tongue as he began to lick Jeff's pendulous balls, but still Jeff did nothing. Bill's tongue traveled slowly over each sac and then headed in the direction of the thick muscular stem, which continued to throb. He ran his tongue up the entire length of Jeff's cock until the tip of his tongue reached the piss slit, then he opened his mouth and engulfed the large head, and began a slow journey down the length of Jeff's cock until Bill's chin nudged Jeff's balls and a slight gasp was heard to emanate from Jeff. With one hand, Bill took hold of both Jeff's balls and gently squeezed them as his mouth began its upward journey along the thick muscle. Throughout this physical contact, Jeff never touched Bill, but lay back and enjoyed the treatment that he was receiving. Bill's mouth began to increase the speed of its journey and the slickness with which his mouth moved was creating an even louder reaction from Jeff, whose eyes were now closed as if in dreamland.

After a while, Bill released his grip on Jeff's balls and began to rub the area around Jeff's winking asshole. Jeff opened his legs wider to allow Bill access and while Bill's mouth continued to work along Jeff's shaft, so his fingers delved into Jeff's exquisite entry. Jeff bucked his hips, clenching his ass muscles around Bill's three fingers, which were trapped inside Jeff's chute, and Bill tickled Jeff's innards. Jeff slid his body a little lower down the chair until his ass hung over the edge of the chair, then he raised his legs into the air. Bill took advantage of this situation and removed his mouth from Jeff's cock and centered on the winking pink hole that had become the center of his attention. He licked around the entrance, lubricating it with his tongue, and making sharp diggings into the opening with his tongue, teasing Jeff.

Suddenly Bill stopped and Jeff opened his eyes to see why. Bill was now standing over Jeff, his shirt removed and the thickset muscular body heaving with excitement at the prospect of entering the wonderful world of Jeff. He took a condom and Jeff watched as Bill seductively unrolled it along his length, then he slicked it with some lube and aimed for Jeff's waiting hole.

Bill's cock head was poised at the entrance. He slowly pushed forward, trying to break through the entry, but it had clamped shut. Undeterred, Bill continued to advance. Slowly his cock head began to slide into the entrance until the head slipped through the magical gates. Jeff gasped, tensed and then relaxed as this happened. Bill held his position as Jeff did this, and then he slowly resumed his journey. He sank a few more centimeters into the confines, feeling the tightness encompass his cock. Slowly he slid deeper, but instead of a warm feeling surrounding his stem, Jeff's chute felt cold, but this was not about to upset Bill, now that he had acquired full access to the young man's body and was deep inside, up to his balls, which gently slapped against Jeff's ass.

Bill took hold of Jeff's waist and pulled him closer to him, sinking himself deeper into the young man, and then he began the slow, rhythmic thrusts and pulls as he made love to his guest. Both men were gasping and sighing with each thrust and soon Bill had built up a rhythm whereby they thrust against each other to ensure depth of penetration. Bill's speed was beginning to increase and perspiration was building up on his face and chest, but Jeff still remained cold to the touch. Although Bill was frantically pounding into Jeff's ass, and Jeff was meeting each thrust with an equally determined thrust with their bodies crashing against each other's, still Jeff remained cold and dry of perspiration.

The more intense and frantic Bill's thrusts became, the louder were Jeff's gasps and for the first time that evening, he took hold of his long-stemmed cock and began stroking it with enthusiasm.

"I'm getting close!" exclaimed Bill, trying to thrust even deeper.

Jeff gave a deep gasp that sounded almost like a growl and his white love juice fired from the tip of his cock as it throbbed. Bill became excited by the sight and increased his pace, bringing himself closer to reaching his climax. Suddenly he pulled out of Jeff, ripped off his condom and began stroking himself. He grunted, tensed and fired. As both men coated Jeff's taut body with love juice, their passion was extended to Bill leaning across Jeff and placing his lips on Jeff's. Their mouths fought for domination while they emptied their seed. Once Bill had began to relax, he lowered himself across Jeff's lap so that he was sitting across his crotch, their cocks lying together oozing the last drops, while their tongues fought together in each other's mouths.

After they released their grip on each other's mouth, Bill sat back, smiled at Jeff and whispered, "Thanks buddy that was great."

Jeff smiled back but said nothing. Bill continued to give Jeff gentle kisses on his lips and neck.

"You're still cold. Do you want to put some clothes on to get warm?" enquired Bill, standing and picking up the towel that Jeff had used, to clean them. He gently wiped Jeff's stomach and chest, removing the last of their juices, and then he cleaned himself and began to get dressed. Jeff did likewise.

Once Jeff was dressed, he said, "I think I'd better be going."

"Where can I take you to?" asked Bill. "I'll give you a lift home if you like."

"Don't worry about me. I'll be fine. If you can just drop me off at the bus stop, that will be fine with me," replied Jeff.

Bill was a little concerned that his new young friend would be out in the cold and wet again, and suggested that he drive Jeff home, but Jeff rejected the offer.

"Please, just drop me at the bus stop. I'd appreciate that."

"Oh well, if you insist, but I'm not happy doing that; not on a wet night like tonight," answered Bill.

The two men got into Bill's car and headed back to the bus stop. When they reached their destination, Jeff climbed out of the car, thanked Bill for the time together and went and stood under the bus shelter. Bill waved and drove off.

The following week, Bill was back at the hotel to have a drink and wondered if Jeff ever frequented the hotel, so he asked Joe, the barman.

Joe listened intently to Bill's description of the young man, but said that he didn't recognize anyone by that description. Then Bill told Joe how he'd met Jeff, but without giving the details of their evening together, and how he had dropped him off at the bus stop and said that he'd like to get in touch with the young man again.

Joe listened intently and when Bill had finished explaining, Joe replied, "I don't know anyone like that, but maybe one of the locals might. Fred!" called Joe to one of the locals sitting in the bar, and related Bill's story to him

"There isn't a bus stop in a twenty-mile radius of this hotel," replied Fred. "There used to be, apparently, many years ago, but one day a young man was standing there waiting for a bus, when the bus came screaming along the road, out of control, and crashed into the bus shelter, killing the young man who was waiting there. I've never seen it, but the locals say that some nights you'll see the ghost of a young man standing in the shelter waiting for a bus. Apparently he just stands and waits; he was tall and slim."

"What was the name of the young guy who got killed at the bus shelter?" asked Joe.

"Jeff!" shouted Fred to the barman.

Bill's body went cold as he took a swig of his drink.

RIDING FOR PLEASURE

I watched with immense interest, from my lounge window, as the cyclist made his customary daily journey past my house. It was almost like a ritual, a time-setting moment where one could set the time on a clock. He was always exact with his timing, passing my house every afternoon at precisely 16:45 and then returning past it at 17:30. The first time noticed him was six months ago and I had been sitting on the front porch, casually having a beer. At first I saw the rider and bike whiz past at quite a speed, heading in a westerly direction and then forty-five minutes later he whizzed past, heading in the opposite direction. This event didn't really impact on me, until I realized that this had become a daily occurrence, and then I started to take an interest in the rider.

I wondered who he was and what cycle race he was training for. Then I noticed his attire: a bright yellow form-fitting racing shirt, a white cap and tight, pale blue Lycra cycling shorts. It was the shorts that made the greatest impact on me. I could see, as he passed by, his firm ass, closely encased in the thin stretch material, and his sturdy, strong legs protruding from his shorts down to the pedals. He always wore the same outfit, day after day, so I began to wonder whether he had a number of versions of this outfit, or whether it was the same one day in and day out.

He looked to be about six foot tall, but it was difficult to estimate as he was always on his bike, had fairly longish brown hair which didn't quite fall onto his shoulders and a tanned face, arms and legs.

There had been times when I decided at 16:40 to wander out into the garden and pretend I was busy watering the plants so that I could get closer to the road along which my cyclist rode. On these occasions, I noticed how he often ventured a look towards me in the garden, and on a couple of times, he nodded to me as a form of greeting. When this happened, I became elated and wished that he would stop and talk to me, but obviously he had others more pressing thoughts on his mind, such as reaching his destination.

As the six-month anniversary of my first sighting of him approached, I decided that I had to pluck up courage to speak to this elusive and mysterious man, who was constantly playing on my mind.

At 16:30 on a Wednesday afternoon, I went out into the street and looked out for my rider. What was I going to do when I did see him, I wondered? I couldn't very well just run out into the street and accost him, but then why not? Maybe I could pretend I had fainted and lie on the grass alongside the road and hope that he might give me mouth-to-mouth resuscitation – that would be nice! On the other hand, maybe I could just stand on the side of the road and wave, much like one would do in a cycle race – no that's boring. In the distance I saw the bright yellow top heading my way. Panic overcame me because I didn't want to make a fool of myself. Quickly the yellow shirt neared me, was upon me and then gone past. I stood with a hand in the air as though to wave, having heard a quick "Hi!" emanate from the lips of my cyclist as he sped past. I didn't even have time to respond. Now I really felt a fool. I knew that in another forty-five minutes, he would be heading back past my front door. I made my way back to my front porch embarrassedly, went inside to collect a cold beer and then returned to sit outside and wait for him.

At precisely 17:30 a vision in a yellow shirt and tight, pale blue cycling shorts didn't whiz past my front door, instead, the rider and bike came to a halt at my front gate. I was sitting sipping my beer on the front porch when I noticed him smiling up at me from his bike. I almost spluttered when I saw him. Now that he was not whizzing past, I was able to take a better look at him. He looked about thirty-years old, with sweat trickling down his face and arms as he stood smiling at me, and his yellow shirt was unzipped to his mid-chest area, allowing me the opportunistic view of a smooth chest. My eyes trailed down to the flat stomach and then on down to the crotch. Oh my, what a crotch! Although his Lycra cycling shorts clung tightly to his body, both naturally and because of the sweat, I could see that the package that was evident was one that most men would die for. I returned the smile.

"Hi, how was the ride?" I politely asked rising from the chair I was sitting in.

"Great thanks," came the breathless reply.

We both stood smiling at each other, with neither saying anything.

"I'm sorry; it's so rude of me. Would you like to come in and have something to drink? I'm sure you must be pretty thirsty after your ride."

"Thanks very much," he answered, bringing his bike up onto the porch.

Once he was close to me, I could feel the heat that flowed from him from his exertion. His features were pleasing to me: his lips were full, he was solid in build, which I didn't exactly expect a cyclist to be, had deep piercing blue eyes and a broad, friendly smile. As he reached me, he stretched out a hand to shake mine.

"Hi, I'm Vladimir," he said, clasping my hand firmly.

"Hi there, I'm Alex," I replied crumbling a little at the grip he had on my hand. "That's a Russian name isn't it?"

"Yes, but I've been in this country for twenty years now."

"Come inside and let's get you something to drink."

We made our way into the house and headed to the kitchen.

"Soft drink or a beer?"

"I think a soft drink if you don't mind."

As we stood next to each other in the kitchen, I could see steam rising from his body.

I poured him something to drink and then we made our way back to the lounge.

"Would you like a towel or something to put around you while you cool down?"

"Gee thanks, I'd appreciate that."

I went off to the bathroom to get a towel for Vladimir, while he waited for me to return. I handed him the towel and watched as he dried his thick hair. As I watched I was tempted to offer to dry it for him, but I restrained myself.

"Do you mind if I take my wet shirt off?" enquired Vladimir.

Heaven forbid that I should mind seeing his half naked body!

"By all means," I casually replied, feeling my heartbeat increase as he peeled off his shirt.

He had broad shoulders and a tapering waist. I could clearly see that he had a well-developed six-pack stomach and firm biceps and on each pectoral muscle was a beautifully rounded and protruding nipple. Maybe I should ask if he'd also like to take off his cycling shorts, as they were also wet, but perhaps that would be pushing my luck.

"Sit. Make yourself at home," I said, reclining on my couch and spreading my legs wide.

Vladimir was about to sit next to me when he realized that his shorts were wet.

"I'd better not sit because my shorts are all wet and sweaty."

"That's no problem. I can always offer you a pair of dry shorts to put on if you like."

"I'll just fold the towel and sit on that," he replied.

Damn! I was hoping to get a better view of what was lying within the confines of his Lycra shorts. Vladimir did as he had suggested and sat down next to me. As we sat speaking, I found it very difficult to focus on his face, which was extremely beautiful to look at, but found myself attracted to his flat stomach and the package that I was tempted to touch.

"Are you training for a race?" I enquired.

"Yep, in two weeks' time. It's a 150 kilometer race."

"Wow! That's far."

"Not really. When you're on a bike, it seems to go pretty quickly and there are always other guys to chat to on the road, so it doesn't seem that far."

"Do you have many friends that you cycle with in your races?"

"One or two that I'm pretty close to, but unfortunately, they don't live near here to ride with on my practice runs."

I watched with fascination as he held his soft drink glass to his stomach as though to let its coolness adjust his body temperature. Each time the cold glass touched his skin, he drew in his breath, puffed out his pecs and nipples and tightened it his already taut stomach. He knew that I was watching this action because he smiled at me and moved his glass and placed it on his heavy crotch. Naturally, my eyes followed the path of the glass and ended up staring at the bulge that loomed under the Lycra.

"Vladimir, do you mind if I ask you a personal question?"

"Depends on what it is," he smirked.

"You know people always want to know what a Scotsman wears under his kilt…"

"…Yeah?"

"Well do cyclists wear anything under their riding shorts?" I blushed as I said it.

He face broke into a broad smile and then he burst into laughter.

"Some do and some don't."

That sort of answer didn't tell me much about Vladimir and I think he could see my disappointment.

"For me …" he hesitated, "… I don't. I prefer to let it all hang loose, so to speak."

Again I blushed. I could imagine by the bulge in his shorts that there was quite a great deal of Russian muscle that could 'hang loose'.

"Do you do any sport?" Vladimir asked, changing the subject slightly.

"I used to when I was at college, but not any more. I prefer to watch, now."

"Is that why you watch me every day?" came the understated comment.

Today was a day of blushing. I'd been found out. Sure I watched Vladimir every day, but then he was worth looking out for, I thought.

"I wouldn't say every day," I replied, but he just laughed. "So you know, then?"

"From the first time I rode past, I noticed you, and then every time I rode past your house, I would glance in your direction, probably without you knowing, to see if you're here."

I felt flattered that Vladimir took the trouble to look out for me, and at the same time I felt a stirring in my crotch, which had been simmering for some time. Vladimir gulped down his soft drink, and placed the glass on the table next to him.

"I wonder if I might use your toilet?" he asked.

"Sure. It's down the corridor and first door on your left."

Vladimir rose, took the slightly damp towel he'd been sitting on, and headed off down the corridor. Once he was out of sight, I sighed, stretched my legs out in front of me and grasped my crotch. I could feel the start of a hard-on in my jeans and I rubbed my hand along it. I then let a hand trickle over my nipples. I heard the toilet flush and immediately sat up straight on the couch. Vladimir re-entered the lounge, but with the towel wrapped around his waist. In his hand he carried his cycling shorts.

"I hope you don't mind, but I wanted to get out of these wet things," he said, tossing them casually on the floor at my feet.

Instinctively I bent to pick them up. I could feel his warmth and dampness still on them. I held them in my hand, feeling where his crotch had lain. I noticed that he turned away slightly and in that quick moment, I had his cycling shorts up to my face, where I could feel their softness and warmth. I breathed in deeply, taking in the heady, intoxicating scent of his sweaty body. Vladimir turned to me.

"Have you ever worn a pair of cycling shorts before?"

I stammered at being asked this question, wondering whether Vladimir had seen me sniffing his shorts.

"Er, no."

"Try them on; they should fit you."

I hesitated, clutching them to me.

"Go on, let's see whether you'd look like a cyclist or not."

"Here? Now?"

"Yes. Why not. There's only the two of us, or are you shy?"

"No," I said hesitantly.

"Well, go for it."

I stood up and unzipped my jeans. They dropped to my ankles and Vladimir smiled as he saw me standing in my white Calvin Klein's. I was just about to slip into his shorts when he said, "No, take those off. You must wear your shorts like I do, naked underneath."

Again I hesitated, but with a little more encouragement from Vladimir, I dropped my Calvin's to the floor. I stood there for a moment with a semi-erect cock bobbing in the air. I bent over to step into Vladimir's shorts.

"Nice ass," came the comment as I did so.

I immediately sprang upright with shock, my cock getting even harder by Vladimir's compliment. I pulled up his shorts and felt the coolness from his sweat against my body. With the Lycra material encasing my body and knowing whose it was, my cock went vertical. A heavy protrusion showed in the front of the shorts as my cock aimed to the heavens. I tried adjusting its position, but it didn't help. Vladimir rose from the couch.

"Let's have a look at you."

He wandered around me surveying the sight before him. I felt a hand delicately run over my ass.

"Nice fit," he said, patting my ass gently. Let's have a look at the front."

He walked to the front of me and surveyed the scene.

"You're quite a big boy, aren't you?" he smiled, running his hand lightly over the length of my cock.

I gasped at his feather-light touch.

"Does that feel good?"

I wasn't sure whether he meant the gentle touch or the material clinging to my body.

"I like both," I whispered, hoping he wouldn't actually hear me.

"Do you think you could get into cycling?" asked Vladimir.

"With you," I spontaneously answered.

I realized what I had said and instantly tried to correct myself, but Vladimir was having nothing of that. His full lips clamped over mine and immediately his tongue ventured into my mouth as though searching for something. Our tongues entwined and fought to take control of the other's mouth. His strong arms encircled me and he brought me closer to him. Under his towel, I could feel that he too was hard and probably needed to be freed of his constraints. I grabbed the towel and pulled it from him. As the towel dropped to the floor, I felt the warm length of hard muscle rub against my stomach. If he thought I was a 'big boy', then Vladimir was a giant of a man. I broke free from his clutches and looked down to admire his equipment. My eyes stared in awe. Before me was biggest dick I had ever seen. Although it wasn't excessively fat, it was long. He had a foreskin, which had peeled back to reveal a pale pink bulbous head just waiting to be kissed.

I sank to my knees as if in prayer and began to worship his 'spear' that waved before my eyes. I grasped his long shaft and slid my hand up its length, re-covering the head with his foreskin. I inserted my tongue into the hooded area and flicked at the entrance. Vladimir watched and groaned as I treated him gently, and then I slowly slid my hand down towards his balls and at the same time, sank my mouth down his shaft, swallowing his cock. I continued this action for a while, opening my throat a little more each time to accommodate his vast length until I was able to swallow his cock down to the hilt. As his head tickled the back of my throat, I thought I was going to gag, but controlled myself and then returned the upward slide to lick his tip, which was beginning to leak some magical pre-cum.

I felt Vladimir lift me to my feet and let his hand drop to my cock. He dropped to his knees and chewed on the Lycra that covered my engorged cock. He nibbled along my covered length and then licked the area where my cock lay. He could obviously taste his own sweat from his shorts, which seemed to be turning him on as he quickly took hold of the waistband of his cycling shorts, and pulled them down to my ankles. He then took my throbbing cock into his warm mouth. He rolled his tongue around my mushroom-shaped circumcised cock, dragging his tongue down to my balls and then heading between my legs in search of my pulsing hole. On his return journey, he stopped to suck each of my balls into his mouth and roll his tongue over each in turn, then continue his upward trip. On reaching my cock-head, he swallowed my head and shaft and sucked deep and long. The suction and tightness created by his mouth was driving me crazy. I thrust down his throat as he sucked, holding onto his thick hair as I did so.

"Let's go to the room," I gasped in between sighs, groans and slurps.

Vladimir and I headed to the bedroom, our cocks swaying as we walked our arms around each other's shoulder.

In the bedroom I lay on my back on the bed and Vladimir lowered himself onto my body. Our cocks rubbed together and I could feel that the pre-cum that was oozing profusely from him was lubricating us both beautifully. At one stage I took hold both our cocks and placed them head to head and pulled Vladimir's foreskin up and over the heads of both our cocks. I could feel as I did this, that more pre-cum was pulled onto my cock-head, causing the two heads to slip against each other. As I did this, Vladimir pumped his cock against mine, as though trying to fuck it. I could tell that this 'giant' of a man was desperate for something more intense, just as much as I was desperate for Vladimir to slide into me.

Before our passions exploded, I stretched across to the bedside table and grabbed a couple of condoms and some lube. Hastily I opened a wrapper and stretched a condom over Vladimir's bargepole. I was struck by the fact that the condom only reached three-quarters down his shaft because he was so big, but that didn't deter me. I lubed my waiting ass and along his cock, then I lifted my legs above my head, inviting him to take advantage of me.

I watched as he held the long pole and aimed for my pulsating entrance. There was a slight touch of cock against my flesh and immediately my asshole clamped shut, but this was not going to deter Vladimir. With a little exerted pressure, he pushed forward, guiding his cock across the boundary into the realm of pleasure. As he sank into me and slowly continued his journey in and down, I held my breath until I felt his pelvis come to rest against my balls, then I sighed. His chest was puffed out like a proud peacock and I grabbed the two round protrusions on his chest. As I squeezed his nipples, he thrust deeply with short, sharp bursts into me. I gasped with each thrust, but there was never any pain. I pulled on his nipples as though pulling him towards me and as I did so, so he tried to pull away, thus creating some pain for him, but he seemed to get pleasure from this and pounded even harder into my ass. My whole body was shaking from the attack, but for me it too was absolute pleasure. I lifted my head to watch as his length slide effortlessly in and out of my throbbing ass. He grabbed hold of my cock and started jerking me off. I reached for the tube of lube and squeezed some onto my cock, allowing Vladimir to slide his hand easily over my stem.

His breathing was becoming more intense as he rode my ass and jerked me. He was getting me closer to coming and I began riding his cock even more; thrusting onto his length, trying to bury his cock deeper into me. I felt like I wanted his whole being inside of me.

"Fuck me! Fuck me harder," I cried out, sweat pouring from both of us.

He held onto my shoulders and went deeper into me, pounding his balls against my ass as his bargepole sank into my magical chute. I tightened my grip on his cock as I neared the completion of my journey.

"Vladimir, I'm gonna come," I gasped.

My body went taut; I thrust hard onto his length and clamped my ass muscles tightly as I fired. A long stream of warm cum shot from the tip of my cock and sped through the air, hitting Vladimir on the chest. A second followed in equal distance, this time landing on the shaft of his cock. He continued to pound my ass, pushing some of my cum on his cock into my waiting hole.

"Alex, I'm gonna fuck you!" exclaimed Vladimir

"Ride me, Vladimir. Fuck this tight ass of mine!"

He growled much like a Russian bear might, pushed intensely into me with his stomach muscles seeming to explode and his chest expanded, then he cried out and fired. I felt his cock jerk inside of me as the first shots were fired, then another jerk and another. After the third throb from his cock, he rapidly ploughed into me, pumping me full of his love juice. My ass felt tired more than hurt, but I continued to attack he thrust that he made, encouraging him to stay deep within the walls of my chute while he came off from his high and allowed himself the gentle throbs as my ass tried to milk the last drops of warm cum out of him.

I felt him try to pull from the confines of my ass, but I clamped tightly shut.

"Don't go … just yet, please."

We lay in each other's arms, kissing and caressing each other, both our cocks staying hard and bobbing erratically as they throbbed. After what seemed like half an hour, Vladimir's cock slid slowly from its security and flopped next to him. I pulled the used condom from him and threw it into the nearby bin, then bent down to kiss and lick his cock of its remnants. The sweet-salty taste made me want more.

"Would you like to have a shower and stay for dinner?"

"That sounds great."

"Then maybe, if you've got the stamina, you might like to have a second round!"

"For someone who doesn't do any sport, you're pretty fit by the looks of things," joked Vladimir, rubbing his crotch and getting it hard again.

RAINY DAY SPECIAL

I had recently settled in a new suburb – three months ago, in fact – and with it came a change in my creature comforts. Prior to my move, I had always gone to the local gym three times a week, but now, because of the distance to the nearest gym, I had cut back to visiting only on day a week, a Wednesday. I had also convinced myself that my body had reached the perfection that I desired and that I was proud and happy to peel off my clothes on the beach or in front of anyone, so my one day a week visit was seen more as a 'maintenance' workout rather than development. Because of my traveling to the gym on a Wednesday being quite long, it also meant that I had made a point of ordering take-outs on that day so that by the time I returned home, I wouldn't have to start preparing food for myself, as I lived alone.

I had developed a routine on a Wednesday, whereby just before I left the gym, I would phone through my order and soon after I arrived home, my order would be delivered. Each week, a battered yellow Volkswagen car would draw up outside my house, hoot, and Thomas would knock on my front door with my dinner.

Thomas was a very pleasing young student who was working to make money for college by delivering food from *Miguel's* Restaurant to customers. He was twenty-years-old, with an athletic build and had a friendly disposition. After the first few deliveries from Thomas, I would often invite him in to have a chat for a while before he darted off on his next delivery, and on one occasion the inevitable happened between us. I say inevitable, because when one saw the way Thomas looked in his uniform, it was inevitable that that uniform would at some stage been ripped from his body. The uniform worn by the delivery guys from *Miguel's* consisted of a white T-shirt in a Lycra-type material, which stretched seductively over their bodies, and which had the name *Miguel's* emblazoned in black across the front and 'We Always Please' across the back, and tight denim jeans. It always looked as though the guys from *Miguel's* were poured into their clothes because they fitted so snugly, rather than they put them on.

One evening when Thomas delivered my weekly pizza, which was usually a combination of Salami, chilies, tomato, avocado pear and olives, I couldn't resist the temptation. He placed the pizza box on my kitchen counter and as he turned to face me, I stood in front of him and ran my hands over his tightly fitting T-shirt and rubbed his sharply protruding nipples. I couldn't resist the touch. They were hard to the touch and I felt that they needed some gentle attention. Thomas merely stood his ground and a gentle groan was emitted from him as I touched him. Having not received a rebuttal, I took the liberty to let my hands run tenderly across his chest and down over his stomach. He never moved nor did he reciprocate in any way; he only smiled at me. When my hands reached the waistband of his jeans, I thought he might object that I had gone too far, but he didn't. I let a hand wander casually down to his crotch and I could fell the developing bulge. I gave it a gentle squeeze and felt his length, and then I sank to my knees, in worship, as it were. I unzipped his jeans and retrieved the prize, hidden within his briefs. His long slender cock with its mushroom-shaped head waited for me to make love to it.

My mouth worked along his length, lubricating it until it glistened in the kitchen light. As I worked my mouth up and down his throbbing cock, my hands gently massaged his pendulous balls until I could hear his breathing increase in volume and speed.

"I'm gonna shoot," he gasped, after a short while.

I released my mouth from his cock and took hold of it and began to slide my hand along its slippery length. His gasping became louder until he tensed and the first shots of his warm, cum landed on my face. I watched with fascination as his body jerked and he fired load after load of warm, sticky love-juice onto my face.

After that day, I understood the meaning behind Thomas's T-shirt which said, 'We Always Please' – he sure did.

One Wednesday, I had phoned my order through from the gym and set off for home. I got home before the delivery arrived, but I had been exercising a little more strenuously than usual, so I was sweaty and sticky, but hadn't showered or changed. I waited for the customary hoot from Thomas's beat-up Volkswagen, but never heard anything. As I waited, I heard the patter of rain falling on the house roof. It started off lightly but slowly built up in intensity until the rain was beginning to pound on the roof. I stood on the patio, watching the rain pouring down, and waiting for Thomas to bring my usual pizza. I heard the roar of a motorbike engine drawing nearer and then I saw the single light of the bike turn into my driveway and head up towards the house. This was no Volkswagen and certainly not likely to be Thomas. In fact, I had no idea who this might be, but as the rider neared, I recognized the *Miguel's* T-Shirt. It wasn't Thomas.

As the rider got up to the house, I could see that he was drenched. The rain had saturated his T-shirt and jeans.

"Pull into the garage," I shouted, pointing in the direction of the open garage door.

I rushed back into the house and went through the kitchen to the inter leading door from there into the garage. As I enter the garage area, I pressed the garage door remote to close out the wet and the cold and watched as the young man sitting astride the motor bike, pulled off his helmet.

He had short, dark, slightly curly hair and from the wetness of his tight T-shirt, I could see how muscular he was. The wet material was stretched taut across two buffed pectoral muscles, while his biceps bulged to break free from the constraining wet material, and as my eyes traversed his body, I was struck by the tight abdominal muscles that were evident. I could feel a sudden arousal in my gym shorts. As he sat astride the body of the bike, his muscular thighs seemed to be glued to the engine and his jeans seemed to be stretching to their limit.

"Hi! Are you Mr. Blake?"

"Sure," I replied. "But call me Geoff."

"Hi there. I'm Mike. Thomas has told me about you and he asked me to deliver tonight."

I wondered just what Thomas might have told him, but as I watched his thick, muscular legs swing over the bike as he dismounted, I hoped that Thomas may have said good things about me.

"You look incredibly wet. Why don't you take off your shirt and I'll get it dried for you?"

Mike smiled at me and began to try to rid his body of his wet T-shirt, without saying a word. As he struggled to get the item off, I instinctively stepped forward to help. I watched as he raised his arms and in doing so, his stomach muscles went taut and his six-pack became evident. My fingers glanced over his stomach and chest as I pulled his T-shirt free.

"You've got a pretty good body," I commented, admiring his flexed torso.

His chest had a fine layer of hair which he obviously shaved to try to create a smooth look and had two large, round nipples that seemed to beg chewing. On his face he had what was probably a two day growth of hair – nothing excessive, but just enough to make him look sexy and perhaps a little threatening in appearance. I looked down at his legs, with well-built thighs, and noticed that his jeans were also wet through.

"Would you like to take off your jeans and I'll put them and your T-shirt in the dryer for you?"

Again he smiled and said nothing. He unzipped his jeans, but as he began to pull them down to his ankles, I noticed how he watched my reactions. His eyes never left my face. Slowly his jeans slid lower and lower, revealing a pair of white briefs. Seeing the whiteness made my eyes focus on the garment and what was evidently lying within it. Mike had obviously become slightly aroused while standing there because I could see the thick lie of his cock with its foreskin still covering its head. As I looked down slightly, I noticed a tattoo in his left groin area. It resembled a snake.

"That's a pretty smart snake there," I said, not realizing that what I had said could be construed in two possible ways: a reference to his tattoo or to his ever-growing hard-on in his white briefs.

Mike stood there for a moment, allowing me the opportunity of admiring his well-defined body, and then he folded his arms, as one might do if one were cold.

"I'm sorry; can I get you some warm clothes?"

"No, it's fine. I'm not cold," he replied. "It's just a little... well you know..."

Suddenly I realized that he might be embarrassed.

"I just feel a bit naked, while you're dressed, if you know what I mean."

"Hey, I'm sorry. No problem," I responded, pulling off my gym vest and pulling down my gym shorts. I stood there in my running shoes and jockstrap. We stood staring at each other, smiling awkwardly, both of us down to our bare minimum.

"You've got a pretty trim body, yourself," said Mike.

"Thanks," I answered; me now being the embarrassed one.

Suddenly I caught sight of the dryer which I kept in the garage and that broke the tension.

"Hey let me put your things in the dryer and while they're drying you can have something to drink if you'd like."

I busied myself putting his clothes in the dryer and when I had done so and turned around, Mike was leaning against his motorbike, which he'd placed on its stand, with one hand resting casually on his engorged crotch, while the other played teasingly with a nipple. My erection had also enlarged in my jockstrap and was straining to break free.

"Thomas tells me that you're pretty good with your mouth," he said, licking his lips as he said it.

Watching that tongue of his slide seductively across his lips made my cock give a sudden throb, and I thought of his tongue rimming my twitching asshole.

"What else did Thomas tell you?" I enquired, slowly approaching him.

He continued to play with his nipple, tweaking and pinching it, which was clearly sending sensory shocks through his body to his drooling cock. I could see the wet patch beginning to appear as he oozed pre-cum onto his briefs.

"He said you gave good head and he thought you'd be a good fuck. Is that true?"

"You'll have to be the judge of that," I answered, stretching out a hand and taking hold of the nipple that was not being played with. I pinched it gently, slowly increasing the intensity of my grasp on it, until Mike was groaning loudly and puffing out his chest as though to encourage me to pinch harder.

"Yes!" he gasped "I like that, but don't be frightened. Squeeze it hard!"

I did as I was told, and with each squeeze so he groaned and my cock throbbed, knowing that I was giving him pleasure. After a while he placed a hand on my head and pushed me to my knees.

"Take that fuck muscle of mine and treat me nicely," he purred.

I pulled down his briefs and watched as his uncut cock bounced free. I took hold of it and slowly slid my hand down his engorged thickness until his foreskin rolled back to reveal a shiny pink head, waiting to licked and kissed. I ran my tongue lovingly around its rim and then over the top. I licked off some of the salty-sweet pre-cum and licked my lips. I liked his taste and I wanted more. I swallowed his cock-head and stem until I could feel it tickle the back of my throat as my chin rubbed up against his firm balls. As I did this, he groaned softly and gave a gentle thrust. I clamped my mouth tightly on his stem and sucked as I began my return journey to its tip. After repeating my actions for some time, I pulled free and looked up at him.

"Fuck! You're good. Thomas was right," he murmured. "Get up. I want to get a taste of your butt hole and massage my fuck muscle in there."

This excited me. I instantly rose to my feet and Mike manipulated me so that I was now next to the motorbike.

"Sit on the bike facing the back," he said, helping me to get on the bike.

My legs were spread wide across the bike and that in itself was a turn-on for me. He gently pushed me so my back lay on the gas tank, then he lifted my legs and aimed his tongue at my ass. The warmness of his touch was erotic and sent ecstatic waves of passion through me. His tongue lathered my hole and every now and again, I could feel the tip of his tongue push into my hole. I then felt as he inserted a finger where his tongue had been and it began to search my innards. It was now my turn to groan with ecstasy as he massaged my prostate.

"Oh, fuck!" I moaned, feeling another finger slide in.

His fingers worked magic inside of me and I wondered if I'd be able to hold out much longer before shooting my load.

"Mike, you're getting me close."

He stopped for a while and pulled the jockstrap covering my cock and balls away to allow them freedom. He licked some of the juice that was leaking from me and gently ran his fingers over the smooth shiny stem, letting his fingers eventually trail around my cut head. This was tantalizing.

"I want you to come, but I also want to get my fuck muscle in that tight hole of yours," he whispered.

"Please fuck me," I whispered back.

"Not yet," came the reply.

Instead, he leant to the side of his bike, felt in one of the side pouches and pulled out a condom, which he tore open of its wrapper and unrolled it down his long, fat cock. He then stood astride his bike facing me, but instead of sliding his cock into me, he leant forward and took my cock into his mouth. I could feel the tightness of his grip on my stem and warmth that he generated. His mouth started a journey of pleasure traveling up and down my length as I groaned and sighed with each journey. I could feel the gentle tickle of his two-day stubble each time his chin reached the base of my cock.

Soon, I was back to where I had been a little earlier.

"Mike, please slow down, you're driving me crazy."

It was as though he hadn't heard me because he just increased his activity. I could feel my balls rising in their sac, getting ready to fire. I gasped and as I did so, so Mike released his grip to watch a stream of white cum fly from my cock tip and strike him across the cheek. Another followed fairly rapidly, again landing on his face, and another and another. As my supply began to dissipate so he returned his mouth to my wet and juicy cock. He licked the remainder of my cum from the head of my cock and sucked long and deep to extract every last drop, Once he had slowly brought me back down from my high, he prepared me for another high.

Mike slowly slid closer to me, aiming his hard fuck muscle at my waiting hole. I felt the initial touch and didn't fight him. Instead, I opened up immediately and allowed him to sink slowly into my warmth.

"Aargh!" I gasped as he sank deeper and deeper until I felt his thighs rub against my ass and then I clamped my ass tightly around his thick weapon, preventing it from escaping.

The feeling of having Mike's firm, thick cock embedded in me sent shivers of rapture through my body. I could feel the coolness of the gas tank against my back and the heat of Mike's body against my front as he slid in and out of my opening. The motor bike rocked gently with each thrust he made. I stretched my arms behind my head and held on tightly to the handlebars of the bike for support. Our bodies collided together, causing a fine mist of perspiration to develop on Mike's face and chest. I could feel my cock sliding against his stomach as he leaned forward onto me, plowing into me deeply with each thrust. I noticed with his enthusiasm increasing, the motorbike began to rock more intensely; and at one stage I thought we might both collapse on the garage floor. My grunts were becoming more and more audible with each deep thrust and so were his gasps.

Before he had a chance to expend all his energy, Mike pulled out of me, giving me a feeling of emptiness, and said, "Flip around so that you're facing the front."

It felt a relief to be able to lower my tiring legs and to straddle the bike like a normal rider would. Although Mike remained in the same position that he had been in, once I had turned around, he told me to lift myself ever so slightly. I did as I was asked and I felt Mike sidle up closer to me and then he said, "Ease yourself down on me, Geoff."

I did as I was told and as I lowered myself, I felt the hard, stiffness of his cock rub against my ass. I wriggled my ass in an attempt to direct it to my opening, but I had no need to do that, because Mike was already aiming for my entry. I once more felt his cock-head touch my quivering opening, and like a whale's mouth gaping wide to swallow tons of plankton, so I was able to 'suck' into me his long thick cock. With a change of position, I was able to ride Mike as I might a horse. My feet rested on the pedals and as I rose and fell onto his throbbing cock, so he drove into me and then retracted. I felt his thick cock nudge my prostate in regular fashion and the tightness of my chute kept him firmly embedded in me.

"Oh, Fuck!" he exclaimed. "You're so fucking tight, you're going to strangle the life out of my dick until I shoot and fill you up!"

I thrust each time that Mike did; the intention being that I could get him deeper into me with each thrust and so enjoy his control over me. He held onto my waist, pulling me onto him to also increase our contact. His thighs were slapping continuously against my ass and each time that happened, both of us gave a deep groan or sigh.

"Geoff, you're going to milk me any minute from now", he growled, as I felt his arms wrap around my waist and hold onto me and he increased his speed.

"You're gonna make me come again," I groaned as each thrust found its mark against my prostate.

We were both breathing heavily now as we came closer to our climaxes. I suddenly froze and tensed. My cock erupted, spurting my warm juices over the gas tank and as I did so, instinctively my ass muscles tightened their grip on Mike's cock.

"Aw fuck!" he screamed and thrust right up the ass, emptying his load into the sheath that covered his throbbing cock. His body shuddered with each thrust and with it came a deep growl each time he unloaded his juice into me.

Eventually, we both lay exhausted, me across the gas tank, with Mike up against my back, perspiration dripping from both our bodies. As he lay resting against my back, I asked, "Was Thomas right?"

"Sorry. About what?"

"Was I good fuck?"

Mike laughed loudly and rubbed his hands over my nipples, squeezing them both hard between forefinger and thumb, causing my cock to throb as he did it.

"I'd say you're one helluva fuck, and I can't wait to tell him how right he was," answered Mike.

"But Thomas and I have never gone this far before," I said.

"Maybe not, but he was sure that you'd be good, and he was right. Maybe next time you order a pizza, the two of us might deliver it to you."

I smiled at the thought.

Mike slipped from me and climbed from the bike, with me following suit.

"By the way," he said, going to a container on the side of the motor bike and taking out a pizza box. "I think your pizza might be cold by now."

"Not a problem," I replied, "because after being with you, a cold pizza will go down very well with a hot body!"

I paid Mike the money for the pizza, tipped him handsomely and gave him back his warm, dried clothes. I watched as he poured his trim body back into his official *Miguel's* outfit, gave him a goodbye kiss, gave his tight ass a squeeze, as well as his still firm cock, and watched as he sped off into the darkness.

As he left, I decided that every Wednesday I would make a point of praying for rain when I ordered my meal!

VIRGIN ON MANHOOD

Part of the fun of studying at a university is the social life – provided you manage to have some kind. There are always some students, whose role in life is to take their studies seriously, and then there are others whose role in life is to have fun seriously; I was in the latter group. Although I wanted to graduate, I was determined to graduate with the knowledge that I hadn't wasted my time at university remaining a virgin. From the day I arrived on campus, I made up my mind to lose my virginity as soon as possible. You see I had come from a small town with a small town mentality and one's virginity was meant to be kept until one married, and as I had already decided that I wasn't going to be the marrying kind, I thought it was time to abandon all.

Although I had taken a keen interest in sport, I didn't consider myself a jock, although from my physique, others might have. I wasn't on a sport's scholarship, but enjoyed my games of football and swimming, and in the athletic season, I also took up a little running. To tell the truth, the reasons why I enjoyed my sport was the fact that I found the clothes I wore for each sport, sexy; those tight, crotch hugging shorts for football, the equally tight Speedo for swimming and the soft, silky touch of my running shorts, kept me in a state of having a permanent hard-on. Added to this, was my ability to get close to the hunkiest guys on campus.

My room mate, Tim, was, let's just say, plain on the eye. Although he had a runner's physique, which I quite liked, he seemed withdrawn and reserved, not the out-going type that I wanted to associate with. I also wasn't sure as to his sexuality as he paid little attention to either guys or girls. Often I would return from football practice, pull off my top and collapse onto my bed, still in my crotch hugging shorts, hoping he might make a comment or even a pass at me, but nothing ever materialized. Even after a shower I would, on occasions, walk into our dorm with a towel wrapped around my waist, let it fall, casually, onto the floor and stand before him naked, my long cock swaying in the breeze, but he still took no notice. I wondered if Tim was asexual!

Although I was enjoying my stay at university, I couldn't find Mr. Right with whom I could lose my virginity. I know this may sound ridiculous, but I was fussy. I had waited long enough and although I was as horny as hell, I didn't want just anyone.

At football practices, I often eyed the guys especially in the showers and found myself getting aroused quite often by what I saw, but then I thought to myself, 'these are all brawn and no brain; is that what I want?'

Swimming practices were just as bad with all those tight Speedos floating around and the various shape and sizes of cocks on display. With all this muscle around, I was ready to be ravaged. There was one guy who got my attention, by the name of Hank, but he didn't seem to notice me. I often remained behind after swimming practice to shower and change at the same time as he did. I'd watch him under the shower as the water trailed down his tight, muscular body, along the thick ridge of muscle that hung tantalizingly between his legs, its thick head just waiting to be sucked, and then down his tree-trunk legs. Oh how I wished I was that water running over his body. Then he'd soap himself, the white foam suds sliding over his chest and then collecting on his large cock. He'd massage his cock with the soap and I'd see how his man muscle would grow in length and girth. Naturally it would be at this time that I'd beat a hasty retreat as my cock began to take on a life of its own and I didn't want to embarrass myself in front of others.

One evening, after football practice, I returned to my dorm and found Tim sitting waiting for me.

"Gary, are you doing anything tonight?" he asked.

I was a little surprised as we hardly spoke much to each other, except when discussing our studies.

"Er, uhm, no!" I replied.

"I wondered if you'd like to go for a pizza."

"Sure, sure!"

I didn't know what else to say.

"But can I take a shower before we go?" I asked.

"Please. There's no rush. We can go when you're ready."

I grabbed my towel, stripped off my shirt, football shorts and jockstrap and threw them onto my bed. I wrapped my towel around my waist and headed out of our dorm to the bathroom.

As I stood under the cascading water of the shower, I wondered about Tim. What had made him offer to take me to dinner? Was he after something? Perhaps he was just trying to be friendly, and after all, what harm was there in that? After I had showered, I returned to the dorm and found Tim sitting casually on my bed. In his hand was my jockstrap. I didn't say anything, but I did notice how he surreptitiously tried to get rid of the object. I wondered if he'd been sniffing the crotch area of my jockstrap. Hey! That would be quite a turn-on. I dropped my towel to the floor and wandered around the room as though deciding on what to wear, allowing Tim to see my naked body. I wanted to see if he'd react in any way to my nakedness. I noticed how he casually glanced at me every now and then. Of course, knowing that he was watching me, I began to get the start of a hard-on. Do I quickly get dressed before my cock looks like a periscope in search of something to torpedo, or do I let it all hang loose, so to speak? What the hell, let's go for the torpedo; after all, I was proud of my cock and its length. I saw how his glances became more focused on my ever growing cock, but I refrained from dressing. I decided to tease him a little longer. Soon my cock was as erect as it could get and I gently manhandled it, knowing that he was watching me. I glanced his way and noticed that he'd placed a hand on his own crotch. Ah Ha! The boy does have feelings! Something was rising between his legs and he was becoming awkward on the bed as his tight jeans were constricting his burgeoning hard-on. I picked up a T-shirt, held it to my chest, turned to face him, my cock aiming its tip at him and said, "Should I wear this one tonight?" Tim never noticed the T-shirt, but gaped openly at my throbbing cock.

"Tim, it's rude to stare with your mouth open – put something in it if you have to."

He instinctively clamped his mouth shut and looked up at my face.

"Sorry, Gary. I didn't mean to, but it's just that… I've never seen anyone with such a big cock before."

"I'll take that as a compliment, Tim. But tell me, are you into cocks?"

He blushed and began to stammer.

"I…I… I'm sorry. I… didn't mean to… you know…"

"…no I don't know."

"I… I… think we'd better get going, if we want to have dinner," replied Tim, standing up abruptly, his now fully erect cock bulging through his jeans.

"That looks like a pretty healthy size you've got there in your jeans, Tim," I said, advancing slowly towards him, my cock waving like a search light seeking something to target.

Tim backed away, fear written across his face.

"You don't have to be shy, Tim. We're guys and guys get a hard-on. I'm sure that you've seen other guys in the shower, for example, with a hard-on."

Tim's face moved from my waving cock, to my face, and then back to my waving cock. I took hold of my thick stem and squeezed my cock. The bulbous head seemed to become inflamed and a drop of clear pre-cum oozed from its tip. I ran a finger over my piss slit and scooped up the liquid, stuck out my tongue and licked my finger. I was sure I saw Tim's cock throb in his jeans as I did this. I squeezed my cock again but this time when I scooped up my juice, I offered it to Tim.

"Open your mouth Tim. Taste this. You'll like it."

Tim seemed to panic and almost fled, but curiosity got the better of him and he stood his ground. I walked up to him, the tip of my finger glistening with pre-cum and as my cock jabbed at his crotch, so my finger went up to his lips. Gently I wiped the clear liquid onto his lips and instinctively, he licked his lips, taking in my juices.

"That wasn't so bad was it?" I asked, almost whispering the words.

He never replied, but stood staring at me as my cock continued to jab at his crotch. My hand went up to his neck and I slowly pulled his face towards mine until our lips met and we started kissing, ever so gently. I tried to insert my tongue into his mouth, but without initial success, however, I soon found an opening and our tongues were fighting to take control of the other's mouth. I felt Tim grab my cock and squeeze it hard. Although I was somewhat taken by his swift action, his touch was firm and pleasurable. I reciprocated by grabbing his engorged crotch and feeling for the zipper to his jeans, unzipped them and found his wet cock waiting to be manhandled.

Tim was not small in the crotch area and I became excited at the prospect of losing my virginity to Tim and his heavy manhood. I knelt in front of him and swallowed his cock head, lathering it with my tongue and rolling his foreskin back; then I sank down on his shaft, pushing it to the back of my throat. I heard Tim groan as my mouth sank down his length. He obviously did like what I was doing to him, but then I knew that many straight guys liked to be sucked off and maybe Tim was one of those. I felt his hands under my armpits as he lifted me to my feet.

"Please fuck me," he whispered when our faces were close again.

Oh Fuck! Here I was hoping to lose my virginity to this man and now I had to play the active role for big Tim. Hey, I'm not unduly worried about playing that role, it's just that I was desperate for someone to attack my ass and give me a good pounding so that I'd shoot and shoot and shoot!

I pulled Time to my bed, stripped off his shirt and jeans and hoisted his legs into the air. My tongue aimed for his tight pink hole that was constantly winking at me. I could see that this boy was desperate to have his ass plugged with a long, fat cock, and I was only too keen to oblige.

Between my tongue and my fingers, Tim's asshole was quivering with expectation of my onslaught. Every time I inserted a finger or two, I could feel how tightly he clamped his ass on them.

"Do you want my hard cock in you," I growled as he started to ride my fingers.

"Oh yes," groaned Tim. "Please fuck me, hard!"

I retracted my fingers, slipped on a condom, lubed my throbbing cock, held my firm stem and guided my rod into his waiting hole.

He anticipated my attack and never rebuffed my advance. My cock slid effortlessly into the warmth of his tight chute. In fact he was so tight I thought I was going to shoot my load there on the spot.

"Fuck, but you're tight, Tim."

"Do you like that?" he asked, groaning as I inched my way deeper and deeper into him until I felt my balls rub up against his smooth ass.

"Oh yes," I sighed as I came to a stop and let him enjoy the feeling of me inside of him.

I began a slow rhythmic thrust and withdrawal movement, watching Tim's face change from tension to pure joy. I knew that he was in ecstasy and that pleased me. I slid my full length deeply into his warm, tight chute, slapping my hefty balls against his ass each time I sank in. Even though it wasn't my ass that was getting a working over, I knew that both he and I were enjoying this immensely. Soon, Tim began thrusting his hips to meet each of my thrusts, in an effort to try to get my cock deeper into his fine ass.

"Oh fuck, but you're good, Gary," he groaned, his thrusts becoming more urgent each time.

"Be careful, Tim, you're getting me close. If you keep squeezing my cock like that with that tight ass of yours, I'm gonna be shooting everywhere."

"I like the sound of that," joked Tim, now beginning to lose that 'shyness' that seemed to be evident earlier.

I took hold of his throbbing cock and began stroking it rapidly. His breathing had increased and a sweat was forming across his forehead and chest.

"Stop it, Gary!" he cried.

I couldn't. I had built up a fast rhythm on his cock and I wanted to see him shoot his warm cum over his chest.

"Come Tim! Shoot that fucking load of yours," I yelled, increasing my thrusts into his ass.

I saw his cock swell and immediately there was a gasp followed by a cry and the first of a stream of thick white juice spewed from the tip of his cock. Load followed load and I began to wonder if this kid was ever going to run dry. His stomach and chest was a wash of white, and with each shot, so I felt the tightness of his asshole clamp around my cock shaft. Suddenly I pulled out, ripped off the condom and stroked myself until I too filled his stomach and chest with warm gushes of my cum. We were both gasping and moaning and our bodies shuddered together, then our mouths found each other's and we kissed. As our exhausted bodies returned to some form of normality, I leaned across Tim's body and we lay in each other's arms, whispering words of thanks in each other's ear.

"That was awesome," said Tim, "but I must tell you something."

I lifted my face from his and looked into his soft eyes.

"You're my first guy."

I smiled at the knowledge. I knew that Tim would always remember me, just as many others also remembered their first time, but I still had to enjoy my first time of having my ass rammed.

"You're damn good," continued Tim, "you must have done this many times."

"Not really," I answered. "In fact, can I tell you a secret, I'm still a virgin."

"What do you mean a virgin?"

"I've never been fucked, so I don't know the pleasure that you experienced."

"So do you swing both ways? I mean are you active and passive?"

"I don't know. As I say no-one has ever fucked me so I don't know whether I'd like it, but I sure would like to try it."

Tim giggled.

"Sorry I can't oblige, because I'm a bottom and I like it that way, but I know someone who might be able to help you out."

My face lit up. "Who?"

"My cousin," replied Tim.

"What's he like?"

"You'd like him very much. He's your build and into sports and I know that he's hung like a proverbial horse, if size is what you want."

I didn't want to sound like a slut, but of course size was most important. In fact the bigger the better if I wanted to experience the full feeling.

"Do you think he'd be interested?"

"I'm sure he would. I'll speak to him tomorrow and get back to you. Now, are we going out to eat or not?"

We dressed and headed out for pizzas; two very different people from what we had been earlier.

The following evening, as promised, Tim returned to the dorm with news from his cousin.

"He says he'd like to meet you and if it is what you say you want, then he's more than willing to oblige you."

"Does he sound keen?"

"Absolutely. He likes nothing more than a tight ass to plow his big cock into."

"So when am I going to meet him?"

"I told him to come round to our room at nine tonight, but don't worry, I'll go out and come back later."

I respected Tim's offer, but I didn't like 'chasing' him from his own room.

"I'll go to movies or something," Tim said, "then you two can be alone to enjoy what I enjoyed, that is, if you're interested."

"You bet, I'm interested," I answered.

Tim and I went off to shower, him preparing for movies and me for my blind date. At 20:00, Tim went off to movies, saying he'd return at midnight. I appreciated his offer although I wondered what he'd do for hours after the movies came out. I was left lying on my bed waiting for 21:00 to arrive. I had pulled on a pair of shorts but didn't bother with a shirt as it wasn't cold. At 20:45, there was a gentle knock on our room door. I leapt from the bed, checked myself one more time in the mirror and then opened the door. There standing in the corridor was my date - my fuck, the guy who hopefully was going to take my virginity.

"Hank!" I exclaimed. "What are you doing here?"

It was Hank my swimming dream.

"Tim said that you needed servicing."

"Are you Tim's cousin?"

"That's it. So aren't you going to invite me in?"

"Please, please come in," I stammered closing the door behind him.

I was a little embarrassed as I knew that Hank had been aware of how I had admired his body in the showers and at the pool, now he was here in my room.

"Tim was telling me that you had a good scene with him last night. You're lucky, because I've been after that tight ass of his for some time, but never managed to get it."

I smiled knowing how much I had enjoyed plowing into Tim's ass.

"You know, I've always admired your physique, Gary. I've watched you in your Speedo and seen the package that you carry, and admired that too."

His talk was getting me hard and the more he spoke about how sexy he'd found me, the harder my cock was getting.

"Looks like that package is growing," said Hank, making a firm grab on my crotch.

I felt my balls being squeezed and although a sharp pain ran through my body as he did that, it also made my cock throb with anticipation. Instinct kicked in and I grabbed his package, feeling that he was already hard. I rubbed my hand across the coarse denim material of his jeans and traced the outline of his long, thick stem. I gripped the zipper and slowly pulled down, opening up his jeans and fumbled inside to find his naked cock waiting to be taken. I pulled his length into view and admired the helmet-shaped pink head and the long, thick shaft. My hand gripped it and began stroking it, bringing a little pre-cum to the tip each time. I knelt before him and licked off the clear liquid, then sank my mouth over his length, like I had done to Tim the night before. This was a weapon of size that he had and I wanted that deep inside of me.

I released my grip on his cock and looked up into his face. He was smiling down at me.

"You are going to use this on me aren't you?" I queried.

"I can't wait to get my rock hard rod deep in that ass of yours. I've waited quite a long time to do that."

Clothes were disappearing rapidly and being thrown onto the floor. Arms and hands were exploring bodies while tongues fought duels in each other's mouth. Our chests heaved against each other's as our cocks rubbed together, being lubricated by the constant flow of pre-cum emanating from both of us. Hank pushed me onto my bed and sank between my legs, lathering my cock, balls and eventually, my waiting ass hole. His tongue did wonders, in and out of my throbbing hole, lubricating me for his attack.

"You got a rubber?" he asked.

I told him to look on the side table next to my bed as I had got everything ready for my blind date. He unrolled the condom down his thick length then, taking hold of his firm shaft, directed it towards my waiting ass. I tensed as I felt his cock touch me, but he slowly placed pressure on me and pushed his cock past the entrance. The pain that flooded through me, because of his size, was excruciating, but I was determined to lose my virginity.

"Slowly," I gasped as I felt his shaft slowly becoming embedded in me.

As he sank deeper, the feeling changed from pain to utter ecstasy; in fact I wanted him to go even deeper if it were possible. Once I felt his thighs rest against my ass, he smiled at me.

"Now fuck me hard," I said, smiling back at Hank.

He didn't need an invitation to do that. His prowess and fitness were proof that this guy knew how to use his cock to good effect. He pounded into my ass, then slid me onto my side and lay on the bed next to me as he sank deeper into my throbbing ass. All the while, he stroked my cock, milking it with clear liquid, which made his strokes slide even more easily. He then rolled me onto my stomach, spread my legs wide and rammed his way in again. This time, with each thrust, I could feel my cock rub against the bed covers and the friction was driving me crazy.

"Careful, Hank. If you carry on like this, you'll have me shooting."

He pulled out of me and the sudden feeling of loss was probably the most painful feeling I had experienced so far. I urged him to slide back in, but I needn't have worried as he had plans already. He pulled me to the edge of the bed and once again hoisted my legs into the air and slid his cock back into me. Except, as he did this, so he bent over me, took my cock into his mouth, and began sucking. As he thrust deeply into my ass, so his mouth worked wonders on my shaft.

"Oh fuck!" I cried. "This is the most awesome feeling I've ever had. Hank I'm gonna come."

He increased both his thrusts into my ass and tightened the grip with his mouth. I could feel my balls rising in their sac, getting ready to fire. I groaned then gasped and fired. My body shuddered with each load that I sent down Hank's throat, but he never released his grip. He tried to swallow as fast as he could, but I could see some of my love juice ooze out of his mouth and dribble down his chin. His thrusts had become more urgent and hard, which made me feel excited as he pounded my tightening ass. Suddenly he let go of my cock and shouted, "Fuuuck!"

He froze for a moment, and then rapidly fucked my ass as he shot his load into me. Our breathing was heavy and amidst the groans and grunts, our mouths managed to find each other's. With our arms clasping each other, we kissed and fucked until we lay exhausted together on the bed, Hank's cock still firmly embedded in me.

As our breathing returned to normality and our kisses became gentler, we opened our eyes to each other and smiled.

"Wow, that was the most incredible feeling," I said, kissing him gently on the mouth. "Now I know what Tim felt when I had him last night."

"Thank you, Gary. For a virgin, you're fucking awesome, but I hope that now that you're no longer a virgin, that doesn't mean I can't have access to that fine ass of yours?"

I laughed. "You can have my ass anytime, Hank."

With that we both fell asleep in each other's arms.

At midnight, the door opened quietly and Tim entered. He saw Hank and me in each other's arms on the bed, stripped off his clothes and climbed on the bed with us. Soon I felt Hank's cock prodding at my ass while my cock slipped effortlessly into Tim's waiting hole. The three of us became connected and pounded each other's ass until we were panting heavily and shooting our load.

That night, very little sleep was had by the three of us as we pleasured each other and brought our friendships closer together.

THE ICEMAN COMETH

Each day I would hear the jingle playing in the distance and would run to my mother and ask her for money; money for an ice cream. That jingle that I heard each day was a melody coming from the approaching ice cream van. I was probably the best human version of a Pavlovian dog. When the music played on the van, I reacted, salivating for the ice creams.

Each time I would rush out into the street and wait for the driver to pull up outside of our house and would then expect a full explanation of what flavors were available that day.

Mr. Banducci was the driver, a stocky man who obviously enjoyed a great deal of pasta, and on some occasions, he would be accompanied by his son, who was about my age. Mr. Banducci always made an effort to see that there were some of my favorite flavors left by the time he reached our house. There were even occasions when Paulo, his son, and I would sit on the sidewalk eating our ice creams together.

As time went by and I grew older, I still heard Mr. Banducci's van drawing nearer and I would jog out into the street to await the vehicle, but now there was no Paulo as he was at college.

"How's Paulo, Mr. Banducci?"

"Doing well, Mike. He's made the college swim team."

"That's great. Please give him my regards."

Paulo had grown into a strapping young man, very Italian looking with dark brown hair, deep blue eyes and hadn't been fed too much pasta like his father. He was tall, slim and had developed an athletic physique. He had the most charming smile and would make a good husband to any woman. Paulo and I had grown close as we got older and while we went to the same school, we were best of friends.

A month passed and I realized that I hadn't heard the tinkling jingle from the ice cream van. I thought maybe Mr. Banducci had come past when I was out and that was why I hadn't heard the music. Then one afternoon, far in the distance, I heard the melodious jingle playing. I smiled as memories flooded my head, grabbed some cash and waited out in the street for Mr. Banducci to arrive. As the van pulled up, I saw the distinctive good-looking Paulo sitting behind the wheel.

"Paulo, what are you doing here?" I asked, surprised at seeing him.

"Didn't you hear? My Dad passed away."

"I'm so sorry to hear that, but it was only like the other day that I spoke to him about you."

"It was very sudden, but I wanted to keep on his tradition, so when I finish college in the afternoons, I get behind the wheel and do his old rounds."

I was pleased to see Paulo again. He had really turned into a very good looking guy, the sort of guy that I could intimate with. Although I had always been attracted to boys, seeing Paulo only reinforced my attraction more.

"What have you been doing with yourself?" asked Paulo, scooping me a tub of Rum and Raisin ice cream.

"Working. I've got myself a job in a sports shop," I replied. "It's not bad and at least I get to meet various people. I know that you're at college, but tell me, what's your love life like?"

Paulo laughed.

"I'm not like I was at school. I've quietened down a lot."

"And the girls?"

His tanned face blushed and his puppy-dog eyes drooped.

"Oh I don't have time for that."

Paulo seemed embarrassed having said that and I wondered why. He had killer looks and a fantastic body, so attracting a woman would be easy for him.

"What about you?" asked Paulo.

At no stage during our growing up together had I ever revealed to Paulo my liking for boys because I thought he might take offence, but now that we were adults, admitting to my desires wasn't a problem for me.

"I'm not interested in girls," I answered.

He looked a little surprised by my comment and raised an eyebrow.

"What do you mean?"

Looking him straight in the eyes I replied, "I prefer boys, Paulo."

I waited for the reaction, thinking it would be negative or result in the end of our friendship, but all Paulo said was "Oh!"

The topic wasn't discussed and I ate my ice cream while Paulo chatted about life in general. When I had finished eating, Paulo said it was time for him to continue his route, so we said our good byes and I watched as the van disappeared into the distance. I stood for some time on the sidewalk, thinking about what I had said to Paulo and wondering what in fact had been going through his mind at the time.

The following week, I received a phone call at home. It was Paulo.

"Hi Mike, it's Paulo."

"Hi there. How're things?"

"Fine thanks. Listen, I was thinking … are you doing anything this weekend?"

"Actually no. I'm not working either, so my weekend is free, why, what did you have in mind?"

"I'm taking my mother away for the weekend to the coast and I wondered if you'd like to join us?"

"That would be great. I'd like that."

"Is it OK if I pick you up on Saturday morning, say at nine and then we can head off?"

"Sounds great to me. Must I bring anything?"

"Just yourself and some clothes. We'll supply everything else. I just thought it would be nice for my Mum to get away from the house for a while."

"I like the idea," I replied.

This is what I liked about Paulo. He was such a caring person and that alone made him appear more beautiful. A sense of excitement filled me when I put down the phone; it would be so good to spend time with him again.

Saturday soon arrived and Paulo and his mother arrived on the scheduled time. I greeted them both, giving Mrs. Banducci a hug and a kiss on both cheeks and formally shook Paulo's hand, but managed to see how deeply he looked into my eyes when we shook hands. The journey didn't take long, but was made even more enjoyable by the banter and chatter we had in the car. Paulo's mother was short and comely, with a lively spirit and a delightful sense of humor.

"You boys must enjoy yourselves when we get to the hotel," she said, with a twinkle in her eye.

I caught Paulo grinning at me in the rear view mirror when his mother said this, and he winked at me.

"I have booked you two in a room and I have my own, but you don't have to spend all your time trying to entertain me," she continued.

"Are we staying at a hotel?" I enquired.

"Yes, my Mum insisted that we stay at a hotel where we could be waited on hand and foot."

I began to feel somewhat embarrassed because this would cost them money and had not been prepared to be staying in a hotel. I thought that they might be staying in a holiday home of some sort.

We duly arrived at our destination, unloaded the car and booked into our rooms. As we walked into our room, I couldn't help noticing, but said nothing, that we had a double bed and not two single beds. I wondered if this was planned or accidental, but I wasn't going to ask Paulo. Instead I thought I'd see what his reaction might be, but he wasn't at all worried by this fact.

"Which side do you want?" asked Paulo.

"Pardon?"

"Which side of the bed do you like sleeping on?"

"Oh, I don't really mind."

"I like the right side, if you don't mind," said Paulo.

"No, no not at all."

"Come on, let's get changed and go for a swim," suggested Paulo, as he began to strip off his shirt.

He had developed a beautifully defined body thanks to his swimming training. He was tanned and in shape with tight abs and broad shoulders. He unzipped his jeans, pulled them down and folded them, placing them on his side of the bed. As he stood there in his stark, white briefs, against the tanned skin, I couldn't help thinking how I would love to get this man into bed with me for a moment of passion. I could see the firm, package in the front of his briefs where his pendulous balls and thick cock lay, then he shucked his briefs to the floor, picked up his Speedo and pulled it on, tucking his cock and balls elegantly into the confines of the Lycra material. As I looked at Paulo, I wondered whether Michelangelo had such a beautiful specimen to copy from for his statue of David. I quickly undressed and slipped on my Speedo, grabbed towels for us and we made our way down to the hotel pool.

There were quite a few people lying there tanning, so we found a spot for ourselves, threw down our towels and lay back to relax and enjoy the sun. I sprayed some tanning lotion onto my chest and massaged it in. While I was doing this, I noticed how some of the other guests, mainly women, constantly looked at Paulo, admiringly. A couple of young women even walked past us, staring long and hard at his well-defined torso and large package on display.

"You seem quite a catch for the women here, by the looks of things," I commented.

Paulo merely grunted, disinterestedly.

"They can look as much as they like," he said, without opening his eyes to take notice of them.

I smiled to myself and wicked thoughts flashed through my head. What would happen if I rolled a little closer to him when we were in bed tonight, I wondered? Might I get lucky?

We enjoyed the warmth of the sun and the freshness of the swimming pool water. When we did go for a swim, Paulo was like a fish. His strong, muscular body glistened in the sun when he climbed from the pool and the water trickled off his body. His Speedo clung tightly to his hips and from the front, one could clearly see the entire outline of his thick cock and his hefty balls. He was well aware of this and didn't try to adjust them or rearrange them; he was proud of what he'd been blessed with.

At lunch time, Mrs. Banducci joined us for something to eat and asked how we were enjoying ourselves.

"It's lovely thanks, Mrs. Banducci."

"Mike, please call me Maria and not Mrs. Banducci. You are like family to me and Paulo, so no more formality, capeesh?"

I grinned boyishly at her and Paulo and replied, "Yes Mama!"

"That's better," came her retort. "You like your room?"

I looked to Paulo to answer.

"It's lovely thanks Mum."

"You have two single beds or a double?" asked Maria.

"Double, Mum."

"Good!" was her reply.

And that was the end of the topic of beds. She was more than happy that her son and I would be sleeping together, but I wasn't sure how her son felt about it.

After a light lunch, Paulo said, "I don't know about you, but I think I'm going to have a little rest after lunch. Maybe later I'll go for another swim. What are you going to do, Mike?"

Maria looked at me, waiting to hear my answer.

"I think I'll join you for a lie down as well," I said, obviously to Maria's pleasure, because she nodded and smiled.

Paulo and I made our way back upstairs to our room. Paulo pulled off his shorts and T-shirt that he'd been wearing and lay down on the bed in his white briefs. I did likewise and lay down next to him. We lay there like two dead bodies, neither moving. I wanted to touch him, but was scared to make the first move. Probably Paulo was thinking the same, but I wasn't sure. I felt the bed move as Paulo turned onto his side and lay facing me.

"You've got such a fine body," he said as he gently ran his finger tips over my chest.

A tingle ran through my body and I could feel my cock take on an instant liking to his touch. I turned to face him and let my fingers run over his nipples.

"So have you, but then you've always had a good body."

My fingers hovered over each nipple. My index finger and thumb took hold of a nipple and gently squeezed it. Paulo smiled and puffed out his chest.

"Do you like that?" I asked.

"Hmm!" he purred.

I could see that his package in his briefs was growing distinctly larger.

Both our hands began to explore the other's body until I reached down and ran my hand over his briefs where his cock lay. I could feel its hardness and then felt the softness of his balls. I gave them a gentle squeeze, and then Paulo's hand found my crotch. His hand slid into my briefs and I felt his fingers wrap around my stiff shaft. It was my turn to moan quietly as he stroked my shaft. We kept this up for some time, still smiling into each other's eyes, then I began to pull down his briefs. I watched as his cock was released from its constraining material, then I adjusted my position so that I could get access to his cock and balls with my mouth.

My tongue licked up along the underneath length of his cock shaft until I reached the tip. His foreskin was pulled over his cock head, so I slowly began to roll it back to reveal his moist, pink head. I licked the tip and then, opening my mouth as wide as possible, I slowly sank down his shaft, taking him further down my throat. Once my chin touched his balls, I held my position and let my tongue salivate the base of his cock. Paulo gave a slight upward thrust and moaned as he did so, then I began my upward journey, licking all the way up until I once again reached the tip where I inserted my tongue into his piss slit, tasting some of his early, clear juice.

I released my grip on his cock and slid my body up over his until our cocks rubbed together and our mouths found each other's. Paulo rolled me onto my back and proceeded to lick over my chest, my nipples, nibbling at them, and then headed down to my cock. His tongue circled my cut cock head and then he wrapped his mouth around the top of my cock, licking at it with his tongue. I thrust upwards, so that he could take my whole shaft down his throat, but he continued to lather my cock head. His tongue was making my cock head swell and become sensitive. This Italian stud was driving me crazy. His mouth moved from my cock to my balls, taking one into his mouth and then the other and sucking on them. His tongue then continued its journey in search of my pucker. By now he was crouched between my legs, which he'd lifted high into the air and was massaging my ass hole with his tongue. My breathing was hastening and becoming deeper and I took hold of my cock and started stroking myself. Paulo saw what I was doing, stopped giving my ass a tongue washing and said, "Don't. I don't want you to come just yet."

I immediately stopped and let him take control of everything. His mouth resumed its washing and teasing of my balls and cock, until I felt Paulo get himself closer to inserting his hard, long cock into my waiting hole. I felt the tip of his cock massage my hole and then felt him push forward ever so gently. He didn't need to be gentle with me, because I desperately wanted him inside of me, so I thrust forward to meet his thrust. I felt his cock break through my opening and his shaft sank into the warm depths of my chute. Paulo gasped as he sank into me and so did I, but we both kept pushing until he couldn't go any deeper. I felt his throbbing cock nudge my prostate and that feeling sent my head in turmoil. My eyes felt as if they were rolling back into my head and an ecstatic rush went through my body. My Italian stud was truly in where I felt he belonged. For years I had admired him as a friend, and now we were together in passion.

We began to build up a rhythmic thrust and pull movement, breathing heavily as we made love to each other, our mouths sending waves of passion to each other. Paulo continued to plow into my tight ass and as I lay there taking this man into me, a feeling of overwhelming joy came over me.

His muscular arms supported my legs in the air and my ass clamped as tight as possible over his thick shaft.

"Mike you're getting me close," he gasped.

"Me too," I said, although he had not touched my cock. It was the constant massaging of my prostate by his thick cock that was bringing me closer to shooting my load.

He lifted my ass high up so that he almost had me resting on his lap.

"Paulo, I'm gonna come," I groaned.

He immediately took hold of my cock and started stroking it frantically. A stream of warm, white cum shot from my cock as it began to throb, hitting me on the chin, and then another followed spraying across my chest. With each throb of my cock, my ass muscles tightened around Paulo's thick cock, almost strangling his shaft in me. I felt his cock head expand and then as he gasped, so I felt the first of his load empty into me. With each thrust, he grunted and gasped, and with each of these grunts, so part of him entered me.

Our bodies were wet with sweat and before Paulo could escape my tight clutches, I held him and rolled him onto his side so that we lay facing each other. He remained embedded in me and as our mouths touched, so we dozed off into our dream world.

When we awoke two hours later, we kissed and fondled each other again bringing our erections back to life.

"Let's go for a swim before we start something we'll never finish," suggested Paulo.

I smiled at his phrasing and both of us quickly showered to clean ourselves of the evidence of our love-making, pulled on our Speedos and headed to the pool, but this time with a light tread to our step.

That evening at dinner, both Paulo and I were in a very happy mood and Maria obviously was aware of this.

"I'm glad to see you two are getting on so well. Did you have a good rest this afternoon?"

Paulo and I grinned at each other.

"Eventually," responded Paulo, winking to his mother.

"I'm very glad," she continued. "You're a good boy, Mike and I think you'd be good for Paulo. You know, keep him on the straight and narrow and away from these terrible women who keep trying to come into his life."

"Don't worry, Maria, so long as I'm around there won't be any women coming into Paulo's life, except you; that I can promise."

Maria stretched across the table and took me by the hand. "Promise me that you'll always look after Paulo if anything happens to me."

"I promise," I replied.

Saturday night was spent in each other's arms. Paulo tried every conceivable position with me and this we did all night, making love then falling asleep only to awaken with one of us stroking the other and bringing him to another hard-on and then making love all over again. I think that throughout the night, Paulo must have screwed me at least five times, and when we did get up on Sunday morning, we both looked so haggard from a lack of sleep, that all we wanted to do that day was sleep.

Until we booked out of the hotel, Paulo and I spent every minute in our room, him deeply embedded in me, and me pushing down onto his swollen cock as hard as I could with my tight ass, until we were both firing our loads again and again.

When Paulo and his Mum dropped me at home, she said, "Please don't wait for an invitation to come to our house. In fact, you and Paulo must discuss this, but if you'd like to move in with us, I would be very happy and I'm sure that he would too."

I liked the idea, but chose not to move in with them just yet, but I did help Paulo with his ice cream rounds in the late afternoons, and not even the cold freezers in the van could stop the heat that was generated between me and my Italian stud. Then one month after our return from the weekend away, Paulo asked if he could move in with me.

Now my ice man cometh virtually every night and my tight ass remains the property of my Italian stud, whose mother sees to it that we stay together as life partners.

.

SPEEDO SALESMAN

The feeling of having a tight Speedo encasing one's torso can only be described as sensuous, mellifluous and silken to the touch, in my opinion. However, others might call it castration! From the moment you pull the Speedo costume up your legs, feel the smooth, soft material clasp onto your ass and feel your cock fit snugly into the front pouch, your whole attitude changes. You might feel sexier, more manly or just plain fuckable! On the other hand, you might feel an idiot.

There are of course many guys who refuse to wear a Speedo, for reasons known only to themselves, but to my mind, I think it's because they're cockshy. I know that that's a rather blunt statement, but it's amazing how much emphasis men place on the size, not of the Speedo, but of the cock – simply watch them in the change room shower! However, there are many guys who look good in a Speedo but don't necessarily have a large package to fill the pouch.

I had seen other guys wearing Speedos and I found them sexy, but I had never had the courage to wear one because I didn't think that I had the physique to go with the bikini-style swimming costume. All the guys I had seen wearing a Speedo tended to be muscular and the Speedo served to enhance their beauty, which I found attractive, but I was never blessed with muscles, except for the one between my legs; instead I was tall and slim, with an athletic physique.

I remember the first time I ever went to buy a Speedo.

I plucked up the courage, walked into the sports shop and a young, dark-haired, tanned man walked up to me smiling a beautiful smile.

"Can I help you, sir?"

I noticed the full lips, the twinkling eye and from his well-fitting clothes, I could tell that he had a good body. With all those assets, I was sure that he could help me.

"Yes," I stammered. "I want to buy a swimming costume." Just saying that made me feel a little stupid. Not that it was stupid to buy a swimming costume, but I knew in my mind what type I wanted.

"No problem, sir. If you'd like to follow me, I'll show you what we have in stock."

He led me to a section near the rear of the shop where a number of various types of swimming costumes were situated. As I walked behind him to the beachwear section, I couldn't help but noticing the perfect roundness of his bubble-butt and in my mind's eye, I could see this young man standing in front of me wearing nothing but a close-fitting Speedo. It took a great deal of concentration to follow him without crashing into shop displays. When we arrived at the beachwear section, he turned to me and saw my smiling face staring at him.

"Is something wrong, sir?"

I was suddenly jolted back to reality.

"I'm sorry, but my mind was elsewhere," I confessed, blushing.

"Well, what type of swimming costume did you have in mind, sir?"

I hesitated at first, then, looking more like an embarrassed schoolboy and knowing that I were blushing, said rather softly, "a Speedo."

"No problem, sir, we've plenty to choose from. What size do you wear and did you have any particular color in mind?"

Oh, God, how was I to know what size or what color! It was bad enough merely asking for a Speedo. What was on my mind was wondering what he would have looked like in a Speedo.

"I don't actually know what size I am because I've never bought a Speedo before."

"What size waist are you, sir?"

"About a 32 inch, I think."

"Well I'll get a couple of different sizes and we can try those on to begin with, then we can decide on the color."

I liked the idea of "we" can try them. I waited at the counter while the young man went off to find the required sizes. I watched as he walked to a rack containing a variety of Speedos. He had an air of confidence as he moved, and as he bent over at the rack to select various Speedos, I noticed how his jeans stretched taut across his beautiful butt.

He returned with four different styles of Speedos and led me to the change rooms, which were situated near the rear of the shop and consisted of two cubicles, each with a door and a mirror on the adjacent wall. He handed me the costumes and opened one of the cubicle doors for me.

"Please shout if you need any help," he said, smiling as he closed the door behind me.

I took off my shoes, unzipped my jeans and let them and my briefs fall to the floor. I took the first of the Speedos, which had very narrow sides, and stepped into them. I pulled them up and adjusted the position of my cock and balls. I looked at myself in the mirror and then turned around to admire the back view – I decided I looked good – in fact I thought I looked bloody good, not to mention sexy. I ran my hands over my smooth butt and then caressed the bulge in the front. I decided I needed my salesman's opinion, so I opened the door and saw him talking to one of the other salesmen at the counter, but managed to get his attention. I then closed the cubicle door and waited for him. There was a gentle knock on the door. I opened it and asked him to come in. He entered and closed the door behind him.

"How does that feel, sir?"

"It feels great to me, but how does it look to you?"

I stood looking into the mirror while he stood behind me. He lifted my T-shirt away from the waistband of the Speedo, so that part of my back was revealed to him.

"Looks good to me," he said. "How does it feel here?" he asked, gently letting a hand slide over my butt.

"It feels snug," I replied, quivering as he touched me.

"Turn around, sir, and let's see the front."

I did as I was told. Once I was facing him, our eyes met and his soft blue eyes hypnotized me. He knelt in front of me and, running a finger on the inside of the waistband, said, "Does this feel tight? You look a bit cramped in there."

I knew what he meant because every time he touched a part of my body, I felt my cock grow another inch and it was becoming restrained in the Speedo.

"Maybe you need to try a larger size, sir."

"OK, let's try this one," I said, picking another of the Speedos.

My salesman opened the cubicle door to leave but I quickly said, "You don't have to go, I won't be a minute."

He stayed and closed the door again. I turned my back to him, looked into the mirror and saw him staring at me. I hooked my fingers into the waistband of the Speedo I was wearing and slid it down to my ankles. As I bent over to step out of it and pick it up, I felt his crotch press up against my butt and I felt something long and hard rub against the crack between my ass cheeks. I stood up and placed the Speedo on the wall hook of the cubicle, while I smiled at his reflection in the mirror. I then took the new Speedo and bent over again to step into it. Again I felt his hardness rest against my butt while my cock had grown to its full length and stood erect against my abdomen. As I attempted to pull the Speedo up, I lost my balance. Immediately, my salesman grabbed hold of my hips to stabilize me. His grip felt strong as I steadied myself and pulled the Speedo up to try to cover my embarrassment.

"Thanks," I said, smiling into the mirror.

"It was my pleasure, sir." His eyes lit up and glowed with a sense of mischief in them. I tried to tuck my cock into the Speedo, but it wanted to pop out above the waistband.

"How does that feel, sir?"

"Awkward," I replied sheepishly, wondering if I should burst into song, "June is busting out all over!"

"Take off your T-shirt and let's see what it looks like."

I started to remove my T-shirt, but the salesman finished the job for me and let it fall to the floor.

"Turn around and let's see how this one fits you."

I turned slowly, hoping that the blood in my throbbing cock would subside, but I wasn't having much success.

When we came face-to-face, his eyes never left mine, but I felt his hand glide very gently over my swollen cock. I felt a finger run over the tip of my cock which was sticking out about an inch above the waistband, and still his eyes stayed fixed on mine. I gasped with pleasure at his touch. His finger ran over the piss-slit and collected a glob of pre-come. He raised his finger to his mouth and inserted it between his full lips. He smiled at me, groaned, and then added, "I think your Speedo's a bit too small. Either we have to get a bigger one, or get this smaller", he said, squeezing my engorged cock.

He knelt in front of me and ran his tongue over the soft material that tried to cover my throbbing cock. He then did the same using his lips. His tongue moved to the tip of my cock, which protruded from the Speedo. I closed my eyes and gave a low groan as the roughness of his tongue glided over the growing head of my dick.

I felt his fingers go into the waistband of the Speedo and slowly pull it down, releasing my swollen dick from the constraints of the tight material. As I felt the Speedo fall to my ankles, I felt the warm cavity of his mouth encompass my cock. He held his lips over the top of my cock, while his tongue encircled it. Slowly he lowered his mouth over its length until his nose was buried in my pubes and my eight-inches were embedded down his throat.

He pulled up slowly, dragging his tongue along the underside of my cock, causing a gasp to emit from deep down inside of me. I ran my fingers through his hair and then gripped onto his head, forcing his head movements to increase in speed.

After a while, I pulled my throbbing cock from the warm protection of his mouth, put my hands under his arms and lifted him up. When we became face-to-face again, I placed my mouth over his full lips and began to suck on them. I darted my tongue into his waiting mouth where our tongues began to do battle with each other. As I held my left hand behind his head, I let my right hand wander over his chest, searching for his nipples. I felt the hardened rise of his left nipple and gently squeezed it between my fingers. His kissing increased with passion as I squeezed, but soon I let my hand drift down his chest, over a firm abdomen, onto the hard length I had earlier felt rubbing against my butt. Once I felt its length, I gave it a hard squeeze and he groaned into my mouth. Without releasing our mouths, I felt for the zipper of his jeans and unzipped them and letting them fall to the floor of the cubicle. I rubbed my hand over what underwear he was wearing, but its texture didn't feel like that of material used in the manufacture of briefs or jockstraps. I released my grip on his mouth, kissed those full lips of his and looked down to see what he was wearing. When my eyes caught sight of it, my cock pulsed with excitement – he was wearing a pale blue Speedo. I immediately fell to my knees and began to give him the same pleasure that he had given me by running my mouth along his glorious length. There was a fairly large wet patch staining the front of his Speedo where he had been oozing some of his pre-come. I licked over its wetness, savoring the relatively sweet taste, and continuing to run my lips and tongue over his length. Eventually I released his prisoner from its confines where it sprang to life.

I placed my moist lips over the head of his cut dick and slowly lathered my way down to its base. As my mouth and nose neared the base of this huge, swelling manhood, I caught the luxuriating aroma of his manliness. My mouth remained at its base while I used my throat muscles to constrict around its girth.

"Oh fuck!" came a low whisper as he pushed on the back of my head as if to try to force more of his dick into my throat. Just as I thought I might gag, I began the slow journey back to the top, but no sooner had I reached his tip, when I felt his hands on the back of my head, forcing me down his shaft again, but this time he was adding his own upward thrust as well. Soon we had a rhythm going which was giving me great pleasure and I was determined that I was going to bring him off and give him the same pleasure that he was giving me.

His breathing became more intense and I placed the palm of my left hand under his nuts while my right hand kneaded his bubble-butt. I continued to work on his throbbing cock until I felt him tense and his nuts move up to the base of his cock, then Vesuvius erupted. With a deep growl, he thrust all seven inches of beautifully thick cock down my throat and fired a salvo of warm cum into my throat. I squeezed his nuts and he fired again and again into the confines of my throat, filling me with joy. I held onto him tightly so that he wouldn't leave the warm safety of my mouth as I sucked the last of his tasty love-juice from him. I then rose and placed my lips gently against his, letting his tongue wander around my mouth, tasting the remains of his own sweet juice. My hands rested on his butt and I felt my still throbbing cock rest against his now subsiding length. I pulled him closer to me as our tongues dueled with each other. I felt him pull away slightly from me and I opened my eyes, which had been closed while our mouths had fought.

"Wow! That was great. Thanks," he whispered.

"It was all my pleasure," I replied, smiling at him.

I felt his hand rest on my dick and give it a squeeze.

"What about you? Can I please you, sir?"

"You have already, thanks," I said, pulling him closer to me.

"But I really want to please you. Is there some way that I can do that?" he asked, kissing me on the lips.

I squeezed both cheeks of his beautiful butt and said, "If you really want to please me more, I'd love to fill that beautiful butt of yours."

He smiled again, bent down and fumbled in the pockets of his jeans, then rose to face me holding a condom wrapped in foil. He tore open the wrapping without taking his eyes from mine and removed the condom. Holding it between two fingers, he trailed it across my bare chest, down to my cock and proceeded to unroll it over the length of my cock. He then stood facing me again. He inserted two of his fingers into my mouth and when I had salivated over them, he removed them and inserted them into his fine ass, lubricating it for me. He then turned his back on me, held the base of my cock-shaft and, spreading his butt-cheeks, slowly pushed back onto my shaft. I felt a little tension as my cock-head touched his asshole, but he continued to push back. I felt his sphincter relax and suck my cock into his depths. The tightness squeezed around my swollen cock and I felt his warmth. Once he had become accustomed to my being in him, I began a slow rhythmic pelvic thrust in and out of his beautiful butt. I slid my hands around his waist and felt his hardening cock. I began to pump him with one hand, the other rubbed over his left nipple, teasing it to hardness. After some time I could feel myself getting close to the edge.

"I'm getting close", I breathed in his ear as I thrust forward.

"So am I", he gasped, meeting my thrust.

"Aaargh! Oh, fuck!" I groaned as the first of a number of shots fired from my cock, filling and expanding the condom. I felt a sudden tightening around my shaft as his muscles clamped my cock in his bubble-butt and he sprayed a shot over his Speedo lying on the floor. He tilted his head back and our lips met once more. As we kissed, so we both continued to explode, sending forth our warm juices. When I had fired my last load, I leant across his back and kissed the back of his neck.

"Thanks buddy. That ass of yours is really great", I said, slowly pulling my still swollen dick from its protected warmth and removing the condom. He turned around, bent down to my cock, and, taking it into his mouth, milked it dry and cleaned it of any cum, then he rose and gave me a brief kiss on the lips, allowing me to taste my own love juice.

I pulled my clothes back on and he pulled up his Speedo, which was wet with his cum. I ran my hand over his wet bulge and gave it a last squeeze before it disappeared under his jeans. We stepped from the cubicle, and holding the Speedo that I had been wearing when our fun had started, I said, "I think I'll take this size, but in pale blue like yours, if you have one."

"Certainly, sir. That is a very good choice. Would there be anything else?"

"I don't think so – for the time being."

"Well, should you need anything else, or if you wish to exchange this item for something else, please don't hesitate to see me."

"Thanks," I smiled, thinking how soon it would be before I made my way back to the store to change my Speedo for a size bigger.

"You never know, I might see you tomorrow", I said, squeezing his hand warmly as I shook hands with him, and with the other hand I clutched my new cock-hugging Speedo and left the shop, glowing.

The following day I was back to buy another Speedo – also in pale blue, and whenever I pull one of my many Speedos on to go for a swim, I feel my dick become harder as I think of my salesman.

OAKRIDGE

A gentle breeze rustled the leaves of the lone oak tree as I stood under its foliage, at the foot of the freshly covered grave - the mound of freshly dug soil holding a roughly hewn wooden cross in its grasp. Alongside me, lost in thought, stood Joe.

....

Oakridge Ranch was a small oasis amidst a barren country littered with rocks and sparse shrubbery. Although there was a stream that ran through the ranch area, there were a few bushes around the main buildings, but no trees, other than a lone oak tree, which stood atop the ridge and which in winter resembled a skeleton, having lost all its leaves. I had inherited the ranch from my parents, when they had died some five years earlier in a motor accident, and had continued rearing horses for stud and rodeo purposes. The staff that had worked for my parents remained loyal to me after their deaths and had continued to support me in my efforts to maintain the running of the farm. In fact, we became like one big happy family.

I remember well the day that Joe and Billy arrived on the ranch. I was seated in my office den going over some documents when one of my stable hands came in to tell me that two men had arrived on foot at the ranch. At the time I thought it odd that someone should be walking and not be on horseback, particularly as we were so far out in the country, away from any towns.

"Do they look like trouble?" I enquired.

"I'm not sure, but the one guy is enormous," came the reply.

I suggested that they be brought in to meet me, and that the stable hand hang around in case there was any trouble brewing. When the men entered my office, I was more than surprised to see that the description 'enormous' was in fact a mild understatement.

The man, who I eventually found out, was Billy, was a giant of a man. He was over six foot tall, aged about early to mid forties with short cropped hair, just graying at the temples; biceps as thick as an average man's thigh, a broad chest and long legs, resembling tree trunks, that were tightly encased in his faded Wrangler jeans. His chiseled face was rugged and stern, yet I perceived what might be the signs of a caring person under this facade. His partner, Joe, was at least twenty years his junior. He was a young, good-looking man with a well-defined body and piercing blue eyes. Although he was incomparable in size to Billy, Joe was no slouch. I could see the athleticism in his physique and wondered whether he'd ever been a budding rodeo rider. Billy, on the other hand, would have made a name for himself in the arena, riding bareback, his strong, long legs clasped tightly onto the sides of the horse, his ass pounding heavily on the horse's back as he fought to remain seated.

I invited them to sit.

"How can I help you guys?" I asked.

Billy spread his legs out wide as he stretched his body in the chair and I noticed how tight his jeans squeezed his legs and crotch. The denim material resembled a second skin, and down the left upper thigh I noticed a thick, elongated mound, suggesting a full package hidden under his Wranglers.

"We were wondering if you had some work for us. We've been traveling for some time and we wanted to take a rest."

I looked into the deep blue eyes of Joe and wondered why a young man like him would be traveling with a much older guy; but that was actually none of my business. My attention then reverted to Billy, who had let a hand drift nonchalantly onto his crotch, as though to scratch an itch. I noticed how his hand rested on the elongated mound and every now and again, I was sure that he applied some pressure on the mound with his fist, and I was equally sure that the mound was beginning to grow in size. If it wasn't, I knew that my own crotch was doing just that. As I glanced from one man to the other, I felt the growing resurgence of an erection I had felt earlier in the morning when I had awoken. Both men were undoubtedly attractive but in different ways; Billy for his ruggedness and Joe for his innocence.

I rose from behind my desk and went around to the front of it and sat on the top of the desk facing the two men. I knew that both could determine my arousal from the tented front of my jeans, but I chose not to hide it. As I sat there facing them, I noticed how Joe followed Billy's earlier repose and stretched his legs out, revealing his tight crotch. I felt a throbbing in my jeans.

"I might be able to offer you some work," I replied staring at both in turn and smiling at each. "Have either of you ever been involved in rodeos?"

Billy stretched his legs, tightening his thigh muscles as he did so.

"We both have," replied Billy. "I was a bronco-rider and Joe here was my student. I was teaching him the skills involved."

"That's good to hear," I answered. "I can see from your legs you must have been a good rider with the ability to grip onto the horse for some time, hey!"

Billy smiled wryly and pressed down on his swollen crotch as he acknowledged my compliment. In the meantime, my cock was hard and fighting to free itself from the confines of my jeans.

"What about you Joe? Are you keen on becoming a bronco-rider like Billy?"

"Sure I'd like to be like Billy, but I don't have the muscles that he has to grip onto the horse."

"What he lacks in grip in his legs, he sure makes up for in other ways," suggested Billy, cutting in on Joe's conversation.

I wondered what the 'other ways' might be to which Billy was referring, but I chose not to broach the subject. Instead, I thought it better to cut short the 'interview' before I did my cock any harm.

"I think you guys will be very happy staying here," I said, sliding from the top of the desk and resting my ass against the edge of the tabletop. By now my erection was clearly outlined in my jeans for both men to see. I too let a hand drift onto my engorged mound and as I did so, both men reciprocated by doing likewise to themselves; it was almost like a mutual signal.

We discussed a few other details such as salaries and living conditions and then I led them to the office door.

"I'll take you guys along to one of the cabins where you can drop your kit and move in, and then I'll get one of the hands to show you around the ranch."

Both men rose from where they were sitting and I saw how Billy towered over both Joe and me. He moved slightly closer to me and I saw how his own hard-on extended down along his thigh. He stretched out a hand to shake mine and as I grasped it, I felt the strength and firmness in his hand. His smile was endearing and I felt a slight increase in the squeeze of his hand. Joe followed suit and although his hands were smaller than Billy's, he too had a strength of firmness. I led them out of the building and headed towards an empty cabin, which would become their home. Along the way I encountered Pete, whom I regarded as my best work-hand.

"Pete, this is Billy and Joe. They're starting today and I want you to show them around, please."

Pete stared at the giant of a man and his young companion then followed us into the cabin.

"Guys, this is your home from now on. Make yourselves comfortable and should you need anything, don't hesitate to ask."

"Thanks, sir," answered Joe.

"The name's Clint," I said, trying to make him feel more at ease. "Well I'll leave you guys to settle in and you can tell Pete when you're ready to have a look around the ranch."

I made my way back to the main house and my office, allowing my erection to slowly diminish.

....

During the time that Billy and Joe stayed on the ranch, we attended many rodeos with all three of us taking part, but I could see that Billy was by far the better rider of the two of them. It seemed as though when he rode his bronco, he was glued to the horse's back; his strong, firm legs tightly gripping the horse's flanks. Soon I found myself being drawn closer to the two drifters. They were friendly, hard-working, good riders and they seemed to enjoy their time at the ranch.

One evening at around 10.30pm, I was making my way from the main house to one of the stables, when I noticed the bedroom light on in the new guys' cabin. As I ventured closer, I saw through the window, the naked top half of Billy's muscular body. I stealthily moved towards the light. My being in the dark made it difficult for those inside to see me. As I neared the window I saw Joe on his knees unzipping Billy's Wranglers. He slid a hand into the opening and scooped out two hefty pendulous balls, accompanied by an enormously flaccid hooded cock. I crouched, amazed at the length of Billy's manhood, and watched as Joe drew it into his mouth, sliding its full length down his throat. While Joe slid his mouth along the slowly hardening length, I noticed how Billy's foreskin slid back to reveal a glowing pink head. After a few minutes, Billy withdrew his cock from Joe's mouth and I was able to admire it's full length and thickness. There was undoubtedly no one on the ranch who could match Billy's cock in either length or girth: this was a literal bargepole.

Billy began rubbing his nipples while Joe went back to salivating along Billy's cock, allowing it too glisten in the light. Billy's nipples were large and protruded a good half an inch. I watched with fascination as he pinched the tips of his nipples, creating a feeling of lust which caused him to thrust deeply into Joe's accommodating mouth.

Joe unhitched the top button to Billy's jeans and let them drop to the ground. Billy's upper thighs were magnificently well-developed – the type to crush anything that got between them. I was becoming aroused.

My hand went down to my crotch and I unzipped my jeans, pulling my hardened cock from its cover. I slowly began stroking it, allowing my fingers to glide over my cut cock-head and then squeezing my stem. As I worked on myself, I saw Billy lift Joe to his feet and the young man place his mouth over one of Billy's nipples.

"Eat it!" I heard Billy say, as Joe began to chew on the protruding flesh.

Billy writhed in pleasure, thrusting his buffed pecs into Joe's face. The young man lathered, chewed and nibbled at the flesh while Billy's arms surrounded him, crushing him closer to the older man.

"Suck me!" growled the older man, pushing Joe back to his knees and puffing out his mighty chest.

By this time, Billy's large cock was fully erect, almost rubbing up against his flat stomach and I could clearly see that this must be a good nine or ten inches long. I increased my action on my own cock, bringing myself closer to pleasure. Suddenly I felt a warm mouth enwrap itself around the tip of my cock. I almost shouted out with fright. I glanced down and caught Pete smiling up at me as best he could do with a fair-sized cock embedded down his throat. I gave a gentle thrust and began face-fucking him, but watching every move that Joe and Billy made. I wanted to shoot my load at pretty much the same time that Billy sent his flying. I timed my thrusts with Billy's, but watched intently as he twisted and pinched his robust nipples, wishing that he was doing that to me. I tried to slow Pete down because I could feel myself getting closer to the edge. I suddenly heard a loud gasp emanate from the bedroom and watched as Billy fired shot after shot of ropey white cum across Joe's young face. As he fired, so I let rip into Pete's warm mouth, feeling my hot cum shoot to the back of his throat. He never released his grip on my length and sucked and licked until I was completely dry of my load.

My slowly subsiding cock slipped from Pete's mouth as I watched Billy lift Joe to his feet, run a finger across the young man's face to scoop up his seed and place it seductively into his mouth. He then repeated his action, but this time inserted his cum-soaked finger into Joe's mouth. The young man sucked on the finger, glowing as he did so.

I zipped up my jeans, helped Pete to his feet and the two of us disappeared into the darkness, but not before I had made up my mind that I had to have Billy.

During the following weeks, I noticed a strong bond between Joe and Billy and I often spent a dark evening outside of their bedroom window watching as the two men gave each other pleasure, and every time that I watched, it puzzled me that they always chose to leave the bedroom light on.

One evening, as I wandered around the ranch, I noticed Billy sitting alone on the steps leading up to his cabin.

"Where's Joe?" I enquired as I neared the steps.

"I don't know. He just said that he was going for a ride on the new horse that you got."

"Has he been gone long?"

"Probably for half an hour. Would you like to come in and have a drink, Clint?"

"Thanks Billy that would be great."

I made my way into their cabin, which they'd made very comfortable for themselves, and sat down on the double seater couch they had.

"Beer do?" asked Billy.

"That's great, thanks."

Soon both Billy and I were sitting together on the couch, deep in conversation.

"Do you have anyone in your life?" asked Billy, taking a deep slurp from his beer.

The question took me quite by surprise, but I replied that I didn't.

"Pity because you seem a really decent sort of guy, the kind who'd make a good partner."

"What about you, Billy?" I asked, hesitantly, not being sure what he might think.

"I'm a drifter. I can't stay in one place too long so it would be unfair for the woman."

I wondered if he really meant this or whether this was a cover-up, after all I'd seen how he reacted with Joe.

"What about Joe?" I ventured.

"Do you mean does he have someone?" asked Billy.

I actually didn't know what I'd meant when I had asked.

"I just wondered what was with you two wandering around the country together."

"You mean him and me being a team?" asked Billy.

"Well, I suppose if you put it that way, yes."

"I met him at a rodeo. I had been riding and we had asked for a volunteer from the audience to try his hand at riding and Joe came forward. We put him on a horse and let them loose. Well poor Joe lasted probably five seconds if he was lucky and then went flying through the air to land rather hard on the dirt. He just lay there, having been winded from the fall, so I ran over to where he was and picked him up in my arms and carried him to my trailer. He hadn't broken anything, fortunately, but he seemed a little dazed by his adventure. And you know, one thing led to another and soon we were friends."

I was silent for a moment and then I smiled.

"That's a great story," I commented. "And was he happy with the treatment you gave him?" I asked with a glint in my eye and a throb in my crotch, thinking of them together in the trailer.

"You bet!" laughed Billy. "That's why we're still together."

I felt myself becoming a little embarrassed because I could feel myself getting harder the more we spoke of their relationship.

"But you know about our relationship," smiled Billy.

"What do you mean?"

Billy put down his beer and rose from the couch.

"Come to the room for a moment."

I rose and followed the big burly man. As we left the lounge area, he switched off the lounge light and as we entered the bedroom, he switched on that light.

"Come here," ordered Billy, who stood casually next to the window.

I moved towards him and as soon as I was alongside, I felt his powerful grip on my biceps as he pulled me closer to him. His mouth found mine and soon his tongue was searching the confines of my mouth. I tried to pull away, but he held firm.

"I know that you've wanted this for a long time, so don't fight it."

I certainly wasn't about to fight it, but I did think of Joe. What would he think if he walked in and saw us together?

I could feel his muscular chest crushed tightly up against mine and his hardening cock pressed against my thigh. My hands instinctively slid down to his waiting meat. I slid my hand along its length, which seemed to be never-ending. I squeezed it and felt its hardness; then I found the magic zipper which would allow me access to this wondrous object. My fingers fumbled to get the zip down, but eventually, I managed. All the while, his mouth and tongue worked wonders with mine.

I inserted my hand into the warm confines of his jeans. No underwear to fight with, only warm, hard skin. My fingers wrapped around his girth and I pulled the bargepole free through the opening of his Wranglers. I broke away from his kisses in order to view this work of art. If I gripped my hand at the base of his cock, I could have placed another hand above it and still there would have been cock protruding from my hands. I immediately sank to my knees as in worship, taking his length into my warm mouth in one gulp. I forced his foreskin to roll back and as I did this the funky taste of sweat and piss entered my mouth. I slurped and licked until he was well lubricated, then I moved to his balls. They were large and firm, like two oranges, full of juice, just waiting to be sucked dry.

I felt his large hands under my arms as he lifted me to my feet and pushed me onto his bed. My jeans were ripped from me quicker than I had taken to put them on in the morning and I lay on my back, naked in front of this giant of a man. I looked up into his chiseled face as I spread my legs and allowed him access to my pucker.

The sharp tip of his tongue teased my entrance, flicking my hole. I lifted my legs higher and closer to my shoulders, allowing Billy better access to my hole. I desperately wanted this man. His tongue moved like that of a snake, flicking in and out, wetting my hole, and then licking my balls. My cock was leaking pre-cum and I wanted him to sink deep into me.

"Aaargh! Fuck me Billy!" I groaned, as I felt the warmth of his mouth encompass my cock. His tongue licked off the pre-cum, and then licked my shaft until his mouth reached the base of my stem. The more I groaned, the more he taunted me with his mouth and tongue, moving from cock to balls and then to asshole. He was getting me so worked up, that I was beginning to shudder. I wanted to come but I didn't know how I wanted it – whether for him to fuck me or suck me or just carry on teasing me with his mouth.

The warmth of the mouth; the sharpness of the tongue and the constant working on my pucker suddenly stopped. I froze in anticipation of what might be about to happen. I looked up at Billy and saw him smiling. He snapped a condom onto his cock, which only covered three-quarters of his length, then he held the firm stem and slowly guided it towards my waiting, pulsing entrance. I felt his cockhead touch my entrance and immediately it clamped shut. Billy placed two fingers in his mouth, lubricated them and then slowly inserted them into me. I took them with ease and felt as he maneuvered them inside of me, stretching my ass to allow for his impending entry. As his finger slipped from me and before my ass muscles could contract, the fat tip of his cock pushed into my opening. Although I fought the pain, I wanted him inside of me. He pushed forward slowly while I groaned in agony, feeling his every inch slide further into the warm confines of my body. The pain was excruciating, but I was not about to disallow him entry. Eventually, I felt him break through my sphincter and delve into my depths. I gave a long, low growl as I felt his size stretching me, but fuck it felt good. My hands automatically clasped onto his firm ass and I pulled him closer so that he sank deeper into me. At last I could feel his pelvis and balls slap against me and I knew that he was mine. Once I had become accustomed to his enormity, I began pushing to meet each of his thrusts. His action increased in speed and he pounded my ass, grunting and groaning as he did so and then he almost pulled right out of me, but I clamped my ass muscles to prevent his early departure, but he had no intention of doing that. Instead, with his cock once more deeply embedded in me, he bent over and took my cock in his mouth and began a double action of fucking and sucking me at the same time. To be given absolute pleasure like this was causing my body to reverberate. His cock was stretching my ass while his mouth remained tightly encompassing my throbbing cock.

After bringing me to heights of pleasure, the kind of which I had never before experienced, Billy released his grasp on my cock, looked me in the eyes and said, "Do you want to ride this bronco?"

Before I could reply, but obviously based on my facial expression, Billy placed his arms under my shoulders, lifted me from the bed but remained embedded in me and told me to wrap my legs around his waist. I did as I was told. Once we were standing, I wrapped my arms around his neck while his hands were placed on each of my ass cheeks for support. As he turned to sit himself on the edge of the bed, I felt as a finger on each hand slid into my hole alongside his bargepole, creating an even tighter fit. He then placed his broad shoulders on the edge of the bed and lay back. I was now sitting on his pelvis with his cock still impaling me. With his shoulders on the edge of the bed for support and his feet firmly placed on the floor, he said, "Now you're in for the ride of your life."

I wrapped my legs around his waist again and grabbed onto both sets of nipples.

Suddenly Billy began to buck like a wild bronco. With each upward thrust of his pelvis, I felt him penetrating me deeper, and with each of these thrusts, I was rocked and bounced on his bargepole. The more I was pummeled, the more I gripped onto his nipples, squeezing and pinching them, exactly as I had seen Joe do.

"Oh Fuuuck!" cried Billy. "That feels sooo good! Ride my dick, kid. This is good!"

Calling me kid made me think that he might be thinking of Joe, but the pleasure that I was getting from him wasn't going to make me worry what he called me.

"Fuck me! Fuck this ass! Harder!!! Buck this ass!! It's waiting for your hot cum. Aargh!!" I cried out as I sweated and ground my ass onto his long, thick cock.

His enormity was creating havoc with my prostate and I knew that because of his size, he would bring me to a climax very soon. I warned Billy, but he seemed to be in a trance. His actions continued without any interruption until I felt a sudden surge of thrusts and realized that he too was nearing his climax.

"Aaaargh! Fuuuck!" I growled, pinching onto Billy's nipples and squeezing.

We both fired together; me getting my first load across his face, but as he gasped when he fired his first shots, he gripped my nipples and pinched. The sudden pain sent shock waves of pleasure through my body and I wanted this to continue.

My cum was splaying across the both of us while he pounded my ass.

Neither of us wanted to stop our action, but once I was spent, I almost collapsed across his heaving chest.

Billy's breathing was heavy and his massive chest expanded and contracted rapidly as he tried to regain his breath. We lay across each other, my warm cum mixing with his thin layer of chest hair as our bodies returned to a restful state.

"Thanks buddy, that was fucking awesome," said Billy, whispering the words into my ear.

"No, you were the fucking awesome guy," I replied. "No wonder Joe stays attached to you. You're one helluva fuck!"

As we lay in each other's arms, regaining our breath, Joe walked into the bedroom. I looked up and saw him. My immediate reaction was to break free from Billy, but with his strong arms encircling me, it was difficult. He looked up and smiled at Joe, who returned the smile.

"That was some awesome performance, Clint," said Joe, sitting on the bed next to Billy and me.

"Were you watching?" I asked, embarrassedly.

"Just like you," he replied.

"What?"

"The same as you do when Billy and I hit it off. We know that you watch from the window and that's why we always leave the light on, especially for you. But don't move. I can't resist this opportunity."

I wasn't sure what Joe meant, but before either Billy or I could break free, Joe had stripped, stroked his cock to get it hard, although it appeared pretty hard already, slipped a condom over his hardened cock, grabbed some lube and aimed for my hole. I felt him nudge the entrance and I panicked.

Joe was going to try to enter me while Billy's bargepole was still embedded in me. I had never experienced a double fuck before and so it was understandably frightening, but I had nothing to fear; I trusted them.

Joe was gentle and exerted just enough pressure to slide his cock head into me a little way. There was some resistance, but with all Billy's pounding, I had been loosened up and soon Joe was comfortably inside of me, sliding his length against Billy's.

"You want to ride a bucking bronco, now's your chance to ride two at once," said Joe, pushing me slightly forward to allow him deeper penetration.

I had thought that Billy's work on me had been wondrous, but having both of these beautiful men inside of me was beyond thought. Not only did I enjoy the tightness of two men inside me at the same time, but I knew that Billy and Joe were getting it on with their cocks rubbing against each others while deeply trapped inside of me. It didn't take long for both Billy and I to get as hard as before and all three of us were soon enjoying the pleasure that the others were giving.

Outside the window, a gentle rustle of bushes was heard, but we never bothered to stop; we were now in our trance-like state of bliss.

As both men filled me with their hot cum, and I sprayed my warm love juices over Billy again, I hoped that Pete, outside in the bushes, had enjoyed his voyeurism as much as I had enjoyed both Billy and Joe.

On completion, Joe slipped gently from my confines and I slid from Billy. All three of us lay on the bed, allowing ourselves the comfort of returning our bodies to a normal breathing pattern. Gentle kisses were shared among us and as I lay there I thought how strange it might seem to others to see three cowboys being passionate together in bed.

Many a night after that, the three of us would get together in Billy and Joe's cabin for a session of passion, and undoubtedly, Pete would be in the bushes peering through the open window at us. There was never any jealousy between us nor was there any feeling of possessiveness. In fact we developed a good relationship which bonded us for another three years, until the day that our world was shattered. Billy was killed in a riding accident.

We had spent the day at a rodeo which was being held near the ranch and at which both Joe and Billy had decided to take part. I had been most impressed with Joe's advancement as a bronco-rider and he made both Billy and me very proud of his achievements. When it was Billy's turn, for some reason he lost his usual firm grip on the horse and he had been thrown from it striking his head on one of the poles surrounding the arena and breaking his neck. There was a gasp from the crowd as the blood from a gash on his head oozed into the golden sand and he lay in the arena he had enjoyed so much, his life ebbing away. Joe and I tried to comfort him, but we knew that we had lost a friend.

....

As Joe stood beside me under the large, single oak tree on the ridge, I stretched out my hand to clasp his. We stood staring at Billy's grave, our hands linking us to each other as we came to terms with our loss, and down each face ran a single tear.

DESIGNING MEN

I had spent many nights watching TV programs relating to style and interior design, drooling at the sight of someone else's home and wishing I too could enjoy such luxurious interiors, but never had the finances nor the time to do anything about it. That was until I inherited a substantial sum of money and decided there and then to spend some of it on upgrading my home.

Step one: find someone to design the interior.

I ran my fingers through the Yellow Pages in search of an interior designer. Names followed names and none seemed to jump out at me, although I didn't know what a name was going to do because that on its own meant nothing. In desperation, I phoned a friend who I thought might know something or someone related to interiors.

"Brian, I need an interior designer."

"Don't we all," came the reply.

"This is serious. Do you know any designers who aren't going to rip me off but do a good job?"

"I do actually. Have you got a pen and paper handy?"

"Yep, give it to me."

"The guy's name is Chad and his number is 567 265890. He's very good and has the added bonus of also being able to do some building as well."

I thanked Brian, replaced the phone and then dialed Chad's number. The phone rang and rang, until the answering machine kicked in.

"Hi, my name's Brad and I got your number from a friend of mine. I want to do some changes to my place and wondered if you'd be interested in meeting me to discuss them. My number is 824 542790. Thanks. Have a nice day." And I put down the phone. There was nothing more for me to do than wait for a call back.

An hour later my phone rang and a deep, well-articulated voice was on the other end of the line.

"Is that Brad?" enquired the voice.

"Speaking."

"Hi, there. It's Chad here. You left a message on my machine."

"Oh yes, Hi. I was wondering if you'd be interested in doing some alterations to my place. I've drawn up a few ideas but I'm no interior designer or builder."

"Whereabouts are you living?" asked Chad.

I gave him my address and explained that I was in no urgent hurry. After all I hadn't had the money before so another six month wait would be no harm to me.

"May I call round tomorrow after noon? Say 3.30pm?"

"That sounds great," I replied. "See you tomorrow, then."

I replaced the phone and thought to myself, "He sounds quite nice. Don't know what he'd look like, but we'll know tomorrow."

The following day, at precisely 3.30, the front doorbell rang and there standing outside was a six-foot, dark-haired man, with a T-shirt and denim jeans. He smiled and immediately I was hooked by his smile.

"Hi, I'm Chad, are you Brad?"

"Yes, please come in."

As we shook hands, I felt the firm grip on my hand and saw his bicep bulge as he held tightly onto my hand. He wasn't what I had imagined an interior designer to look like, but then I don't want to sound stereotypical. To me he looked more like an average All American boy from next door.

"Can I offer you something to drink?" I asked, leading him into the lounge area.

"Thanks. Anything cold, please," he replied, sitting on my two-seater couch.

I bustled off to the kitchen to get us both something to drink and soon returned with two beers.

"Is a beer fine with you?"

"That's great, thanks."

I sat down next to him on the couch and 'clinked' my bottle to his.

"Here's to us working together," I said.

He smiled his beautiful smile once more and took a swig of beer.

"Right, show what you have in mind."

I took a couple of drawings from a folder on the coffee table in front of us and spread them out before Chad. My plans were simple: I wanted an en-suite bathroom in the main bedroom and I wanted both the kitchen and lounge extended, where possible.

"I thought you wanted interior designing done for you?" questioned Chad. "This looks more like full-scale building operations."

"I'm sorry, but I thought you might be able to do some building for me as well as the designing."

I didn't want to lose this hunky, good-looking young man.

"I can do some building construction, but I'm going to have to get someone to help me with that."

"Not a problem," I answered, excitedly, knowing that he would be able to do the job for me.

Chad scrutinized my drawings and said that he thought it wouldn't be a problem for him to do, but it wouldn't be done quickly.

"I'm in no rush, Chad. All I would like is to get it done. Would you be willing to take on the job?"

"I don't see why not. Can we have a look around so I can get some idea of where alterations need to be made?"

We got up, leaving our beers on the coffee table and I took him on a tour of my home. I led the way, but whenever I had the chance, I found myself admiring his taut physique and the tight ass that was encased in his jeans.

The kitchen, he felt, wouldn't be a problem as there was plenty of outdoor space which could be utilized to extend a wall or two and the en-suite bathroom also seemed to be very little problem. When we returned to our beers in the lounge, Chad made some suggestions about rearranging the lounge, which I liked.

"So we don't need to extend the lounge?" I enquired.

"I think with a few changes in your décor and a mirror here and there, we can create the feeling of space, but I'd like to bring a friend around to confirm my suggestions about the building alterations, if that's OK with you."

"No problem. Would tomorrow suit you?"

"I'm sure it'll be fine for both of us, say in the morning."

We went back to downing our beers and chatting generally.

"Do you live alone?" asked Chad.

I wasn't sure what his motive was for asking a question like that, but I told him that I was alone. I did, however, notice a smile develop once he heard my answer.

As I sat drinking my beer, I cast my eyes down his long legs which were snuggly fitted into his tight jeans, then slowly lifted my eyes until they reached a decidedly firm bulge in the crotch. I looked up and saw that Chad was watching me and obviously knew where I had been looking. Once again he smiled and adjusted the way he was sitting, so that his legs stretched out in front of him, emphasizing the bulge area. I could feel myself becoming slightly hot and took another swig of beer, emptying my bottle.

"Would you like another?" I asked getting up and allowing him to see that I had become aroused by his presence.

He looked at me, smiled and shook his head.

"Unfortunately, I have another appointment, so I'll take a rain check on that."

I knew that I showed disappointment on my face, but as he rose to leave, I noticed how his hand slid across his swollen crotch, as though to try to adjust the lie of his cock.

"I'll see you tomorrow, then," he said as he departed, again giving my hand a firm squeeze.

I was saddened by his departure, but at the same time, excited with the knowledge that I would see him again the following day.

True to his word, Chad arrived the following morning, with his friend.

"Hi Brad, this is Mike. He's a builder-cum-plumber and I've asked him to come and have a look at our possible plans."

Mike was slightly more muscular than Chad probably as a result of his construction work, but was equally good-looking. The two young men seemed to complement each other in their looks and physiques.

I followed them around admiring both physiques and wondering if perhaps I might strike it lucky with one of them.

After a quick inspection of what was planned, both Chad and Mike left, leaving me with a feeling of emptiness, but that feeling soon vanished an hour later when Chad phoned.

"Hi Brad. I just phoned to tell you that Mike is willing to help me and so, if it's fine with you, we'd like to start next week."

Hearing this excited me and I was only too pleased to have them start work on the alterations.

"Great! Will you guys be here on Monday?"

"First thing in the morning," answered Chad. "We're going to start with the kitchen and then move on to the en-suite bathroom, so if you'd like to start clearing out cupboards in the kitchen, I'd appreciate that."

"Consider it done," I replied.

On Monday morning, both young men arrived in separate vehicles but simultaneously. Mike had on a pair of overalls which had buttons down the front to crotch level while Chad had worn a pair of denim shorts and T-shirt. The shorts were worn either to taunt me or to show off his long, muscular legs; either way, I was impressed. I made coffee for the three of us and after finishing their drinks, they set to work. I did offer to help, should they need me, but found myself unable to focus on any task that was given to me.

"I think perhaps you keep us in coffee and we'll do the work," said Chad noticing how much time I spent eyeing them and admiring their sweaty bodies.

As the morning progressed, I found myself out in the garden, away from the dust and dirt that was being created by the smashing down of walls. I had decided to slip into my Speedo and spend some time lying next to the pool wh8ile the guys got busy in the house. Every now and then, I would look up to see Chad watching me as I lay tanning on the grass.

Because of the intense heat, I plunged into the pool, swam a couple of lengths and then got out to dry in the sun. My Speedo clung to my body, revealing clearly my outlined cock, and the moment I turned towards the house, I noticed how Chad was staring at my form and smiling. As we stood watching each other, I felt the start of an erection inside the Lycra material that covered me. I chose not to hide it, but let my cock take on a life of its own, until it had swollen sufficiently to break free of the top of the waistband to my Speedo. I looked down and noticed the tip of my cock protruding from the material, but chose not to try and cover it. Instead, I lay down on my back on the towel and closed my eyes, hoping that by not seeing Chad, my erection might subside.

"Would you like something to drink? You look very hot out here." said a voice, suddenly making me open my eyes.

Chad stood above me, shielding my face from the sun, looking down at my prone body. My cock had still not subsided so I was aware that he could see my predicament.

"Thanks, Chad. That's very sweet of you."

He never moved, but remained looking down at me. My hand went to my Speedo and for the first time, I tried to cover my protruding cock.

"Don't," he whispered. "It looks good!"

I dropped my hand to my side and lay looking up at him. I was aware that there was a distinct growth in the crotch area of his shorts, so I would say we were getting on equal terms.

"Is Mike still busy?" I enquired.

"Yes. He's also in the kitchen."

I knew that there was nothing we could do with Mike hanging around, so I pushed the idea of Chad and I rolling around together on the grass out of my head. After a moment, Chad turned and headed back into the kitchen, only to return with a cold beer.

"I thought you might like this," he said, handing me the bottle.

"What about you?"

"I'll have one later."

Chad then headed back to work and I never saw him until I felt hungry and went to see what I could get for us to eat for lunch. On entering the kitchen in my Speedo, I could see the mess of rubble scattered around. I also noticed how, for the first time, Mike looked at me in my Speedo; a long lingering look.

"You know it's rude of me not to offer, but would you guys like to have a swim. It's incredibly hot, so if you'd like to have one, please, be my guest."

"If I'd known, I'd have brought my costume," said Mike, having unbuttoned his overalls to just above his navel.

"I can lend you one if it'll fit you."

"Don't bother Brad; he can swim in the nude. He often does that," replied Chad.

My heart skipped a beat at the thought of Mike swimming in the nude.

"Same for you, Chad. If you want a costume I'm sure we can arrange something."

Chad merely smiled, pulled off his T-shirt to reveal a buffed chest and tight abs, pulled down his shorts and the jockstrap that he was wearing, and raced to the pool, diving in as he reached it.

"Oh well, Mike. If you want to do the same, go for it."

Mike unbuttoned the remaining buttons so that his overalls dropped to the floor, revealing a naked, muscular, trim body. His flaccid cock bounced as he ran to the pool and as he dived in I noticed how his heavy cock hung in the air; he looked like a shark accompanied by a pilot fish. Both men splashed and laughed in the cool water.

"Come on in," shouted Chad to me in the kitchen.

I couldn't resist the invitation, so I hurried back to the pool to join them, but just as I was about to dive in, Chad shouted, "Take it off!"

I froze.

"What?"

"If we're naked so must you be."

I pulled down my Speedo and both men could see the semi-erect, hefty, engorged cock, bobbing in the air as I dived in. We splashed around and a couple of times Chad dived under the water and I felt him graze my legs, causing me to become even more aroused. At one stage as we stood at the side of the pool in the water, and as I glanced down into the water I could clearly see that he too had a hard-on, but I was afraid to touch him, in case Mike noticed. Eventually, when my erection had diminished somewhat, I climbed out of the water in order to get towels for them. When I returned to the pool with the towel, both men had emerged from the water and were standing in the sun drying.

"Here you go guys," I said, handing each a towel.

They toweled themselves dry and continued to stand in the sun, but without the towels draped around them. This gave me ample access to admire their beauty. Both were well-endowed and both had obviously spent a considerable time at the gym, working on their torsos, but I was also aware that I mustn't stare at them like at had done on the first meeting.

The guys slipped back into their clothes, except Chad kept his T-shirt off and Mike's overalls remained buttoned to just on the navel, allowing me a wonderful view of them. When they had completed their day's work, both thanked me for the lunch and the swim and left.

The following day, both arrived at work again and completed the new kitchen wall. Chad then said he would get started on the en-suite bathroom. This wasn't going to be a difficult task as there was a bathroom just outside of my bedroom. All that was needed was to break through the wall and incorporate it into the bedroom area.

I busied myself covering furnishings in my bedroom while Chad began bashing down the dividing wall between bathroom and bedroom. When I had the chance, I watched as his arms pounded at the wall with a hammer. I could see his biceps bulging with every stroke as his back muscles tensed. I could feel myself being aroused by the sight of his muscular body straining with each blow. He was demolishing the wall from the bedroom side, so I got a back view of him regularly. His ass muscles tightened with each blow and his legs strained to take the force that was being exerted every time the hammer hit the wall.

I ran a hand over my burgeoning crotch and felt my hard cock straining to break free from my running shorts. The sweat was beginning to trickle down Chad's back and I was tempted to go and lick it off. I lay back on my bed, watching, my hand resting on my hard-on, squeezing it gently. Chad stopped for moment to rest and turned towards me, seeing my hand stroking my hard-on.

"That looks great," he whispered.

I never said a word, but continued my stroking over my shorts.

He walked towards me and stood at the foot of the bed, where he grabbed his crotch. I could see the outline of his large cock clutched in his fist.

"Is this what you want?" he asked.

I licked my lips as if to say 'yes!'

He lowered the hammer he was carrying and knelt on the bed between my spread legs, and then he lowered his mouth to my engorged cock. His tongue ran the length of my cock, wetting the silky material of my running shorts. I closed my eyes and lay back to enjoy the pleasure he was giving me. I felt him slide the waistband of my shorts down, releasing my swollen cock. I opened my eyes and watched as his mouth sank down my shaft, allowing his tongue to run along the underside of my shaft as he did so. A soft moan emanated from me, as I felt the tip of my cock touch the back of his throat. He stopped and held his position without gagging, and then he slowly moved up my length until he reached the tip and licked the pre-cum from my leaking piss-slit.

My shorts were shucked to my ankles and then pulled free. He placed his arms under my thighs and lifted my legs into the air, attacking my pulsating hole as he lifted me. I felt his tongue dart in and out of my asshole and my groans became more regular and louder. Chad's tongue stopped washing my ass and he slid up my body to find my mouth. Our mouths made contact and our tongues dueled with each other's. I could feel his hard cock pressing against my stomach, so I felt for the zipper to his cut-off jeans and released his throbbing cock. I then rolled Chad onto his back and sat up, removing his shorts and jockstrap at the same time, then I settled my mouth onto his long, thick cock, lubricating its length. As I was busy doing this, Mike had entered the doorway to my bedroom and stood watching us.

"I think you might need this," said Mike approaching us on the bed and carrying a condom.

"Wrap that on Chad's cock and ride him," instructed Mike.

I did as I was told, sliding the sheen condom down the thick length, then I positioned my quivering asshole over the tip of his cock and began a slow, but firm downward move onto the waiting projectile. A gasp escaped my lips as I sank down, feeling the thickness of Chad's cock expanding my chute. I could feel him going deeper and deeper until I felt my ass rest on his balls, then and only then did I take a breath.

"Now ride him," said Mike, who had by this time stripped and was encouraging us.

I started to rise and fall on Chad's length, feeling the stretch with each downward movement. God, the feeling was ecstatic and I didn't want to pull off his cock and lose the contact.

Mike, in the meantime, had positioned himself above Chad's head and inserted his cut cock into Chad's mouth. Both Chad's hips and mouth were moving in unison, one thrusting upwards while the other sucking Mike's cock, down his throat. Watching Mike's cock disappearing down Chad's throat was turning me on and I increased my thrusts onto Chad's cock; then Mike pulled out of Chad's mouth, climbed from the bed and came around the back of me.

"Lean forward, Brad," said Mike, giving my back and shoulders a gentle push.

I lay across Chad's chest and felt the tip of Mike's cock nudging my asshole, seeking entry along with Chad's cock. I'd never had a double fuck before, but having these two hunky men wanting to get inside of me, never fazed me and I opened up to let Mike in. I felt his cock slide in along Chad's and both men gasped as they felt the tightness engulf their cocks. I cried out in pain as they entered me, but it was more a cry of pleasurable pain, and soon I was relaxed and enjoying their thrusts. My builders were building up my climax and I warned them. Chad took hold of my throbbing cock and began to slick it up with my pre-cum. His hand slid effortlessly along my length, stroking me faster and faster until I couldn't hold back any longer.

"Ah! Fuck! I'm gonna come!" I shouted.

My cock erupted spraying my warm come over Chad's chest and stomach while my ass muscles clamped tightly around the two cocks buried inside of me. My body rocked and shuddered as I fired load after load and frantically rode both stiff rods.

"Fuck! I'm gonna shoot!" cried Mike, holding onto my hips and increasing his speed.

Chad's face was grimacing as Mike's cock slid fiercely against his. I could feel Chad's hips lifting me higher with each thrust. I tightened my ass muscles on their stems and rode them hard, bringing both of them to climax at the same time. The sounds that were escaping from the three of us could have woken the dead as our bodies thrashed together, sweat pouring freely from each of us. I could feel the deep thrusts from Chad and Mike and then slowly they diminished until Mike lay exhausted across my back while had sunken onto Chad's chest. Our bodies heaved as we tried to regain our breath, and my chest became sticky from the come that I had shot on Chad's chest.

When our breathing had returned to some form of normality, I felt Mike's cock slide slowly from my warm, tight chute. It was a pity to have him escape, but I clung desperately onto Chad's throbbing cock, still embedded in me. I didn't want to lose him, so I gently rocked up and down his length in an effort to keep him hard. He smiled at me as I did this.

"You're quite horny, aren't you?" he quipped, giving me one last deep thrust before pulling out.

"I can't help it when I've got two great guys in bed with me."

The rest of the day was put on hold as we showered together, swam together and made love over and over, together.

Naturally, the building construction came to a halt that day, and it was a unilateral decision to go slow with the building so that we could spend more time together and not get the job over with in a hurry.

I still keep in touch with Chad and Mike and often find excuses to suggest alterations to my house, but they've told me not to bother about that – "Just pick up the phone and call us," said Chad.

HARNESSING

Phil Granger turned the pages of the magazine admiring the pictures, rather than reading any of the articles. It wasn't that he couldn't read it's just that he preferred the visuals which turned him on. Sure, he did read stories which had an influence on him, but to see the pictures seemed to have a greater effect on his reactions.

Phil reached the centerfold and sat staring at it. He could feel a tingling sensation in his groin but did nothing about it. He could feel the blood rush to his cock causing it to become slightly hard, but still he did nothing about it, other than look at the picture. It was a color photo of a man in his late thirties or early forties, dressed in leather. The man was staring directly into the camera, much like the look of the Mona Lisa and no matter which way you moved, it seemed as though the eyes followed you. He had narrow, dark eyes, cropped black hair, was slim yet muscularly proportioned, shaved chest, pumped pectoral muscles, a washboard stomach, designer moustache and goatee and wore a leather waistcoat which was open in the front and from the waist down, the man's legs were encased in tight leather jeans which molded around the skin and an unbuttoned fly out of which hung a generous, pendulous, uncut cock with heavy balls.

Phil stared for some time at the picture before turning the page. Over the page were a series of photos of the same model, but in different stages of undress. Phil glanced at the photos and then his eyes fell on the one in which the model was posing minus his waistcoat, but with the buttons of his leather jeans still undone.

Next to this was a photo of the guy in a studded jockstrap. Phil stared intently at the picture, and then ran a finger gently over that section of the photos where the jockstrap was situated, almost as though he were touching the real thing. His eyes seemed to glaze over as he stared at the photo, as though in a trance, but what was happening between his legs was definitely not in a trance; his cock was very much awake and alive. It pushed against his own jockstrap that he was wearing, trying to break free.

Phil turned the pages once more and there appeared four more photos of the same model, but this time sans clothing. The mystery of what was under the leather clothing had been revealed and Phil admired what he saw. To him everything on the model was rightly proportioned for a leather man. Phil dragged a finger down one of the photos, tracing a line from the model's mouth, across his chest to the strong stomach and on down to the long, heavy uncut cock, where his finger halted. He held it there for a moment and then subconsciously lifted his finger and placed it in his mouth as though sucking something from it. He glanced down at his own cock, still encased and noticed the wet spot which had appeared. He wiped his finger gently across the wetness and again inserted his finger into his mouth, tasting the salty-sweet taste of his pre-cum which had oozed from his stiff cock.

Suddenly the silence of the room was broken by the shrill sound of the telephone. Almost in a daze, he picked up the receiver, but still stared at the pictures.

"Hello."

"Hi Phil, it's Joe. What you doing buddy?"

"Nothing," came the response in an almost trans-like monotone.

"Are you OK buddy; you sound a bit strange."

On hearing this, Phil snapped out of his trans-like state.

"Sorry, Joe, I was just deep in thought. What can I do for you?"

"I just wondered what you were planning on doing over the weekend."

"What did you have in mind?"

"There's a new bar opening downtown and I thought we could go and see what it was like; but if you don't want to go, I'll understand."

"No, that sounds like a good idea. What time were you thinking of going?"

"I'll pick you up about 10.00pm," replied Joe.

"I'll see you then."

Phil and Joe had known each other for about five years when they had a three-month relationship but broke up because Joe had to move away on business and neither wanted a long-distance affair. However, now that they were both back in town again, they had renewed their friendship.

On Saturday, at precisely 10.00pm, Joe rang the doorbell to Phil's apartment and after the two friends had greeted each other and had a quick drink together, they set off to the bar.

The bar, The Factory, was decorated a-la-industrial. The décor was minimalist with metal piping scattered around and bare lighting hanging from the roof, thus giving it a feeling of detached coldness. The bar area was large with a horse-shoe-shaped bar counter at one end and a number of high metal tables and stools scattered around. At one end was a spiral metal staircase which led to an upper level. On this level, partitions had been erected, creating a variety of different sized areas, and within these areas were a variety of spaces dedicated to certain activities, such as a maze with glory holes cut into the walls, a sling area, a St Andrews cross and an area which contained a rack, whips and other accoutrements.

Joe and Phil entered the bar, which had quite a number of customers already enjoying themselves. Above the bar counter were two TV screens which constantly played videos of cartoons on the one and hardcore leather sex on the other. The guys found this juxtaposition humorous and stood watching them for some time until they decided to order drinks.

Joe picked up the drinks for himself and Phil and together they found a couple of empty stools at one of the tables. They sat surveying the people around them and occasionally focused on one of the TV monitors above the bar counter.

"This looks quite a nice place," commented Joe, "But what about those TV screens," he chuckled.

"But what do you think is up those stairs?" asked Phil, pointing to the metal staircase.

"I heard they were going to create theme rooms upstairs," replied Joe.

"You mean like a backroom," suggested Phil.

"I suppose you could say that. Do you want to go up to have a look?"

"Sure."

They picked up their drinks and ascended the metal staircase. Upstairs it was a lot darker than the downstairs section, but not unduly so. Subtle lighting had been installed in each of the partitioned off areas.

They entered the sling area where the sling, hanging from chains attached to the roof, hung in the center. Joe watched as Phil walked over to the sling and ran his hand soothingly over the leather attached to the chains.

"Have you ever been in one of those?" asked Joe.

Phil looked at Joe trans-like, as if deep in thought.

"Hey Phil, I'm talking to you."

"Sorry, what did you say?"

"I asked you if you'd ever been in a sling before."

"No, never," came the reply.

"Why don't you climb in and try it; it's actually great."

Phil looked at it once more then ventured towards one of the other areas with Joe following.

In the rack room, Phil picked up one of the whips and cracked it. A sharp sound reverberated around the area. Joe picked up a couple of paddles and a leather harness which was hanging from a hook on the wall. He held the harness to his chest.

"How's this look?" he asked turning to Phil.

Phil had seen pictures of leather men wearing a harness, but not over a shirt.

"I thought it would look much better without a shirt," said Phil, picking up some of the other accoutrements.

After having wandered around the upstairs area, and both being impressed with the layout and what was on offer, they returned downstairs to the bar area, which had by now become very crowded. Their stools and table had been occupied, so they found a corner to have their drinks and watch people.

By midnight the music was pumping and people were in a very festive mood. The bar was filled to capacity with leather men, ordinarily dressed men and some really out of the ordinary.

As Joe and Phil stood admiring the crowds around them, Phil noticed a muscular guy in leathers leaning against the bar counter. Although there were many muscular guys in leather, this one in particular caused Phil to take note. He had on a leather cap, well-fitting leather jeans and a leather waistcoat. He looked about forty-something with a designer stubble moustache and goatee. Phil's heart hastened on seeing the man – he was the exact image of the centerfold of his magazine. Could it be he wondered? His focus remained on the man until the man caught his eye. The two stared at each other, without any facial reactions.

Phil watched the man for what felt like an eternity. The man gulped down his drink, placed his glass on the bar counter, eyed Phil once more and moved towards the metal staircase. As he ascended the staircase, the man hesitated, looked in Phil's direction, and then continued upstairs. Phil put down his glass on a table and also headed towards the staircase.

"Hey Phil, where're you going?"

"Upstairs," came the reply.

"Have you spotted something?"

Phil merely smiled and Joe fully understood.

Phil reached the upper floor and silently moved around the partitioned sections, looking for the man. There were a number of other guys up there already in various rooms and in various situations.

Phil moved about slowly, watching what the others were doing, but couldn't see the man. As he entered the rack area, he saw the man positioned at the far end of the area, standing with his legs akimbo, thumbs in his waistband and his huge fingers splayed across his bulging crotch. Phil's heart almost skipped a beat. His body became excited and he could feel his mouth becoming dry. He licked his lips to create saliva, but the man interpreted this in another way. On seeing Phil lick his lips, the man pushed his crotch forward, clenching his ass as he did so.

Phil slowly sidled into the room which was devoid of other men, and made his was to where the accoutrements were situated. He casually picked up a leather paddle and pretended to admire it, but in fact his attention was focused on the man who had not moved from where his feet were planted. Phil replaced the paddle and took the harness from its hook. The man watched him.

"Put it on," came a deep resonant voice.

Phil was initially startled, and dropped the harness to the floor, but without loosing eye contact with the man, undid his shirt and peeled it off. A slight smile developed on the man's face when he saw Phil's shirtless body.

"Nice body," said the man.

Phil bent and picked up the harness from the floor and fitted it over his chest. As the cold leather touched his skin, knowing the man was watching him, he felt his cock begin an upward and hardening journey.

"Drop your jeans," instructed the man.

Phil never hesitated. He unzipped his jeans, which dropped to the floor and then he stepped out of them, leaving him only in shoes, socks and his white jockstrap.

"Really nice body," said the man, still standing where he'd been all the time.

Phil stood with his hands in front of his crotch, trying to hide his hard-on. For the first time the man moved. He moved to Phil and tightened the harness around his body, symbolically suggesting his control and power over Phil. Although the tightening of the harness was not painful in any way, it was constrictive to Phil's expansion of his chest, if breathing in deeply. Slowly the man then circled Phil, admiring the sight in front of him and then went to pick up one of the leather paddles.

He admired the young, firm ass supported by the two white straps of Phil's jockstrap. He gave the young ass a gentle thwack with the paddle. Phil never flinched. The man repeated his action, but this time a little harder, but still Phil stood his ground; he still stood subservient with his hands covering his now leaking cock.

"Do you like this, boy?" questioned the man, sending another thwack onto Phil's ass.

Phil merely nodded.

"I didn't hear you," said the man, meting out another spanking, so that even in the subdued lighting, one could see how pink Phil's ass was becoming.

"Yes," came the timid response.

"Yes what!"

"Yes, sir."

"That's better. Have you ever done this before, boy?" asked the man, moving to face Phil. He looked into the young man's eyes and saw within a sense of desire rather than fear.

"No, sir, I've never done anything like this before."

"Then I'll teach you," came the response as the man crossed over to where the accoutrements lay, picked up a pair of nipple clamps and together with the paddle, he took Phil by the arm and led him out of the rack area into the adjoining sling area which had just been vacated.

"Get into that," said the man motioning towards the sling.

Phil climbed on and immediately felt the warmth which had been recently left by the last occupant. The man lifted Phil's legs and rested his feet against the chains hanging from the roof, thus spreading Phil's ass wide.

The man stood between Phil's legs and admired the cleanly shaved asshole spying him.

"Nice pucker!" said the man, stroking the paddle seductively down Phil's ass crack and then administering another thwack.

The sling swung gently as Phil lay there passively.

The man put down the paddle and picked up the nipple clamps. He moved to the side of the sling and clamped them onto Phil's protuberant nipples. Although no sound escaped Phil's lips, the facial expression revealed the initial pain he felt. Phil's stomach muscles tensed as the man exerted pressure on each nipple and he felt an exhilarating feeling dart through his body, ending at the tip of his cock as more pre-cum was exuded.

As the man pinched Phil's nipples, Phil instinctively put out a hand and ran it over the packaged crotch in the leather.

"Who said you could touch?" demanded the man.

A slight whimper was heard to come from Phil.

"Please sir, may I touch you?"

The man gloated and unzipped his leather jeans and pulled out a long, thick semi-hard uncut cock. His foreskin covered most of the head and was in the process of rolling back. He dangled it close to Phil's mouth, so close in fact that he could feel Phil's warm, heaving breath on it.

"Suck on it, boy," came the command.

Phil couldn't wait to engulf this piece of man-meat. He took the man's whole length into his throat and created a tightening suction around its girth. The man moaned when he felt the warm tightness and began thrusting.

"You've got a hot mouth, boy."

Phil merely eyed the man and continued to get him harder. When the man considered himself hard enough, he pulled away from Phil and moved between his legs. He bent down and began an ass wash. His tongue ventured around Phil's twitching asshole, lubricating it. He then inserted two fingers which instantaneously were clenched by Phil's ass muscles. The two fingers manipulated Phil's innards, twisting and expanding his chute. Phil gasped, and in so doing, he felt the constriction of the harness on his chest. Throughout, the sling swayed too and fro from the man's hand movements. Once he felt Phil's ass relaxed and open, he stood up, felt in a pocket of his jeans, pulled out a condom, rolled it onto his now fully erect cock, pushing his foreskin right back, aimed at the anticipating entry and drove forward.

Phil gave a deep, guttural groan as the man's thick cock sank straight and deep. There was no compassion, only sheer lust. The man took hold of Phil's harness and began swinging the sling while he stood fixed in one place. The result was a series of deep insertions and withdrawals.

The more the man pounded into Phil, the more Phil's cock was milked, spilling pre-cum into his jockstrap which was battling to keep his throbbing cock securely encased.

Phil held onto the chains for support and let the man and the nipple clamps provide all the pleasure. Throughout, the man never let go of the harness and used it as a means of swinging Phil back and forth.

As their passion unfolded, so a few guys came into the sling area to watch and then left, but one remained; Joe stood at the entrance to the sling area, both intrigued and surprised. He stood watching his buddy take a pounding and rubbed his hand over his own growing hard-on. Should he join in with his buddy or not? He decided instead to remain the voyeur.

Both Phil and the man's breathing were becoming deeper and more intense. The man, using his free hand, grasped one of the nipple clamps and squeezed hard. The pain reverberated through Phil's body and he cried out. As he did so, a flood began to fill his jockstrap. Phil's cock throbbed with each ejaculation. The man, seeing the wet patch on the front of Phil's jockstrap growing, and feeling Phil's intensity, thrust quickly and deeply until suddenly his stomach muscles tensed and he released a long growl as he emptied his seed into Phil.

Once the sling had slowed its swinging, the man, who was still attached to Phil's harness, leant forward and rubbed a hand across the wet patch, up Phil's stomach to the nipple clamps and gave another tight squeeze. Phil's body once again reverberated with pleasurable pain and he clamped his ass muscles tightly around the man's still hard, throbbing cock.

Joe remained in the shadows quietly watching; his own cock hard and wanting to be milked.

The man slowly pulled out, pulled off the condom and threw it on the floor, walked to the side of Phil and once again placed his cock near Phil's mouth. The exhausted young man instinctively opened his mouth and took in the head, licking and tasting the sweet-salty taste of the man. The man then removed the nipple clamps from Phil and helped him out of the sling.

"Thank you, sir," came the subdued voice.

The man held Phil in his arms and undid the harness, removing it and placing it on the sling. Phil was now free but elatedly satisfied.

"My name's Marco," said the man, still holding onto Phil, "and yours is?
"Phil, sir."

Marco laughed a hearty laugh and hugged Phil.

"Would you like me to teach you more?"

"Yes please, sir," said an elated Phil.

As the master and the student dressed, Joe melted into the shadows and made his way back downstairs. The master and student descended the stairs to the hubbub of noise in the bar below to where Joe was now waiting.

"Joe, this is Marco," said Phil introducing the two.

"I've seen you before somewhere," said Joe, shaking hands.

"Probably in my magazine," interrupted Phil. "He's my centerfold."

Marco burst out laughing.

"Don't tell me you've got that picture!"

"Yes, but now, even better, I've got the real thing."

Joe sidled up to Phil and whispered into his ear, "You never told me you were into leather."

"Always. But I never had the guts to get involved, and now Marco's going to show me the ropes."

"Do you think he'd like another slave to teach?"

"Only with pleasure," came the response from Marco who had heard their discussion. "In fact, I think you learnt a little upstairs just now."

Joe was surprised by this statement and blushed; he'd been seen.

"I'll tell you what, let's have a drink together and then I'll take you both upstairs for your first proper lesson!"

THE HOLE IN THE WALL

Summer Park was a favorite place for people to have picnics, take their dogs for walks or to meet other people, depending on your pleasure. The picnics were usually restricted to Sunday afternoons and the dogs' walks to early evenings, but the meeting of other people was never restricted. You could go there any time of the day or early evening, and you would find cars parked under the trees with people sitting in them, not doing much, other than watching other people.

The park covered a large area of trees and grass with a duck pond in its center. Situated to one side of the park, next to a road, were two sets of public toilets, one for men and the other for women. These had become a very popular place for guys meeting other guys and it was accepted that the people who were there for their picnics seldom frequented these toilets.

The men's toilet cubicles, of which there were two, had a wooden wall dividing them, but a small hole had been made in the wall, and over time this hole had been worked on and made bigger until it reached a diameter of almost 15 centimeters. On the walls there was various graffiti, which made for interesting reading, and the doors to the toilets couldn't be locked, but could be closed.

Mike, my best friend, and I went for a drive to the park one Saturday and parked the car under a shady tree near the toilets and watched to see what happened. At the time there were three other cars parked there, each with a driver. Everybody simply sat, but where we were positioned, we could see who went in and out of the toilets. After having sat there for what seemed like eternity, Mike said, "This place is dead. Nothing seems to be happening here."

Just as he said this, a car pulled up and stopped about twenty meters from where we were parked. In the car were two young guys of about nineteen or twenty years of age.

"They don't look too bad," I remarked.

The passenger door of their car opened and a young blonde guy in tight jeans got out and walked towards one of the toilets.

"That really looks good," I said tapping Mike on the leg.

"Go for it, then," he replied. Mike has always been one to encourage people.

I watched as the young guy entered the toilet and closed the door behind him.

"Should I?" I questioned, "But what about you?" I asked Mike.

"Don't worry about me, but go before somebody else moves in next door to him and you lose him."

I climbed from the car and moved towards the other empty men's toilet. I don't think most of the people in their cars saw me do this, but the young guy who was sitting in the car that the blonde guy had got out of, saw me. I entered the empty cubicle, undid my jeans, pulled them down around my ankles and sat on the toilet seat.

As I sat there, I turned my head to look through the hole in the wall. I saw that the blonde guy was doing the same from his side of the wall. His right hand then went down to his dick and I could see that he was playing with himself as he sat there. I could feel my cock getting harder as I watched him. I leant slightly sideways and saw through the hole that he had a nice, cut dick. I put my left hand through the hole as a movement to suggest that he put his dick through the hole. He rose from the toilet seat and turned to face the hole.

I sat and watched as his hardened dick swayed towards the hole. Slowly he pushed his dick through the hole. This was a beautiful sight and my mouth went to greet it. As I wrapped my mouth around his cock, I heard him give a soft groan from the other side of the wall. My warm mouth moved slowly up and down the length of his shaft until he eventually pulled away and I rose to my feet and put my cock through the hole for him to do what he felt with my cock.

I felt his warm breath as his face neared my cock, then I felt a wet tongue run along the length of my cock. Soon the wetness came from more than just his tongue as his lips wrapped around my length. I pushed forward as far as I could, and then slowly pulled back again. This continued for some time and then there was a pause. I left my cock in the hole to wait and see what would happen. I felt the warmth of a mouth around my cock again, but somehow the pressure used by this mouth was not the same as the previous one. I hadn't heard a door open, but I wondered if someone else had moved into his cubicle.

After a few moments, I slowly pulled my cock from the hole and bent down to look through. As I looked through I saw that there were two people in the cubicle and that the other person was the blonde's friend who had been sitting in the car.

The new guy pushed his huge uncut dick through the hole for me to admire, and I kissed it with admiration, taking it all the way to the back of my throat. I heard this guy give a deep groan as I did so and felt him thrust his cock as far into my throat as he could. Again, after a while, he pulled from the hole and beckoned me to put my dick through the hole.

Once my cock was through the hole to the other side of the wall, I could feel a tongue licking my length and then I felt something strange being done to my cock. I pulled back to see if I could see what was happening, and as I did so, I saw that one of them had rolled a condom onto my cock. So that was it, I thought, one of them wants me to fuck them. The next time I looked through the hole, I saw the young blonde guy turn his back towards the hole and aim his ass at the hole in the wall. I saw this beautiful opening waiting for me to plunge into it. I held onto the base of my cock and slowly pushed against his entrance passage. I felt a little resistance and then my cock slipped easily into the warmth of his passage. It felt so tight in there that I thought I was going to come straight away. I held it there for a moment so as not to excite myself too much, and when I was ready, I started to push forward.

Just as I had started pushing into him, the door to my cubicle opened and in came Mike. He stood for a moment surveying the scene, then felt in his pocket and pulled out a condom. As he pulled his jeans down, I grabbed his cock and started getting him hard. Meanwhile, I could hear a slurping sound coming from the other cubicle and realized that his friend must be sucking off the blonde guy while I was fucking him.

Mike pulled the condom onto his now swollen dick and I wondered what he was going to do.

"Do you want to take over?" I asked.

"No," was the reply. "You carry on; because it's your ass I want."

Mike came behind me and I felt him pull my ass cheeks apart and then felt the head of his bargepole touch my entrance passage.

Mike had fucked me many times so I was well used to his size, but it still sent shivers through me every time he entered me. I pushed back onto Mike's cock and felt it slide into me. As Mike began to pound my ass, so the pounding went through the wall into the ass of the blonde guy who then pounded his cock into the throat of his friend. This continued for quite a while with a fair amount of vocal sounds coming from the four of us. Suddenly I heard somebody gulping, and from the tight feeling around my cock, I knew that the blonde guy was shooting his load down the throat of his friend who was guzzling it down and enjoying every bit of it as he did so.

No sooner had the blonde come, then he slowly slid from my cock and I had this empty feeling, but not for long. Before I had a chance to check what was happening I felt another ass slide onto my hard dick. Mike's pounding increased with speed and obviously my pounding went through to the ass on the other side. I knew that I wouldn't last for very much longer because the ass that I was fucking now seemed tighter than the previous one and this was creating a thrilling sensation in me.

I pounded as hard as I could until I could feel a swelling up in my balls as I got ready to fill that condom.

I leant my head back and whispered into Mike's ear, "I'm gong to come. Fuck me harder!" Mike did as I asked and as the first shots of my load splattered into the condom, I gave a low guttural sound. The guy on the other side pushed further onto my cock and I heard him say to his buddy that he was going to shoot and felt his ass muscles squeeze tightly onto my cock. I continued to pound his ass until there was nothing left in me, and I felt him gently pull away from my cock. Suddenly our toilet door flew open and there stood two large, burly cops, one Latino and the other White, in full uniform.

The guys next door to our cubicle made a very hasty retreat and we just heard all the cars that had been parked in the area, start up and drive away. The cops stood in the doorway, looking at Mike and me with our jeans around our ankles. Obviously, as the door had opened, Mike had pulled his dick from me, but there he stood, in all his glory with his dick wrapped in a condom.

The White cop looked down at Mike's bargepole and a look of admiration crossed his face.

"Were you using that on your buddy just now?" asked the cop.

Mike stared the cop in the eyes and said defiantly, "Yes, is that a problem?"

"It's a problem if you were wasting it on him," replied the cop who stretched forward, pulled the condom from Mike's swollen dick and threw it into the toilet bowl.

"What are you going to do?" I asked, trying to pull up my pants in the confined space of the toilet cubicle.

"I'm going to fuck you," was the brusque reply. The White cop stood in the open doorway and unzipped the fly to his pants. His right hand went into his briefs and pulled out a flaccid, fat, cut dick.

"Suck on that, kid," he said pointing at me.

I moved forward and knelt on the floor in front of him admiring his cock length. In the meantime, Mike was standing behind me next to the toilet bowl, watching, along with the Latino.

"Take this meat and get it hard," shouted the White cop, thrusting his cock into my face. I opened my mouth and began to swallow his length. As my mouth moved up and down its length, wetting it, I could feel him getting harder. All this time, Mike stood behind me watching and playing with his dick. At the same time I noticed that the Latino was also caressing his crotch.

"That's what I like to see," said the White cop to Mike, "get that thing hard, because you're going to use it soon."

The White cop pulled me to my feet, pushed past me and entered the cubicle. He stood staring at Mike and Mike's growing cock, while I and the Latino stood in the doorway.

"How big do you think that thing of yours is when it's hard?" snapped the cop, pointing at Mike's throbbing cock.

"I don't know, but I think it's about 8 inches," said Mike looking down at his bobbing cock.

"Crap! That looks more than 10 inches to me, and I want it," snorted the cop. "Sit down on the toilet seat," snapped the cop again.

Mike did as he was told and sat on the toilet seat, facing the door.

"Get in here," commanded the White cop to me, and I scuttled into the cubicle closing the door behind me.

There we were, the four of us with Mike sitting on the toilet seat and the two cops and I standing by the door.

Suddenly the White cop undid his pants and let them drop to his ankles. His cock was now very erect from the sucking that I had been doing.

He looked at Mike and snarled, "Do you want this ass?"

Mike didn't know what to say.

"I asked if you wanted this ass."

"Yes, please," stammered Mike.

The cop bent down and pulled a condom packet from his pants. He tore open the packet and put the condom onto the tip of Mike's cock. He then turned to me and said, "Put that on your buddy, but with your hot mouth."

I moved to Mike and using my mouth, I slid the condom over his hard dick, making it wet as I did so. When I had completed that, I stood up.

The White cop turned towards the hole in the wall and pushed his erect cock through the hole.

"You and my buddy there go next door. Joe, I want that Latino ass of yours, and you," he said pointing to me, "you give my buddy the best fuckin' blow job. You," he said turning to Mike, "you're gonna give me the best fuck ever."

Mike rose from the toilet seat and aimed his erect dick at the White cop's waiting ass. He held his stiff rod and pushed slowly into the White cop's pucker.

"Aargh! Fuck," he groaned as Mike's cock slid into his ass passage. His face contorted as if in pain and he continued groaning. "Oooh, that's good," he groaned. The full length of Mike's dick was now embedded into the cop. On the other side of the wall, the Latino cop dropped his pants and briefs, pulled a condom from his pocket and unrolled it onto his buddy's cock, then positioned his ass where the White cop's cock protruded through the hole. The Latino slowly slid onto the fat cock and his face revealed the pain as he did so. I watched his face the whole time, in a way, feeling sorry that I wasn't on the receiving end of the White cop's man-meat.

The White cop put his hands behind his back and pulled Mike closer into him and started to ride Mike's cock. As he pushed back and forth, so his cock entered and retreated from his Latino buddy. Mike and the two cops were now beginning to enjoy their positions. As soon as the White cop had got used to Mike's size inside him, he began to relax and his rhythm became more even and so did the Latino's.

"Kid, come here and wrap those hot lips of yours around this throbbing dick," said the Latino cop pulling me towards him and pushing me down onto my knees. I was positioned between his spread legs and lowered my mouth to meet his bouncing cock. My tongue ventured under his foreskin and my mouth nibbled gently at the surrounding skin. My Latino groaned as I did this and thrust forward encouraging me to take his whole cock into my warm mouth. I did as he wanted.

As the White cop got pounded by Mike's cock, so the Latino cop's cock slid in and out of my mouth. I tightened my grip on his dick and pushed down deeper over it. While I was doing this, I marveled at how deep Mike must have been fucking the White cop. As I sucked the Latino, I gently inserted two fingers into his ass, letting them run along the length of the White cop's cock as it slid too and fro into the warm Latino cavity.

The White cop began to squirm and grind on Mike's cock and so did my Latino as he felt both a cock and some fingers entering his ass. His thrusting increased, just as my sucking did, and soon I could feel his cock swelling, getting ready to fire his load.

"I want to shoot on your face," he shouted to me, so I pulled my mouth free from his cock and wrapped my hands around it and worked it ferociously, pulling his foreskin to the tip and then pushing it right back to reveal his glistening cock-head. The other two heard the Latino and increased their pace.

"I'm coming!" grunted the White cop.

"So am I," breathed Mike as he pushed deeper into his cop's ass with his cock.

All four of us were working frantically.

The Latino suddenly shot his warm cum which hit me on the cheek and I could feel the next shots hitting all over the face as I closed my eyes and he continued to grunt and groan in pleasure.

"Fuck me! Fuck me harder and deeper," the White cop kept saying as he felt the Latino's ass muscles clamping tight around his cock. Mike thrust deeply and emptied his load into the cop.

When the two in the other cubicle had come, the White cop merely relaxed up against Mike's chest, while on the other side of the wall, my Latino stretched out a hand, grabbed my hard-on and pulled me towards him, and then he sank to his knees and took my throbbing cock into his warm mouth. It felt so good to be in the warm confines where his tongue maneuvered around the length and head of my dick, bringing me to pleasure.

"Aargh! I'm coming," I gasped, but he never left my cock. He continued to suck until every last drop was extracted from me. Eventually he released my cock once he had cleaned it with his tongue. I helped him to his feet and looked into his deep brown eyes.

"Thank you," I whispered, hoping the two next door wouldn't hear.

"Thanks, kid, you were great," said the Latino.

When we had finished and cleaned ourselves and left our respective cubicles, Mike turned to the White cop and I heard him ask, "What happens now?"

"Do you two come here often?" asked the White cop.

"Not that often," was Mike's reply.

"Well, how about us making a date to come here again?" said the White cop, looking at his Latino buddy. I looked at the Latino, who smiled at me. He obviously liked the idea.

"What do you mean?" I asked.

"Maybe we can swap around next time. You can go with my buddy while I fuck your buddy or my buddy can have me while I fuck you, but we'll make a plan…"

"Sounds cool to me," said Mike. "When are we going to meet?"

"How about tomorrow?"

Mike and I looked at each other. "Tomorrow?" asked Mike.

"Yep, or is tomorrow too soon for you guys?"

"No not at all," I replied.

"Sorry guys, it's just that we like a lot and when it's good, like it was today, we like it even more often," said the White cop putting his arms around our shoulders and escorting us from the toilet. "Now, don't let me see you two hanging around here for the rest of today, get home and get some rest because you'll need it tomorrow."

As Mike and I headed towards our car, we looked at each other and burst out laughing.

"Do you realize, we could be sitting behind bars now," I said as we got into the car.

"Yes, but we're not, so long as we keep these guys happy, and we can keep up the pace!"

IN THE DARK OF THE NIGHT

A steady rain fell on the tarred road leading through the center of town. The street lights illuminated not only the desolate buildings, but also the wet, empty streets. The sleek, black Cadillac slowly glided along the neon-illuminated street, as though it was in search of something or someone. The tinted windows disallowed one to peer in but because of the car's steady movement, there had to be a driver inside. The vehicle made its way up and down the deserted streets until it reached a section of a street where there was an element of shelter for people. This shelter took the form of an overhang of a building and there in the light from the shop-front windows stood a tall, slim young man of about mid-twenties in a pair of tight denims and a white T-shirt. The Cadillac slowed to a crawl until it was adjacent to the young man and then stopped. The driver's window slid slowly down to reveal the black capped face of the driver. The strong face of the driver turned to the young man.

"Are you waiting for a ride?"

The young man never moved but stared back at the driver. He could see, from where he was standing, that the driver had on a black leather waistcoat but no shirt. The bulging biceps were evident as was part of the driver's pectoral muscles. The young man couldn't see anyone else in the car, but that was understandable as the back windows remained closed. The young man contemplated walking over to the car, but something made him hesitant, so he remained where he was. Once more the driver asked a question.

"Would you like a lift somewhere?"

The young man once again hesitated then shook his head as if to reject the offer. The driver's window slowly made its way back up, closing the inside world of the car from the outside world of the rain, and the car moved off slowly as if in search of something else.

The car circled the block and slowly drove past the young man still standing under the shelter, but this time when the car came past, there was another young man standing talking to the first. This second young man looked younger than his friend and, although he looked pleasant enough, his appearance was a little disheveled. He had on a pair of cut-off jeans that fitted snugly to his cute ass and wore a plain white vest which revealed the pleasant young torso.

The car came to a stop adjacent tot the two young men. Once more the driver's window slid down and once more the driver asked if they wanted transport. The new young man turned to his friend who merely shrugged his shoulders, and then he strode confidently towards the driver's window.

The young man peered into the car, but there was a dividing glass between the driver and the back of the car, so he couldn't see if anyone was sitting there.

"Hi!" said the young man, admiring the driver's taut body.

"Are you looking for a ride?" asked the driver, smiling slightly at the young man.

"Maybe," came the reply.

The two men smiled at each other but said nothing more. The young man in the street leered down at the crotch of the driver and saw a hefty package encased in black leather jeans, between the driver's thighs, and then he looked up at the driver's face. The driver gave an indication with his eyes that there was someone sitting in the back of the car. The young man realized that the pick up was not with the driver but with another client.

"Are you alone?" asked the young man, innocently.

The dividing glass between driver and passenger slid down and a voice came from the back of the car.

"No, he's not alone. Would you like to join me for a ride?"

The young man leaned in through the driver's window and peered into the back of the car. A smartly dressed man of about fifty sat on the back seat, smoking. The young man looked at the passenger and then turned back to the driver. In his mind he thought he'd rather spend an evening with the driver, but it was money that he was after, and he had been undergoing a rather lean period.

"How much?" enquired the young man.

"I'll give you $1000 to spend the night with me," replied the middle-aged man.

$1000 was a great deal of money for the young man, so without hesitation, the young man moved to the back door which opened for him and he climbed in alongside his client. The car slowly started off as the driver's window slid closed again.

"Call me Jack," said the middle-aged man, eyeing out his young visitor.

"Hi, I'm Clint," replied the young man. "Nice car you've got here."

"Thanks," answered Jack. "Nice body you've got."

Clint smiled at the compliment and ran a hand subconsciously over his buffed pecs.

"How old are you, Clint?"

"Twenty."

"Hm. Nice and young. I like them young," replied Jack, still letting his eyes glance over his young passenger.

Where Clint was sitting, he could see through the glass how the driver eyed them in the back seat. He also noted that Jack, although middle-aged seemed to have a buffed body. As he sat there watching the driver's eyes and glancing every now and again at Jack, Jack's hand slid across the leather seat to rest on Clint's thigh.

"Hm. Nice firm legs you've got. Are you an athlete?"

"When I was at school I took part in sport, but since leaving, I've done nothing to keep fit."

"And your friend there on the street that we left behind?"

"What about him?"

"Do you two work together?"

"Sometimes, but not often."

"He looks older than you."

"Yes, he's twenty-five," replied Clint, feeling Jack's hand moving higher up his thigh and under the cut-off jeans legs.

"Is he like a pimp for you?" enquired Jack, still trying to slide his hand up under the denim material.

"No. It's just that he looks out for me," answered Clint.

Jack found it difficult to get his fingers higher under the denim material to grasp Clint's balls so instead he grabbed the bulge that confronted him between Clint's thighs.

"Nice package by the feel of things," said Jack, grinning at Clint.

Jack then took hold of Clint's hand and guided it towards his crotch, allowing the young man to feel his erection hidden under the suit pants that he was wearing.

"Unzip it and suck my cock," said Jack, forcing Clint's face onto his crotch.

Clint did as he was told and unzipped Jack's pants, releasing his hard-on. The middle-aged man had been blessed with a fair-sized cock that was thick, heavily veined and uncut. Clint leaned over and took the uncut cock deep into his throat causing Jack to throw back his head and groan with pleasure as he felt the tightness of the young man's mouth around his girth. The driver continued to watch in the rear-view mirror as Jack received his night's pleasure. The car continued its slow journey around the wet streets, while Clint continued to take the thick uncut cock as deeply down his throat as he could. The driver continued his voyeuristic driving, one hand on the wheel and the other rubbing his own engorged cock inside his black jeans.

After what seemed like an eternity of Clint sucking on Jack's cock, which was now oozing pre-cum, the driver was instructed to head for home. The drive from the city center to the edge of town and 'home' didn't take long. As they neared the wrought-iron gates of the driveway leading up to the baronial mansion, Jack pulled Clint's blonde hair from his raw, glistening cock and zipped up his pants. Clint sat up and peered out of the car's window into the night. The house was well lit up and once they had come to a halt, the driver jumped out and opened the door on Jack's side of the car. Jack slid out and Clint was about to follow, when the car door was slammed shut on him.

"Max will bring you up to my rooms," said Jack as he ascended the steps leading to the front door.

Max, who was obviously the driver, returned to his position behind the steering wheel, smiled into the rear view mirror at Clint, winked and sped off to the back of the mansion.

Once the car had been parked, Max opened the back door of the car, allowing Clint to alight.

With Max standing next to him, Clint could see the driver was tall, lean and muscular. Everything about Max was tight – his jeans, his stomach and the grip on Clint's arm, as he ushered the young man into the warmth of the house.

"We need to get you cleaned up," said Max, leading Clint upstairs to a room.

"Who is this guy?" asked the young man. "Does anyone else live here with him?"

"You seem to ask a lot of questions," replied Max, pulling Clint's vest from his body and throwing it onto the floor.

"Nice trim body. He'll like that. Take off those shorts," commanded Max.

Clint slipped his cut-off jeans to the floor and stepped out of them. He stood looking around the richly furnished room, while Max admired the young body in his tight white briefs.

"Nice ass. He'll like that too."

Clint instinctively rubbed his hands over his cute ass when Max made mention of it.

"I see a little wet patch in the front as well," commented Max, giving Clint's cock a squeeze. "Pretty healthy length too. That he'll like."

"Is there anything that Jack doesn't like?" asked Clint.

"Rude boys that ask too many questions."

"What happens now?"

"You get rid of those little white briefs and we throw you into a shower."

Clint pulled down his briefs revealing a well-hung muscle that lay semi-hard between his legs. Max smiled broadly when he saw the length of Clint's cock.

"Come! It's shower time."

Max escorted Clint to an en suite bathroom off the bedroom and turned on the shower water.

"In you get and scrub!"

Clint climbed under the warm water and let it run over his taut body. He picked up a bar of sweet smelling soap and began to wash himself, and all the while Max stood watching.

"Clean that tight ass of yours," said Max, firmly.

Clint rubbed soap over his ass crack and inserted a finger into his tight little hole and as he did so, so his cock gave a sharp jerk and began to thicken and harden.

"I didn't say play with yourself," said Max, abruptly. "That'll come later."

Clint finished washing himself and then Max handed him a soft towel with which to dry himself. Once Clint was dry, Max handed a thin, cotton caftan to Clint, who put it on over his naked body. Max then led Clint out of the room that they had been in and headed down a long corridor until they reached another section of the huge mansion.

"When you go in, speak only when he asks you something, do you understand?"

Clint looked somewhat blank but nodded.

"And remember, he's your Daddy!"

Clint smiled to himself. He liked to be dominated and although he liked guys of about Max's age and build, he was never one to walk away from an older man. Clint felt that older men were easier to pick up, even though he'd been picked up this time, but he also thought that Jack was pretty good-looking for his age – whatever it might be.

Max tapped gently on the large wooden door and waited, then he heard the voice of Jack.

"Enter."

Max and Clint entered a spacious, elegant bedroom with a large four-poster bed in the center of it. To one side of the room stood a tall wooden cupboard and on another stood a high-backed wooden chair. On the bed lay Jack, naked.

"He is clean and ready for you, sir," said Max, leading Clint to the foot of the bed.

Jack was lying spread-eagle on the bed on his back with his head against three large pillows, watching Clint's every move.

"Max, you know your place."

Clint watched as Max made his way to the high-backed wooden chair and sat down. Max smiled at Clint, who was watching him, and then Max took off his waistcoat that he had been wearing, to reveal a muscular well-defined body. Clint looked from Max to Jack. The older man had a fine body, probably kept toned from daily exercise, and black hair with tinges of grey at the temples making him look sexily distinguished, but to Clint, Max's body was a picture of pure bodybuilding muscle.

"Take off your caftan and crawl to me baby," said Jack, smiling as Clint pulled the caftan over his head to reveal his taut young body and his heavy-hanging cock and balls, and then he knelt on the carpeted floor to begin crawling up onto the bed.

Clint reached the top of the large bed and peered up between Jack's thickly muscular legs. For a man in his fifties, Jack had kept himself trim and this impressed Clint. He slid slowly closer to Jack's crotch, where he could see Jack's cock growing in length and girth while his balls hung loose. Clint reached Jack's balls and was about to lick them when Jack stopped him.

"I didn't say you could touch them!"

"Sorry, Daddy," whispered Clint.

"Breathe on them," continued Jack, spreading his muscular legs wider.

Clint began to blow gently onto them causing Jack to coo like a dove.

"Ooh, yes!"

Clint continued to exhale warm air onto the throbbing cock and sturdy balls while Jack began to writhe on the bed ever so gently.

"Now lick my balls!" came the command.

"Yes, Daddy," replied Clint, with a tone of submission in his voice.

Clint did as he was ordered and with the tip of his tongue, he flicked Jack's pendulous balls like a snake's tongue flicking for air.

Jack cooed some more as his cock became harder all the time.

"Play with my nipples, boy," instructed the older man.

Again Clint did as instructed, pinching and nibbling Jack's protruding nipples. While Jack thrust his chest upwards to meet Clint's attacks of his nipples, he shouted an order to Max.

"The paddle, Max!"

Max rose from his seat and went to the large wooden cupboard where he withdrew a leather paddle and began using it on Clint's smooth ass. As the first blow struck, Clint cried out, more from surprise than from pain, but soon the young man was enjoying the gentle pain that Max was inflicting on his reddening ass.

"Now suck my cock!" ordered Jack.

Clint knelt between Jack's thighs and took the older man's cock well down his throat. Jack writhed and moaned as Clint work his mouth along the length of Jack's throbbing cock and all the while Max continued with the paddle on Clint's ass.

"The clamps, Max!" commanded Jack.

Max stopped his work with the paddle and returned to the wooden cupboard, but this time he returned with two clamps which he placed on each of Clint's nipples.

Clint cried out in pain as the two alligator clamps bit into his nipples. His mouth increased the suction on Jack's cock causing Jack to buck upwards, forcing his cock deeper into Clint's throat. Max played with the clamps on Clint's nipples and as he did so, so his own cock was rising in his black jeans. He was tempted to get involved in their action, but he knew that Jack wouldn't allow that without inviting him to join in. Max admired Clint's tight little ass with its pulsating hole, waiting to be ravaged, but he knew that he couldn't do anything unless he wanted trouble from Jack.

"Rubbers, Max!"

Max reluctantly slid from the bed and made his way back to the cupboard where he collected some condoms and lube.

"Clint, put one of those on my cock! Max, prepare that ass of his!"

Clint unrolled a condom down Jack's shaft while Max gently inserted two lubed fingers into Clint's tight ass and readied it for Jack's assault.

"Now ride me, kid!"

"Yes, Daddy," replied Clint, eagerly.

This was the part that Clint was looking forward to – to be impaled on his 'Daddy's' large bargepole.

Clint rose above Jack's body, held onto Jack's cock and directed the thick shaft towards his waiting hole. Slowly Clint sank down the shaft, taking it inch by inch until the entire solid muscle was buried deep in his ass. The youngster squirmed his ass on Jack's rock solid cock, causing the older man to groan with pleasure.

"Fuck me, Daddy!" said Clint, "Fuck me hard, please."

Instinctively Jack thrust his hips upwards, impaling Clint firmly on his hard cock.

Clint squealed like a pig as the hard rod sank in and hit his prostate, massaging it and causing his cock to dribble some clear pre-cum. Then Clint began a frantic upward and downward movement, riding the hard muscle and playing with Jack's nipples at the same time. The older man's groans could be heard loudly through the room while Max sat watching and slowly rubbing his hand across his engorged crotch. With each downward thrust from Clint, Jack met him with an upward thrust of his hips, hitting Clint's prostate each time and causing the young man to cry in ecstasy. Apart from the constant groans of pleasure from Clint, the young man kept encouraging Jack to fuck him harder.

Jack never touched Clint throughout their passion and it was only when Clint began to stroke his own erect cock that Jack reprimanded him.

"Don't touch yourself, boy! You are here for my pleasure, not yours!'

Clint immediately stopped, but little did Jack realize that Clint was getting his pleasure from the way in which he was riding Jack's cock. He forced the thick cock head to constantly rub against his prostate, knowing that he would soon shoot his load without his cock being touched. All the while, Jack remained flat on his back with Clint on top of him.

"Aargh!" shouted Jack, bucking Clint high into the air. "I'm coming, kid!'

"Daddy, fuck me faster!" cried Clint.

Jack's thrusts became frenetic as he shot load after load of warm cum into Clint's ass.

"Yeah, that's it Daddy, fuck my tight ass. Fuck me harder! Aargh!" cried Clint.

Almost at the same time, Clint's throbbing cock let loose a stream of white cum that shot across Jack's chest covering one of his nipples, and then another stream followed by yet another. As the two men's breathing began to slow down to normality, Jack pulled Clint closer to his face and kissed the young man.

"Now lick up your mess you've made on me, boy" said Jack, caressing Clint's firm ass while he remained impaled on Jack's still throbbing cock.

Clint's tongue lapped up the sweet-salty cum that covered Jack's nipple and nibbled at the protrusion at the same time, causing Jack to give a couple of upward thrusts into Clint's ass. When Jack's body was clean of Clint's evidence, he guided the young man's ass up and off his still hard cock, removed his cum-filled condom and instructed Max to take Clint to his room.

"That made Daddy a very happy man. Now, keep him clean and rested," instructed Jack "and when I need him, I'll call."

Max handed Clint the caftan and led him out of Jack's room and back to the room in which he first went to.

"This is where you'll sleep tonight and whenever Jack needs you, you must go to his room, but I'll be staying here with you," said Max, with a glint in his eye.

Max knew that Jack had an insatiable appetite for young men and sex and that although they had enjoyed each other's company, the night was still young.

"Does he do this often?" enquired Clint.

"Do you mean inviting young men back to his house, or having sex regularly through the night?"

"Both."

"Yes, to both questions," replied Max. "He likes young guys and he likes to dominate."

Max took Clint back to the en-suite bathroom and made him shower.

"Each time you go to Jack's room, you must shower afterwards and put the caftan back on. It's just that Max doesn't want to see his men naked when they enter his room. He prefers the mystique of wondering what's under the clothing. Now shower and then rest."

Clint did as he was told and then climbed into the large, soft bed, ready to sleep.

"Tell me, did you start off like me, on the streets or where did he find you?" asked Clint as he made himself comfortable in the bed.

"Yep, I was like you. He found me on the streets, brought me to his house, fucked me and I've been here ever since. Now go to sleep; you'll need your rest."

Two hours later, Max shook Clint, giving him a gentle kiss on the lips to wake him.

"Clint! Wake up!"

Clint opened his eyes to see a naked Max standing next to the bed. Seeing Max naked sparked a desire in Clint to make love to this muscular man.

"Jack wants you," said Max, helping Clint from the bed and putting the caftan back on.

Clint stood for a moment staring at Max's beautifully structured body and well hung cock with its long thick shaft and smooth mushroom-shaped head. How he wished he could have that instead of Jack, but the older man was paying for his services and so he must oblige.

The two men ventured back into Jack's room to find him standing at the foot of the bed.

"Disrobe!" instructed Jack.

"Yes Daddy."

Clint, now used to the routine, did as he was commanded and stood looking at both Max and Jack who were both naked, waiting for his next instruction.

"Get on the bed and lie on your stomach," instructed Jack.

Clint spread himself across the bed waiting to see what happened next.

"Max, rubbers!"

Max did his customary walk to the cupboard, collected the necessary items and returned to the bed.

"Lube his ass, Max."

Max spread some lube onto his fingers and gently inserted them into Clint's tight ass, maneuvering his fingers in the young man's chute to loosen him up. When he had finished, Jack handed Max a condom and gave him another instruction.

"Put this on and slip in."

Max's face lit up as he unrolled the condom down his thick shaft then climbed on top of Clint, aiming his long cock at the winking hole that waited for him. A sense of excitement filled Clint as he realized that Max was going to enter him. Clint gasped as the enormity of Max's cock sank into his depths. Max continued to slide in until his balls lapped up against Clint's tight ass. Max could feel the tight chute clamped around his length and he gave a sudden deep thrust into Clint which caused the young man to cry out in pain.

Jack then took the lube and inserted three fingers into Max's asshole. Max ground his hips into Clint as Jack lubed him up then the older man sank his sheathed cock into Max's slightly raised ass. The three men were connected.

Max started to thrust into Clint and as a result, his ass dove onto Jack's sturdy muscle that was embedded in his ass. Jack and Max clung to each other as they slid their weapons into the warm chutes that comforted their cocks, while Clint continued to cry out with each thrust that Max gave.

After some time of deep thrusts, Jack rolled off Max who in turn pulled out of Clint. Although Clint was relieved to have Max's long, thick rod out of him, he still longed for it to be back where it belonged – deep inside his puckering ass.

Jack climbed onto the bed and lay on his back then invited Clint to sit on his cock, like he had done earlier. The exception this time was that no sooner had Clint impaled himself on the older man's cock, than Max moved in as well. Max pushed Clint forward slightly so as to open his ass wider, then Max took hold of his hard shaft and directed towards Clint's already filled asshole. Slowly Max pushed forward until his cock slid past the sphincter and joined Jack's cock in Clint.

Clint's face was a grimace as the pain ran through his body. Both Max and Jack pushed their cocks into Clint's tight ass. Max enjoyed not only the tightness of Clint's chute, but also the friction caused by rubbing against Jack's cock. Once Jack and Max had got used to their cocks working together, they set up a constant rhythm, driving in and out of Clint's pulsating hole. Max ran his hands over Clint's shoulders and back in an effort to calm him down and then he found the young man's nipples, which he clamped between thumb and forefinger. Clint forgot about the pain of having two thick cocks embedded in him and concentrated on his nipples instead.

Soon, all three men were oblivious of any pain, and were thrusting and pushing, groaning and breathing heavily until Jack shouted that he was about to shoot his load. Max increased his speed to catch up to Jack's climax and try to come together. He and Clint could feel Jack's cock throbbing as he filled his condom, then Max tensed his body, gasped and plowed deeply into Clint's ass, filling him with his juices. Max continued to plow into the tight opening, pinching Clint's nipples with each load that was fired until the young man's cock swelled, his balls rose up and he fired warm cum over Jack's stomach. Clint fell forward onto Jack's chest, breathing heavily, while Max's massive cock continued to throb in Clint's ass, until Jack slipped from the confines of Clint, leaving the two younger men still coupled.

"Wow! That was fabulous," commented Jack. "Max, take him back to his room and let him rest. I'll not need him again tonight, but in the morning take him back to where he wants to go."

Max nodded and slipped from Clint's grasp.

"Clint, I would like to see you again. Max will see you right and take you home in the morning."

"Thanks Daddy. You really gave me great pleasure."

"Next time you come here, perhaps your friend might like to join you. Do you think he'd like that?"

"I'll speak to him when I see him again, Daddy" replied Clint, slipping his caftan back on over his naked body.

"Perhaps tomorrow night?" suggested Jack.

Clint didn't respond. He just thought of how exhausted he was and just wanted to go to bed.

Max took Clint back to his room where Clint showered once more, but when he returned from the shower to get into bed, he saw Max lying in the bed waiting for him.

"I just wanna tell you that I'm not your Daddy," said Max, enfolding the taut young body in his muscular arms and pulling Clint closer to him, "so you can do whatever you like; that's if you're up to it."

Clint smiled at Max and snuggled closer to him, allowing his growing cock to rub up against Max's already stiff rod.

"How about turning over?" asked Clint, smiling at Max and waiting tentatively for a response.

"My ass is your," replied Max, guiding Clint's long, hard cock towards his already lubed ass.

Early the next morning, Max and Clint made their way in the sleek black Cadillac back to the center of town to where Clint lived. Max gave Clint the promised payment and they agreed to meet at eight that evening to bring Clint, and perhaps his friend, back to the mansion for another night of passion.

Clint smiled broadly to himself as he closed the front door to his apartment, knowing that he was onto a good thing, both financially and physically. As long as Daddy Jack supplied the money, he, Clint, could get his pleasures with Max as well.

RANDY ROCKET AND THE RAVISHING REDHEAD

Willow Creek was a small town with a small population with an equally small mentality. It was an ordinary, dusty town which had the inevitable local hero, who invariably caused trouble for the local sheriff, and the local hero in this case was twenty-year old Charles Randolph William Rocket, commonly known as Randy Rocket.

Randy Rocket was the archetypal cowboy. He was a gun slinger par excellence, was extremely good looking with sun-bleached hair, gentle blue eyes, and had a physique that had the ladies running after him. Randy had everything going for him: he had a personality that exuded charm, a smile to advertise toothpaste products, if they'd been in abundance in those days, and had been blessed with everything a man could want. Yes, his surname said it all. Between his legs hung a rocket both in length and shape, and as for his first name, he lived up to that as well – Randy just couldn't get enough sex; but with all these attributes, one thing was missing – he wasn't the brightest gas lamp in the factory! If it hadn't been for all his physical attributes and gun slinging prowess, he wouldn't have been noticed by anyone in the town. Admittedly, something could be said for the people who chased after Randy, it was obviously pure physical lust and not his intellect they were after. It was all brawn and no brain.

There were some, among the residents, who regarded him with pity because of his lack of basic human understanding, while others merely despised him, whether out of jealousy or sheer frustration, we'll never know. You either liked Randy or you hated him; with him there were no grey areas.

Randy was one of those talented young men who had the ability to hit a pin head with his Colt 45 but couldn't hit on any of the young ladies at Mrs. Turkington's Saloon. Rather, it wasn't that he couldn't, instead it was that he lacked confidence in approaching the ladies. Mrs. Turkington's Saloon was, at that time, the only center of entertainment for pretty ladies and horny cowboys.

Now with all due respect to other gun slingers, I have always been of the opinion that to be a reputable gun slinger requires some skills other than aiming and firing a gun. Tactics are required and for that brains must come into play, so how Randy survived, left me in utter wonder. Having said that, I have to concede that he had remarkable ball-skills – and here I'm not referring to sporting skills! Randy was always playing with or man-handling his pendulous balls, no matter where he was, in public or private. To him it was part of his manly persona, but to others it was often an embarrassment. However, when he was in Mrs. Turkington's Saloon, it was amazing the number of ladies who flocked there to see Randy fumbling with his balls as he tried to explain and demonstrate his recent shooting experiences. He always had his thumbs dug deep into the waistband of his jeans with his fingers splayed across his crotch, from where they jangled his balls and rocket.

Randy's best friend was another cowpoke by the name of Tyrone who was equally blessed with shooting abilities and physical qualities, but added to this was the fact that Tyrone had been given a number of gas lamps, so to speak, and it was up to Tyrone to try and guide Randy along the 'paths of righteousness'. Poor Tyrone would often have to cover for Randy's erring ways and forgetful moments; in fact Tyrone would often have to make decisions for Randy. The result was that Randy relied heavily on Tyrone, and because of this they were the best of friends.

Recently, after winning a shoot-out in the main street, Randy took his friend Tyrone for drinks to Mrs. Turkington's Saloon, where the drinks were flowing freely and so were the ladies. Although the guys went there together, it didn't stop them from inviting others into their group until soon there were about twenty men and women gathered around them, drinking and carousing. While they were chatting merrily together, Randy noticed a tall, slim redhead, whose hair hung long and straight onto her shoulders, sitting up at the bar. He nudged Tyrone and pointed towards the redhead, and then whispered something into Tyrone's ear. Tyrone looked askance at Randy then at the redhead. He put down his drink and sauntered through the crowd to the redhead at the bar.

"Excuse me, Ma'am", he shouted, trying to be heard over the honky-tonk piano and the general noise of the bar, "but my friend over there would like you to come and join us."

The redhead turned and surveyed Randy, who was standing with his thumbs in his jeans and busily stroking his rocket and balls with his finger-tips. She smiled at him and turned back to Tyrone.

"Who is your friend?" asked the redhead seductively.

"His name's Randy."

"Oh my, and is he?"

Tyrone hadn't quite heard properly, or so he thought. "Is he what?" he eventually asked.

"Randy."

When Tyrone realized what had been said, he laughed at the joke, but neither confirmed nor denied the question.

"He's very good looking", continued the redhead, "And he looks oh so big."

Tyrone wasn't sure as to what the 'big' was a reference, whether it was Randy's height or the fact that Randy's rocket was beginning to reveal a hard-on in his jeans, so he merely smiled inanely.

After much coy smiling back and forth between Randy and the redhead, and much ball-scratching by Randy, the redhead chose to remain seated at the bar counter while Tyrone, as the messenger, returned to his group.

"Why didn't she come over?" enquired Randy, looking a little upset that this potential conquest had been unsuccessful.

"She just wants to be alone," replied Tyrone.

"But she's the best thing in this saloon tonight," continued Randy. "I have to have her, so go and fetch her," he commanded.

Randy, by this time could feel the heavy arousal in his jeans and was constantly rubbing his fingers across the outline of his rocket, trying to get it harder.

"Just leave her," said Tyrone trying to take his friend's mind off the redhead and get Randy to focus on the others in their group. "Let's get another drink."

"Good idea," said Randy leaping up and heading for the bar counter with Tyrone in tow. Randy headed straight towards where the redhead was sitting.

"Could I buy you a drink?" he asked, sidling up to the redhead and tipping a finger to his Stetson.

"Why thank you kind sir. Cider, please."

Randy's eyes followed the contours of the redhead as he admired the elegant figure with the shapely ankles and seemingly long, slim legs that seemed to stretch all the way up to…

…a finger rested under Randy's chin and lifted his face so that he met the redhead's eyes.

"You seem to be paying a great deal of attention to my figure; I think you should keep your eyes up at face level," said the redhead, smiling an engaging smile at both Randy and Tyrone, as the drink was delivered.

"Wouldn't you like to come and join our group?" asked Randy, almost like a naughty school boy who'd been found guilty of doing something he shouldn't have.

"That's very kind of you, but I don't think so. Maybe another time."

"Are you here on your own?" asked Randy, now trying desperately to peer down the top of the redhead's dress.

"I was waiting for some friends, but they don't seem to be coming, so I think I'll just finish my drink and make my way home," replied the redhead, knocking back the cider and rising from the bar stool.

"You're new around here, aren't you? Will I be able to see you again?" enquired the brazen, yet sheepishly-voiced Randy.

Tyrone suddenly pulled Randy to one side and whispered into his ear. Randy's face lit up when Tyrone had finished speaking to him. He turned back to the redhead.

"I'm having a birthday party next Saturday night. Would you like to come?"

"Oh my! A party! Who's going to be there?" asked the sultry redhead.

"Just a few friends. Mostly the gang that's over there drinking," replied Randy.

"And will you be there?" asked the redhead, turning her attention to Tyrone.

Tyrone blushed so rapidly that it was obvious even in the dim light of the saloon. He didn't have to say anything, because the blush and a nod of the head said it all. The redhead smiled glowingly at Tyrone.

"Where's the party?" asked the redhead, smiling at Tyrone, but directing the question to Randy.

Randy obviously didn't realize that he was being asked, so Tyrone answered for him and said it would be here at Mrs. Turkington's and what time it would be.

The redhead thanked them for the drinks, gave each a peck on the cheek and glided out of the saloon into the darkness of the night, leaving the two men grinning from ear to ear.

"Did you see how she checked me out?" said Randy delightedly, running his hand across his hardened crotch and hoisting his balls in his jeans.

"Bullshit, she was making a pass at me," retorted Tyrone. "Didn't you see how she focused on me when she asked where the party was being held?"

"I've never seen such a great figure and such a firm body before," continued Randy. "Now *that* I could easily take to bed."

"So could I," replied Tyrone.

"Hey, I saw her first, so hands off," replied Randy, striking an aggressive pose, and pulling out his colt.

"Hey, take it easy," retorted Tyrone, trying to pacify his buddy.

The Colt was replaced in the holster and the two made their way back to the rest of the group to relate what had happened and to inform them of the extra person who would be attending the party on Saturday.

The following Saturday arrived and both Randy and Tyrone, who shared digs together, went out for a ride in the morning and then returned later in the afternoon to smarten themselves up for the evening's event.

As they dressed, Randy commented that his old rocket needed to fire some shots and the redhead was just the right person to receive his load. He stroked his long cock, pulling his foreskin back to reveal his shiny pink head, as he explained his intentions to Tyrone, who watched fascinated as Randy's cock began to grow in length. Naturally, Tyrone found watching Randy's cock grow, stimulating and soon his own cock was rising to the occasion. Both cowboys stood admiring each other's erections. Tyrone stretched out a hand and took hold of Randy's long stem, squeezing it as he did so.

"That's sure one fucking big dick you've got there, buddy."

"…all the better for fucking with," replied Randy, taking hold of its stem and waggling it in front of Tyrone, tauntingly. Tyrone merely smiled at Randy as he watched his friend give a couple of quick thrusts with his pelvis to demonstrate his fucking technique.

At approximately seven-thirty, they arrived at Mrs. Turkington's. By eight the saloon was filled to capacity and most of the guests had arrived, with the exception of the redhead. Both Randy and Tyrone were a little disillusioned that their star guest had not yet arrived, but they were not going to let this get them down. The party was now in full swing. The drinks flowed; the piano beat out its rhythm and the camaraderie was one of jollification for this was Randy's twenty-first birthday.

At exactly ten o'clock, the saloon swing-doors opened and there stood the redhead, tall, elegant and smiling. When Randy saw the redhead through the crowd, he rushed to the door.

"Howdy Ma'am. I thought you wouldn't pitch up," he gushed like an embarrassed teenager.

"I said I would come, didn't I?" said the redhead, surveying the crowd behind Randy.

The redhead glided into the saloon and people made way allowing Randy and his partner to make their way through the lounge to a table. Tyrone made eye contact with the redhead and made his way over.

"Howdy Ma'am, how are you?" said Tyrone automatically tipping his ten-gallon hat.

"Fine thanks," gushed the redhead.

"Can I get you a drink?" asked Randy, almost pushing Tyrone out of the way.

"Thanks that would be lovely."

"What would you like?" asked Randy.

"Surprise me," came the reply, with a twinkle in the eye.

Both Randy and Tyrone were a little surprised by this remark, but Randy rushed off to fulfill the redhead's request.

Being left alone Tyrone took hold of the redhead's hand and held it in his own.

"By the way, I don't even know your name."

"It's Antoinette, but most people shorten it to Toni, T-O-N-I."

"Well, in that case, Antoinette, or should I say Toni, I'm Tyrone," he said squeezing her hand a little tighter and smiling into her brown eyes.

Just then Randy rushed over with a cider which he thrust into Toni's hand, almost spilling it in the process.

"I remember you drinking this in the saloon last time, so I got you the same."

As Randy, Tyrone and Toni huddled together in a group, making small talk about small things, both men kept eyeing Toni's superb figure.

The piano continued to play above the chatter of the guests and Randy asked Toni to dance. The two of them moved into an open space in the lounge where Randy put an arm around Toni's slim waist and pulled her closer to him. Their bodies crushed up against each other's and Toni could feel the rocket pressing against her stomach. As they danced, it felt that the rocket was getting ready for launching. Randy's cock was growing harder as he rubbed up against Toni.

Tyrone watched them enviously for a while and then decided to cut in.

"Can I take over in this dance, for a while?" said Tyrone cutting in and whisking Toni out of Randy's clutches. Randy stood for a while in the middle of the floor bewildered, with a hard-on in his jeans, wondering whether he should take things into his own hands and deal with Tyrone for 'stealing' his date.

Toni and Tyrone danced together for a while and Tyrone soon found himself in the same position that Randy had been. Throughout all this, Toni kept her composure and smiled to all around her. When the music finished, they went over to where Randy had been standing to pick up their drinks.

"Why don't we go where there's less noise," suggested Randy, taking Toni by the hand and leading her upstairs towards the bedrooms of the saloon. Tyrone automatically followed.

The three found an unoccupied bedroom and went in.

"This is a beautiful room," commented Toni. "You even have a good view from the window," she commented, staring out over the deserted dusty street below.

Tyrone moved up behind Toni and put his arms around her waist, thrusting his still hard cock up against her ass. Toni never moved but let him remain in that position. Randy, not to be outdone, moved next to Toni and tried to grasp at Toni's breasts, only to have his hand slapped.

Toni could feel Tyrone getting harder all the time and Tyrone enjoyed the position in which he found himself. He had Toni's attention and Randy didn't.

Not to be outdone, Randy moved in front of Toni, removed his Stetson hat and started kissing her, their tongues dueling together. Toni was sandwiched between the two cowboys. She let a hand slide down towards Randy's crotch and felt the rocket erect, ready for launching. She gave it a squeeze which made Randy sigh. Slowly she then began to unbutton Randy's jeans. She slid her hand into the warm interior of his denim jeans and felt the rocket with its pointed head. She rubbed a finger over its tip and felt a little of the rocket fuel leaking. She eased the rocket from its hiding place and as she did so, so Tyrone watched and felt left out, so he unbuttoned his own jeans and shucked them and his chaps to the ground. He stood there in his briefs still rubbing up against Toni's ass.

"Listen boys, why don't we get comfortable on the bed, that is, if you want some fun?" remarked Toni casually.

Without a second invitation, Randy had stripped off his clothes and was lying naked on the bed, fondling his engorged rocket, and getting his engines going. Tyrone, not to be outdone, peeled off his briefs and joined Randy on the bed. Toni stood staring at the two naked men, lying on the bed, side by side, waiting to see what was going to happen.

In front of her lay two beautiful men with magnificent physiques and both with cocks that would please any right-thinking person. She licked her lips and moved in for the kill. She gently lowered herself onto the bed and positioned herself between the two men, knowing that she could pleasure both at the same time.

"Boys, just lie back and enjoy," she cooed as she lowered her mouth over the tip of Tyrone's swollen cock. Tyrone groaned with ecstasy as she slowly slid her mouth down its full length. After three trips up and down the length of Tyrone's cock, she moved across to Randy, who had been stroking his cock and was oozing pre-cum quite rapidly. The rocket was thrust upwards, and Toni's mouth was ready to take it all, much to Randy's surprise. Her warm lips encased his stem and she sank her mouth down his length until her mouth reached the base of his cock and her tongue massaged the stem. Randy prized himself in having one of the biggest, if not the biggest cock among all the cowboys he knew, and no woman had been able to take his full length, but here was Toni quite happily traveling up and down the length of the rocket with ease, and creating a pleasurable pressure that no other woman had achieved.

"Why don't you take off your clothes?" suggested Tyrone, encouraging Toni to disrobe.

"Before I do, I'd like to see you work on each other," she replied, releasing her grip on Randy's rocket.

Both Tyrone and Randy were startled at this suggestion. They may have compared cocks with each other and seen each other naked, but they had never had any form of sex together.

"You mean…," stammered Randy.

"Yes, I want to see you suck Tyrone's cock and Tyrone, I want to see you take that big dick of Randy's down your throat," smiled the redhead. "After all, you've seen me do it, now it's your turn."

The two cowboys lay looking at each other, each waiting for the other to make the first move. Eventually Tyrone made his move and positioned himself between Randy's thighs. He tentatively licked the tip of Randy's cock, not knowing what to expect, but he didn't remain there long because he soon had it down his throat, slurping like an old hand. It was clear that Randy was enjoying Tyrone's treatment, because his oohing and aarghing was growing louder. It wasn't long before Randy was doing likewise to Tyrone and the two men were at each other like two dogs after a bone.

Toni watched with fascination as the two men, oblivious of her presence, lay sucking each other's cocks, Tyrone gagging occasionally as he tried to take Randy's full length down his throat. Soon Toni stopped them, smiled at the two men, rose from the bed and asked, "Do you have any rubbers?"

At this suggestion, Randy's eyes lit up and he shot from the bed, rocket glistening and bobbing in the air, and hurried to get some condoms from his jeans and return before he missed out on any action. Toni handed each man a condom.

"Roll those on, sweeties," cooed Toni, as she kicked off her shoes and prepared to undress. She moved over to the gaslight and flicked it off.

"Hey!" exclaimed Randy. "Why are you putting off the lights?"

"It's nicer to feel our way in the dark," responded Toni, whipping off her dress.

Soon her mouth was back where it belonged, lubricating the rocket and its partner. Randy's groans reverberated around the room while Tyrone felt for Toni in the dark. Hands were moving in all directions but Toni guided them to where she wanted them. She wasn't sure whether she'd be able to take Randy's length inside her, so instead she reached for Tyrone's cock and guided it towards her ass. Slowly she sank down onto his length. A gasp of air escaped from Tyrone as Toni sank down his full length and held her position for a while getting used to his size, then she slowly began to rise and fall onto this weapon. As she did so, she leant over and continued sucking on Randy's sky rocket.

Once she felt that she had loosened herself to be able to take Randy's length and girth, she climbed off of Tyrone's throbbing cock and sank onto Randy's. By this stage, Randy was bucking like a bronco as Toni rode this wild animal. She felt for Tyrone's cock and started stroking it. Both men were nearing their climaxes, but she wanted to pleasure both equally, so she stopped stroking Tyrone's cock and instead brought Randy to his climax by tightening her ass muscles and squeezing his rocket tightly. Randy gave one enormous upward thrust which had Toni high off the bed and ploughed into her ass as he fired his load. From the sound, Tyrone knew that his buddy was coming, so he started stroking his own cock faster, but Toni stopped him by grasping his hand in the dark. Rising off Randy's cock, she removed Tyrone's condom and guided his cock into her mouth. Toni was also reaching her climax just about the same time that Tyrone was with his. She sucked wildly on his hard rod until both he and Toni gasped with passion and he shot his load deep down her throat. Her throat muscles clamped tightly around Tyrone's cock taking each drop of his cowboy juice deep down her throat until she had milked him dry,

As Tyrone shot his load he felt a warm wetness hit his stomach. He didn't worry too much about it as he was too busy thrusting into the warm cavity of Toni's mouth. As Toni came, so she fell across Tyrone's chest and felt the heaving muscular chest against hers. They lay there for a while catching their breath, then she felt Tyrone's hands come up to her breasts. They searched, but there were none. Tyrone's hands fumbled in the dark around Toni's waist and then he moved them downwards. He felt something hard; hard and long; hard, long and wet. It was exactly like he had; something hard, long and wet. He yelled and leapt from the bed, pushing Toni over in the process. The gaslight was immediately switched on and as they all became used to the light, they saw their ravishing redhead – wig lying on the floor, short brown hair, slim athletic build and an equally large cock with cum still dribbling from its tip.

"A guy!" gasped Randy. "Oh shit! A fucking guy!" continued Randy. "Who the fuck are you?"

"My name is Anthony or Tony for short, T-O-N-Y," came a sheepish reply, not knowing whether he would be attacked. "I'm new in town"

The two guys continued to curse and swear when they realized what they had done, but it was too late, it had been done. Randy even made a move for his gun, but 'Toni' warned him not to try anything stupid.

Tony smiled at both of them, not even thinking that he could be beaten up at any minute by these two egotistical cowboys, and said, "I don't know what all the fuss is about. Let's be honest, you both enjoyed it didn't you?"

The two guys didn't know what to say, other than to continue cussing and swearing. Then they realized that their friends were still in the lounge.

"Shit, if any of our buddies find out that we screwed a guy…!" exclaimed Randy. "…My reputation will be ruined," he continued.

"Well I won't say anything, if you two don't," replied Tony, replacing his wig, cleaning himself up and putting his dress back on.

The other two were in a dilemma and didn't know how to deal with the situation, but quickly got dressed again. When all three had made themselves presentable, Tony suggested that they simply go down stairs as though nothing untoward had happened.

"I don't know about you two guys," said Tony, once again looking stunningly beautiful, "but thank you. I thoroughly enjoyed myself and you are both great fucks; now I'll leave and no one will be any the wiser."

The three cautiously exited the bedroom, the two guys looking a little sheepish as they re-entered the lounge and escorted the glamorous Toni to the saloon door. On the way they heard a few snide comments such as 'hey check, they must have scored with that redhead!' and 'I bet she got lucky with old Randy and his rocket', but the two men chose to ignore the comments. She gave each of them a kiss on the cheek and again thanked them for the wonderful evening, but as she was leaving Randy said, "Hang on a second I just want to get something."

He ran to the bar counter, grabbed a piece of paper and wrote something on it. He then ran back to the door where Toni was still waiting and handed the paper to her, smiling as he did so.

"So long," the two guys said, looking embarrassed as Toni departed and the swing doors closed.

The two cowboys remained at the doorway; obviously thinking of what they would say should any of their friends asked them about the redhead.

"What did you give her?" asked Tyrone.

"Oh nothing much," was the nonchalant reply, as Randy turned to join his friends and once again squeezed his balls and rubbed his hand over his rocket.

As Toni left the saloon and opened the piece of paper, she saw:

Don't tell Tyrone, but I think you were really great.

Maybe we can do it again.

ENGLISH 101

Once I had graduated from high school and headed off to university, I had two aims in life – to get a degree and to lose my virginity; not necessarily in that order. At University, I had landed up in a *Frat House* with a number of other guys who didn't seem to share the same interests or aims as me, so I decided to focus my attentions elsewhere.

I attended my lectures regularly, but found that each of my lecturers seemed to be somewhat dull, unattractive and wizened. However, after my first lecture of English 101, I moved from the back row of the lecture theatre to the front row. Dr Hudson, our English professor was definitely not like the other professors, old fossils. He was middle-aged to start with, and by that I mean he was probably in his fifties, if you call that middle-aged. He was tall, with broad shoulders and a slim waist, long athletic legs, a cute, tight ass and a bulge in the front to make anyone's jaw drop open. Now you might ask how I know all these things; well, by sitting in the front row of his lectures enabled me to take a close look at him. He always wore tight fitting, but smart clothes and it was through the tightness of his shirts and chinos or jeans that I was able to determine his physique. Of course, without his clothes on, I had no idea what his physique was like. His hair was his distinguishing feature for me as it was light brown flecked with gray, and it was the gray that made him look so distinguished He was unlike the other professors who never moved during the lecture. Dr Hudson made a point of walking up and down in front of us as he spoke, which enabled me to see his slim hips and tight ass and of course the bulging crotch tightly packed into his chinos or jeans. Naturally, my mouth was permanently dry whenever I had English 101. I would watch his every movement from the slow seductive walk as his butt cheeks would rise and fall, to the slight increased bulge as his right leg stepped forward, pushing his bulge out further to the left. When he put his hands into his chino pockets, the movement would pull his chinos tight across his ass and I would see the outline of his briefs, then my mind would wander. I wonder what type of briefs and what color they are? Every time we had an English lecture and I was seated in the front row of the lecture hall, I would feel myself becoming aroused as Dr. Hudson walked past. Obviously he was not good for my studies because I could never concentrate in his lectures because I was too busy admiring this man and getting an erection.

Now I must explain that up until going to university, I had never taken much notice of older men; I had often adopted the familiar stance of so many other guys who are attracted to men, that young was better. However, seeing Dr. Hudson had certainly changed my mind.

I thought back to my two aims while at university and decided that perhaps Dr Hudson might be the person to help me achieve both. If I played my cards right, I might get my degree and lose my virginity.

One rainy afternoon, I took myself off to the library to do some research for an English assignment. I found the books that I required and then found a quiet corner to myself. I had probably been sitting there for about half an hour when I suddenly heard a voice.

"Nice to see you doing some work, Mr. Ward."

I looked up into the blue eyes of Dr. Hudson looking especially sexy in a pair of well-fitting faded blue jeans and a casual shirt with at least the top three buttons undone, allowing all to see the smooth chest under the soft fabric. Immediately I felt a tingling sensation in my crotch and put a hand between my legs to squeeze my crotch. I don't know if he saw me, but I really didn't worry.

"Yes, Prof. It's your assignment I'm working on.

"Well that I'm glad to hear. I would have taken offence if it had been another lecturer's."

I smiled, feeling a definite growth happening in my jeans.

"Are you here to do some work, Prof?"

"Yes," he replied, setting down his books at a desk about four feet away from me.

I glanced in his direction when he was seated and realized what a magnificent view I had. Under the desk top, I was able to view the large package in his crotch area and how he had spread his muscular thighs wide, allowing me a better view.

'Oh hell! I can feel myself getting harder and harder and I can feel how cramped my cock and balls are feeling inside my briefs.'

When I think he's not watching me, I slide my hand onto my swollen cock and try to adjust its position. I can also feel a small dampness in my briefs and know that my cock has started a gentle leaking of pre-come.

His face is serene as he studies his books; mine is probably pained as my balls get squashed in the tightness of the denim of my jeans.

I notice, after a while, that his hand slips down to his crotch and I see how he gently rubs over the large package. Maybe an itch; maybe he's also feeling horny! I reciprocate on my crotch and wonder if he's watching me out of the corner of his eyes. I then notice how his hand now goes into the open top of his shirt and I can see he's rubbing his finger tips over his nipples. Oh God! This is such a turn on for me. Now my cock is throbbing and I know the leaking has increased. Fortunately the wet patch is not going to show through my denim jeans, but if I stand up, my erection will definitely show. I stay seated, pretending to do my research, but it's now not research on English, but rather on Dr. Hudson. My mind starts to wander and I begin to wonder what it would be like going to bed with this hunky man. Is he married? Is he single? Maybe he's not into guys. Mentally, I start to strip him of his clothes and imaging what his chest looks like and how he might pull me close to his chest and crush me against it. With each thought, my cock gives a little throb and I rub my hand over the engorged muscle.

This goes on for at least half an hour until I can't handle it any more. I decide I need to go to the washroom. I stand up and try to hide my erection and head off in the direction of the men's toilet. On entering, I find the place empty so I move to the urinal, unzip my jeans and haul out my large cock, which is standing erect like a conning tower on a submarine. Because I'm so hard, I can't piss so I have to think non-sexual thoughts to get it to begin to become limp. While I'm still semi-hard, I hear the toilet door open. I glance over my shoulder to see who's come in and suddenly I get a shock. There is Dr. Hudson heading to the urinal. What if he sees my hard cock? I try as best as possible to hide my embarrassment, but it's about to become worse. He comes and stands next to me at the urinal and unzips.

Oh my God!!! What a size!! He pulls out his thick, flaccid cock with its beautifully mushroom-shaped head and long shaft, and then he scoops out two hefty balls. I can't control my reaction and a short gasp comes from my mouth as I stare down at this wonder of the universe. Dr Hudson catches me looking at his equipment and smiles at me. Now I have a problem because my own cock has taken on a life of its own. Instead of getting softer, it's now become rock hard; so hard I can't even get it back into my jeans if I wanted to make a quick getaway. I look to the ceiling to take my attention away from this beautiful sight that's next to me, but that doesn't help because the leaking is still taking place. I then return my look to see that he has become semi-hard and in the process it looks like his cock has grown another inch or two both in length and girth. I take my attention up to his face to see his soft blue eyes looking at me and an enigmatic smile on his face. Oh boy! What am I to do? Do I drop to my knees and worship this man's equipment with my mouth, or run back to my *frat house*?

Dr. Hudson makes the decision for me. Slowly and seductively he hoists his balls and pushes them back into his briefs and jeans, leaving his massive cock still protruding from his jeans, then equally slowly, he takes the shaft and begins to insert his cock back into his briefs, but he's careful to allow me a last look at the magnificent mushroom head. Instinctively as I see the head disappear, I lick my lips, which he sees. He smiles, zips up and leaves the toilet. Now I have to face him when I exit the toilet.

I make my way back to my books, still with a hard-on, and sit down. I look across towards his desk and notice that the outline length of his cock is visible. I can see now that he has a full erection and my mouth becomes dry again. This is frustrating! The only solution is to pack up my books and head home where I'll have to whack off to bring some relief to me.

I pick up my books and move to go, but I have to have one last look at this magnificent older man. He stops studying, looks up, pushes his seat back, allowing me to see the engorged outline of his cock in his jeans and says, "I hope I see you at lectures tomorrow, Mr. Ward?"

The following day I'm a little embarrassed to sit in the front row, although I really want to be near him. I also notice that there are not as many people in the lecture as usual.

"I think you should all move forward seeing we're so few today," said Dr. Hudson.

Was this his subtle way of telling me he wanted me in the front row? Those of us in the middle and back, move forward. Our eyes connect and I can see that he wants me nearer, so I move to the front row, but having thought about the previous day's event in the library, I've already got an erection.

The lecture is on Oscar Wilde's *The Importance of Being Earnest* but I'm not concentrating very much because I'm wondering what's going through his mind. His behavior patterns are no different from any other day. He walks up and down as he lectures and that wonderful package is still being flaunted in front of me. The only difference is that now he seems to smile at me more often.

The lecture comes to an end and Dr. Hudson asks us for our assignments, which we duly hand in.

"I hope this is brilliant, Mr. Ward," he says as I hand mine in.

As I hand him my manuscript, I feel his hand glance mine. There seems to be magnetic warmth and immediately my cock gives a throb. I really am the horniest creature in front of this man, but I can't help looking; I like what I see. I'm even beginning to question my interest in men; have I overlooked some older men in my past and only woken up to the fact that older men have a certain something that younger men don't possess?

Two days later, I get a message to report to Dr. Hudson's office as he wants to discuss my assignment with me. I don't have a problem with the invitation; it's the time that interests me. He has asked me to report to his office at 6 p.m., which is after most of the other lecturers have left for home.

I'm not sure what to expect, but I'm hoping that something exciting might occur, so I pull on a pair of white Calvin Klein briefs, my jeans and an old T-shirt. The reason I chose an old T-shirt was that it's a bit small for me and therefore shows off my physique. I'm no slouch and am very proud of my body even though I haven't spent years in a gym or doing sport.

I wander across the campus, passing the odd students coming out of their last lectures and heading home. Then I reach Dr. Hudson's office. The wooden door with his name on is closed. I hover outside, plucking up courage, and then I knock lightly on the door.

"Enter!" comes the deep voice.

I open the door gingerly, not knowing what to expect, and enter.

I gasp at the sight.

Dr. Hudson is standing with his cute, tight ass on the edge of his desk, facing the door, and his legs are spread wide, allowing me full access to his glorious bulging package.

"Come in Mr. Ward and make yourself at home."

I slowly walk towards the desk, my eyes glancing from his smiling face and soft blue eyes to his bulging crotch and well-built legs, encased in the flimsiest of cotton chinos.

"Have a seat. I just wanted to talk to you about your assignment."

"I hope it wasn't too bad," I replied, still not taking my eyes off the forbidden package.

"On the contrary, I think it was a very good effort, but I wanted to offer some advice on how to improve on it."

I sit in a chair facing him, waiting. He smiles at me, winks and then crosses to another chair which he pulls up next to mine, so we are sitting side by side. I can feel his warmth and I can also feel the constraints in my Calvin Kleins. He places my assignment across our legs and begins to explain certain features about it to me. I feel his knee touch mine, but I don't show any physical reaction, other than I know my cock is leaking again. I feel a little more pressure being exerted on my leg but I don't move it away. Instead, I exert pressure on Dr. Hudson's leg letting him know that I like the feeling.

After ten or fifteen minutes of so-called discussion, Dr. Hudson rises from his seat and returns to the position he was in when I first entered his office. However, now as he stands there, I can see the thick, long outline of his erect cock in his chinos. The dry mouth syndrome comes again, but now I've had enough; I have to do something.

I put down my assignment and stand up, allowing him to see that I am also equally aroused, and I walk up to him. I let my hand drift gently over his swollen cock, smiling at him as I do so. He sighs and closes his blue eyes.

"You have a beautiful cock, Prof."

There is no answer, but the sighing continues.

"I want to suck you, sir."

Still no reply; but no rebuttal.

My hand feels for the zip in his chinos and slowly I lower it, feel inside his briefs and then feel the solid muscle of flesh. I take hold of it and pull it out into the open for me to admire. Immediately I sink to my knees on the carpet in his office and run my tongue down the length of his thick shaft until my mouth reaches his balls. I lick them and attempt to pull them into the warmth of my mouth, but I am unable to take both in at the same time as he is too big. After a moment, my mouth heads back up along the solid flesh until it reaches the swollen mushroom-shaped head. I lick around the top then swallow it and sink my mouth back down the lengthy shaft. His sighs became groans and then he starts a gentle back and forward thrust. This continues for some time until he feels the need to take a rest, so he lifts me to my feet.

"You're quite a horny student, aren't you?"

I smile and feel his mouth touch mine. Before I know it, his tongue is embedded in the warmth of my mouth and our tongues begin a duel. I thrust my crotch against his, rubbing our cocks together, then I feel his hands unzip and pull down the jeans I am wearing. This is rapidly followed by my briefs until we can feel each other's nakedness, then he sinks to his knees and takes my throbbing cock deep into his throat.

I've had the odd blow job in my life, but nothing like this. It felt like his mouth was a suction taking everything out of me. Thank goodness the staff was all headed home, because the groans that were coming from me were, to say the least, loud, but it didn't seem to worry him.

As his mouth works up and down my cock and he lathers my balls, I feel a finger begin to explore the opening to my ass. As I said earlier, I was a virgin and no-one had ever penetrated me, but I felt ready for this man to be the lucky guy. Two fingers suddenly enter me and I gasp, but soon relax.

"Hm, Mr. Ward, you've got quite a tight little ass; just what I like."

"Please be gentle," I answered, breathing heavily.

He releases my cock and looks up at me.

"Are you a virgin?"

I smile guiltily and nod.

"Would you like that to change?"

My smile becomes broader and again I nod.

Dr. Hudson rises to his feet, crosses to behind his desk, opens a drawer and takes out some condoms and lube.

"Please be gentle," I plead again when I see the condoms.

"I promise," he replied. "This is going to be special for you and for me."

He unrolls a condom along the length of his cock, or rather, as far as the condom would go; lubes up his cock and then gently inserts a lubed finger into my tight ass. It feels really good as his finger slips into me. He then guides me to the top of his desk.

"I hope this is not going to be uncomfortable for you, but lie on your back."

I do as he asks, feeling both trepidation and excitement; it's what I had wanted – to lose my virginity to someone manly and to someone that I had made a move on.

Dr. Hudson takes hold of his thick shaft and slowly guides it towards my waiting ass. I tense as I feel his cock-head touch my opening.

"Relax"

I try and then feel the bulbous head begin to push into my opening. Although I am instinctively trying to prevent this from happening, I am also willing it to happen.

Suddenly I feel the large head break through and enter my chute. What a sensation! The tightness is intense I can feel my eyes roll back and stars begin to appear. If this is what it feels like, I can't wait to experience it again and again. Once he feels me relax, he slowly pushes forward, sinking his hard cock deeper into me until I feel his swollen balls nudge against my ass. Both he and I sigh in unison. He holds his position for a while allowing me to become accustomed to his size, and then he begins a slow and rhythmic thrust and pull motion while he holds my legs, hoisting them high to allow for deeper penetration.

After the initial pain, I am in heaven and find myself encouraging him to go even deeper. He then leans forward so that our mouths cam meet and he kisses me passionately with each thrust. I lie there thinking why I had waited so long to lose my virginity, but on second thoughts, I am glad that it had been with this older, elegant and handsome man.

Because of the size of his cock-head, it rubs ever so gently against my prostate bringing me to an exhilarating climax. I know that I won't last long and I warn him, but he seems to ignore me and continues at his gentle pace.

"Prof, I'm gonna come," I gasp.

He smiles down at me and pushes deeper. Throughout all this, he has not touched my cock, but I know that I am about to shoot my load. I grab my balls and squeezed them hoping I won't come so soon, but to no avail. A hot stream of cum shoots from the tip of my cock landing on my chest, closely followed by a second and third stream landing on my stomach. Still Dr. Hudson continues and I cam see a film of perspiration forming on his face. What amazes me is that even though I have come, my cock remains rock hard and I feel that I want more. I resume thrusting against Dr. Hudson's thrusts, encouraging him to delve deeper and encouraging him to fuck me harder.

My stomach has become sticky from my cum but I seem to have gathered a second breath, because I place my hands behind Dr. Hudson's cute ass and began pulling him closer to me.

"As much as I want to flip you over and take you from behind," he says, "this is so special for both of us that I want to keep looking at your beautiful face."

I noticed that his thrusts have increased in intensity so I know he is getting close, but then so am I for a second time. I have never experienced coming twice so soon after the first time, but it feels like a tidal wave is breaking over me. I have become so used to his large size in me that I am able to take whatever he throws at me. His action increases to a rapid pummeling of my ass, but it never hurts. The noise from our thrusts and gasps echoes around the office, but we are both in such a passionate state that it never concerns us.

I feel his hefty balls swell and rise and then he lets out a loud gasp and thrusts a long, deep thrust into me, then I feel the cock-head flare and begin to throb as he empties his load. At precisely the same time, I begin to coat my stomach and chest with warm cum again. He pounds my ass, thrusting deep and long until he has emptied his balls of his supply. He leans across my sticky stomach and chest and gently places his lips on mine.

"Thank you, Mr. Ward," he whispers softly.

"It's Kevin, sir. But thank you; that was awesome, Prof."

"It's Michael, Kevin."

I feel as he slowly begins to withdraw from the confines of my tightly clamping ass. I don't want him to leave, but once he has, he lies across the desk alongside of me; both of us breathing heavily, and our hands touching, locking fingers.

When we have recovered, I turn to him and smile.

"I'm so glad it was someone like you who made love to me first and that it wasn't in some sleazy place by some unknown person in the dark," I say, squeezing his hand.

"And I'm glad that you made a move on me because I've been eyeing you in lectures for some time, hoping that you would be available."

As we begin to clean ourselves and get dressed, I turn to Michael and say, "Does this mean that every time I do an assignment, I'll be able to see you in private?"

He laughs.

"Certainly not, Kevin. I hope we're going to see much more of each other; at least that's what I would like, if that's OK with you."

What a question!!! My estimation of this so-called middle-aged man has risen, much like my cock does whenever I see him and I can't wait for our next meeting, especially to see what my sexy, 'middle-aged' Professor is going to teach me next, because they say older men are wiser and more experienced!

MIRROR, MIRROR ON THE WALL ...

They say that all that glistens is not gold; but I'm unsure who 'they' are. I say that beauty is in the eye of the beholder; and you're probably wondering what this has to do with 'mirror, mirror on the wall, who is the fairest of them all'? Imagine a room full of mirrors, and I'm not talking about the Palace of Versailles; but instead, a plane large room, filled with heavy metal objects, glistening, and in some cases, heavily built vane men, also glistening. Now don't get me wrong, not all men found in these rooms are vane, but when there is a mirror involved, they invariably are. I had recently joined a local gym and on my first visit, was embarrassed to see all the mirrors on the surrounding walls. I say embarrassed because I didn't have the typical Mr. Universe type build, nor did I actually want one. All I wanted was to bulk up a little to look healthier than to look like I was so big that I had trouble walking or swinging my arms, and all this had to do with my best friend.

My best friend, Alex, had suggested I join him at the gym, where he'd been going for the past five years, but I had always found some excuse to avoid making a fool of myself in front of all those muscle-bound guys.

"You've got yourself a pretty good natural build, Chris, why don't you just bulk up a bit more and get more definition," he'd said one evening as we sat drinking a beer or two while he flexed his muscles to impress me.

I nearly choked with laughter, but I could see he was serious, so I promised I'd consider it. Now like most people, when they say they'll consider something, it doesn't mean that they are likely to agree to do that something, so I was no different.

Alex kept persisting until I eventually relinquished and said I'd make the effort, much to his delight.

"I promise you'll enjoy it," he said.

How could anyone enjoy pain, sweat and strain!

So, I got myself psyched up to face the world of muscles, the world of ego-busting self-indulgence. I had even been told by Alex to get myself an ego-boosting outfit to wear at the gym. Have you ever heard of anything so absurd?

"What constitutes an ego-boosting outfit?" I had asked.

"It must enhance your physical attributes and it must be modern and streamlined," replied Alex, oozing confidence.

"So tell me, what exactly did you have in mind for me?" I enquired, not sure of what constituted 'modern' or 'streamlined'.

"Get yourself a tight-fitting vest, preferably white, as it will enhance your tanned skin, and a pair of Lycra shorts."

"You mean like the kind cyclists wear?" I asked.

"Yeah, but without that crappy padding on your ass," he answered.

"Why? What's the point of wearing skin tight shorts?" I asked bemusedly.

"To show off your legs and what else you have."

I liked the 'whatever else you have' because I knew I had a great ass and a well hung cock, but wearing such tight shorts might make me self-conscious of my attributes.

"Trust me on this, Chris," replied Alex, trying to convince me.

I wasn't totally sold on the idea of the dress code, but when Alex arrived at my apartment one day with a package filled with various colored shorts and a couple of white vests, I knew that he was serious.

"Here, try these on," said Alex handing me the package.

I pulled out the shorts and vest and roared with laughter when I saw what he'd brought.

"You really are serious, aren't you?"

"Stop playing for time, and try these on," he said, sounding as though he was losing patience with me.

I had no inhibitions with Alex as we'd been friends for some time, so I stripped off there in the lounge and pulled on the first pair of shorts, a bright yellow pair.

"Looks good on you," said Alex, wandering around me, admiring the view from all angles, "but you look like a canary in that bright yellow."

I pulled them off and was handed a pale blue pair, which I put on.

"How do those look?" I enquired, turning on the spot for Alex to judge.

"Much better. Do they fit OK?"

"Like a glove, but tell me, should I wear jocks under them or not?"

Alex's eyes lit up at my question.

"For me, I think you should go commando; let it all hang out!"

"Yes, you would, you sex-starved young man," I joked.

With the shorts selected, it was just a matter of finding the right size vest from the few that Alex had brought. Once that was established, I then had to model the complete outfit to meet with his approval.

"Pick a couple of other colors of shorts," said Alex, picking some up from the bundle. "You can't be expected to wear the same ones day in and day out."

"Hey! Who said anything about going to gym day in and day out?"

"Well, you know what I mean."

I chose a white pair, another blue pair and a pale yellow that didn't make me look like a canary.

The afternoon of my first visit to the gym arrived. I had arranged to meet Alex at the gym so that he could show me around and had decided to wear my blue shorts for this first occasion. I knew that I looked good in the tight-fitting outfit, but when I arrived at the gym, I was shocked to see what a fashion show there was. Guys were in an array of brightly colored outfits and I immediately understood what Alex had meant when he said I needed to appear modern and streamlined. There were trim, buffed and very few ordinary looking bodies scattered around the gym. Some were busy with an aerobics class, while others were 'pumping iron'. However, the one thing that struck me more than the colorful array of men was the amount of mirrors that covered the walls of the gym. Everywhere one looked there was shining glass with preening men looking into them. Although the mirrors created the effect of more space, the number of men filling that space was incredible. Although there might have been forty or fifty guys in the large room, with the mirrors, it appeared as though there were hundreds.

Alex took me around the gym, showing me the various areas, which included the change rooms, showers, steam room and massage area, as well as the weights areas. Once he had shown me around, he introduced to some of his buddies who all seemed to show an interest in me, even though I was not as well built as them.

"I think they like you, Chris," Alex had said, with a twinkle in his eye.

"Thanks, but why? I'm not in the same league as them."

"That's what you think," chuckled Alex. "You see it pays to wear those Lycra shorts."

"Meaning?"

"Well look at the heavy package you're carrying in front and that tight ass at the back!"

I laughed at Alex's comments because I couldn't think that this was what the guys came to gym for.

"A lot of these guys are here for one thing only…"

"…and that is?" I questioned.

"A big cock or a tight ass," whispered Alex.

I think I must have blushed when he said that.

"The things that you've got, my friend."

"Well, I'm not necessarily here for that," I replied, heading off in the direction of a bench to do some bench presses.

I found a vacant bench, lay down on my back and proceeded to lift the bar with some weights on. As they were not that heavy, I was able to do the exercise on my own, but soon I noticed a pair of muscular legs standing at my head and when I glanced upwards, I noticed a heavy bulge in a pair of red Lycra shorts standing over me.

"Do you need some help," said a very strong accented voice.

I looked up at the face above me and saw a hefty looking man, muscles seemingly bulging from every part of his body, standing astride of my head. Obviously I couldn't resist the view of his hefty crotch. I felt my heart pound at the sight of this giant-looking man.

"Thank you," was all I could whimper as I lifted the bar.

His hands were at the ready in case I was about to drop the weights.

"You new here," he said, more as a statement than a question.

"Yes," I grunted, hoisting the bar.

"You have nice young body," he continued.

"Thanks," came another grunt.

"Nice legs … and you big boy!"

I knew exactly what he was referring to and the thought of him eyeing out my crotch, was an instant turn-on because I knew that my cock was beginning to enjoy the attention it was getting and was therefore taking on a life of its own.

"Thank you," was all I could think of to say.

"You here by yourself?"

"No, a friend brought me," I replied, thinking that this might chase him off, but it didn't.

"Who?"

"I don't know if you know him His name's Alex."

"Ah, Alex. He good friend of mine."

I was intrigued by the accent so I asked where he was from, hoping to change the subject and thereby take the attention away from my ever burgeoning cock.

"Moscow," was the reply, "but I have lived here for three years now."

As we spoke, I could see that he too was becoming aroused by my engorged cock and every time I raised the bar, my hands grazed his hefty crotch.

"You like that?" he enquired on one occasion as my hand rested on his hard-on.

I wasn't sure what to say as there were others around, but I think my smile gave him his answer.

"Why do we not work on other machines? I show you how," he said, laying the bar and weights to rest on the rack above me.

I sat up and said I would be grateful, so he led me to an area of the gym which was somewhat secluded. I thought it odd that Alex hadn't shown me this area, but then I realized he couldn't show me every nook and cranny. In this secluded area, which was also walled with mirrors, there was a simple bench plus some machines to do arm, leg and abs exercises. He stood on the machine, resting his arms on the armrests and began to show me how to do my abs exercises by lifting my legs in a crunch style. His erection was very evident to me, but this didn't seem to concern him.

"I am Boris, and you are?" he asked lifting and lowering his legs.

As I watched him exercising and seeing his thick cock begin to create a wet patch of pre-cum in the front of his Lycra shorts, I replied and said, "My name's Chris."

"Now you try, Chris," said Boris alighting from the machine and allowing me to rest my arms on the armrests.

"Lift your legs, Chris and crunch your stomach muscles. Ja, that is it," he said, beaming as he watched my wet patch begin to form, darkening the pale blue Lycra.

He could see that after a while I was tiring and my legs were not getting as high as he wanted, so he placed his hands under my upper thighs and helped to lift my legs. Naturally, I felt that on occasions, his hand moved up to my ass and encased it in the palms of his hands and squeezed. I liked the feeling and so did my cock.

"That's good. You have firm ass," he continued.

After a few more repetitions, he allowed me to stop, then proceeded to show me how to exercise my arm and shoulder muscles. He had used the same machine, but was now facing away from me. I was able to admire his ass, which was quite broad, just like his back muscles, but I was also able to admire his thick thighs and muscular calves. Once the demonstration was complete, it was my turn to attempt the exercise. I climbed onto the machine and made a first attempt.

"Let me show you," said Boris moving onto the machine with me.

He stood behind me, helping to lift me by the waist, but each time he touched me I could feel the definite prod of his cock against my ass. At this stage I was no longer concerned about his presence and enjoyed the physical attention he was giving me. Each time I was lifted, so his cock rubbed against my ass, allowing his wet patch to wet the rear of my shorts. When we came to an end, Boris remained behind me, the two of us merely standing still, while he pressed his hefty cock against my ass and then gave a gentle thrust.

"You like that?" he whispered into my ear as he placed his muscular arms around my waist.

I instinctively pushed my ass back against his throbbing cock.

"Yes," I whispered back.

"You want?"

"Yes, I want," I retorted.

Suddenly my shorts were shucked to the ground, I was carried to the bench and laid down and Boris had my legs in the air and his tongue glued between my ass cheeks, his tongue darting in and out of my opening. I glanced to my right and noticed his actions in the wall mirror. I could see how his cock was straining to break free from the constraints of his shorts while my ass remained high in the air, his mouth doing wonders for my ego.

The feeling was so intense that I couldn't help myself.

"Please fuck me," I whimpered as I felt his tongue delve deeper into me, but he seemed too preoccupied to listen.

I closed my eyes and lay there enjoying the treatment that my new Russian friend was meting out to me. As I lay there, his mouth eating my ass, I could hear him pulling his shorts off. I opened my eyes and saw in the mirror his thick, veined cock, his foreskin pulled right back allowing the mushroom-shaped head to appear, waiting to penetrate me. I also noticed that he'd encased his fat cock in as much condom as would fit along his long shaft and then I felt the large round head nudge the opening to my ass. Slowly Boris began push forward and sink into me. I could feel his bulbous cock head push through my sphincter and enter my warm chute. A feeling of ecstasy filled my whole being. Slowly he sank deeper until I felt his furry balls caress my smooth ass cheeks.

"Aagh! You have fine ass, Chris," he said, smiling down at me.

I grinned back, enjoying the pressure his cock was exerting on my prostate.

"I like your hard cock, Boris," I reciprocated.

As if that was the signal to start the action, Boris quickened his pace and began thrusting long, deep plunges into my waiting ass. He held onto my hips for support and grunted loudly with each thrust. As he continued to please both of us, I glanced into the mirrors and watched his cock sliding in and out of my ass. This in itself was a complete turn-on for me, but just as much as it was a turn on, I noticed that we'd acquired an audience. Alex and a friend of his had entered the area and were watching Boris's prowess. I was in my seventh heaven!

Soon both Alex and his friend, Matt, had their cocks out and were stroking them. To see this, along with Boris sliding his massive weapon into me, was enough to bring me to the edge of a climax.

"Oh Fuck! You're gonna make me come, Boris."

"That is good," he replied, thrusting his length deeper into me, as though he were trying to squeeze his balls into my ass as well. "Shoot, my friend!" He exclaimed.

I could feel my balls rising in their sac and without much warning I groaned and a stream of warm, white cum flew from the slit in my cock and landed on my chest, soon to be followed another and another stream, covering my stomach. Boris smiled happily as I fired my load, but Matt was very quick to attack my throbbing cock,

Matt placed his lips around the cut head of my cock and sucked. I could feel every last drop of warm cum being extracted from me as Matt swallowed what I had to offer. While he did this, Alex positioned himself above me and forced his long, thin cock into my waiting mouth. It felt good to have my best friend in my mouth. Although I was still breathing heavily, I was able to take him to the base of my throat, licking and nibbling his shaft as my mouth worked over his length.

Boris continued his thrusts into my ass and from the mirrors around us I could see how each man was enjoying himself with me. Suddenly Boris pulled out and I thought he was going to shoot over me, but he pulled off his condom and moved to above my head, sending Alex to between my legs. Boris thrust his veined cock into the confines of my mouth and I clamped my lips tightly around his shaft.

"Ooh that is so good and tight," he groaned as he began to fuck my face.

At the same time, Alex had slid into my chute that had been stretched by Boris's thick cock and was effortlessly sliding in and out of my well-lubricated ass. Matt, in the meantime had moved to behind Alex and was trying to penetrate Alex's muscular ass. I knew that Alex liked to be fucked occasionally, but it was a really great sight to see two well-built guys going at each other. I glanced into the mirrors once more and noticed that a few more people had entered to watch while the four of us pleasured each other. I felt like a pig being skewered at both ends. Boris had my mouth well and truly plugged with his enormous cock, while Alex was sending me over the edge once more. My cock was bobbing from each thrust that Alex gave me and even though it had not softened after Boris had made me come, I knew that my excitement was building again.

"I am gonna shoot," groaned Boris, taking his cock from my mouth and stroking it.

Both Matt and Alex increased their pace and watched eagerly as Boris's cock head swelled and a stream of white jism shot onto my face. I felt its warmth and immediately I opened my mouth as though encouraging Boris to reinsert his cock into my mouth, which he hastily did. I sucked hard and tight, pulling every last drop of Russian cum out of Boris, while Alex let out a cry and fired into my warm chute, pushing deeply into me and thrusting back to receive Matt's thrusts.

As Alex's eruption subsided, so Matt pulled free from Alex, pushed him forward and shot onto Alex's back, covering it with his sticky seed.

All four of us were exhausted and our heavy breathing could be heard by the voyeurs who were now returning to the main part of the gym.

I lay on my back and smiled up at my three friends, one old and two new and then looked into the mirrors and saw their happy faces reflected, while the last of their erections still throbbed.

"Let us show you the showers," said Boris, pulling on his shorts and trying to adjust his still hard cock.

Alex helped me from the bench and I pulled on my pale blue shorts. I looked at myself in the mirror and smiled. I could see the long outline of my erect cock, still oozing cum into the Lycra material and I realized that I probably would fit into the gym world, but I wouldn't be a Boris or Alex or Matt when it came to build; but I did know that I'd be seen by many guys who'd like to view my ass or my cock either in the mirrors around the gym, or in the privacy of the secluded area. I smiled at myself in the mirror and felt Alex and Boris both give my ass a gentle squeeze.

So, mirror, mirror on the wall, who's the hunkiest of them all?

MR. LEATHER

It's amazing how the leather scene spans age groups and it's the one area in which older guys are accepted openly. I had only recently decided to get involved in the leather scene, not because I had reached a stage in my life where I couldn't pick up guys, but rather, I'd always taken a liking for the feel and smell of leather, the tight leather clothing worn by the guys and the sexuality associated with leather. I wasn't interested in the S & M scene and was more focused on the appearance in wearing leather. I didn't want the whips and chains, nor the bondage or pain; instead I wanted the feel of the leather against my skin, its smoothness and softness caressing my body. Just the touch of leather on my body could turn me on.

I had ventured, rather naively, into a leather shop one day and wandered around admiring all the different outfits, jockstraps, waistcoats, caps and jeans. Everything in the shop was dark and had a sense of mystery about it. A tall, African-American guy of approximately six foot six, in leathers, came up to me and asked if he might help. He had broad shoulders and a trim waist. I looked at him and almost shot a load in my jeans. He was hot, but I was at a loss for words. Eventually I was able to speak.

"Hi. I'm looking for something leather to wear," I said, rather stupidly.

He smiled at me, knowing that I was new to the leather scene.

"Is this your first time of trying leather?" he asked, showing a sense of pity for this idiot who was confused by all the garments on display.

I nodded, like a young child, except I was now thirty.

"I've always had a liking for leather but I don't know what to buy."

"Are you planning to go to the leather bars?"

I hadn't thought of things like that and so was once again dumbstruck.

"I think you must also decide what image you want to portray. How about us getting you a decent pair of leather jeans, because that is the basic item you need?"

"OK," I replied. "I'm a size 32."

"Right, come this way and let's see what we can find for you."

He led me to a section towards the back of the shop where there were rows and rows of leather jeans, and on seeing them, my mind became confused; but I needn't have worried, because he pulled three pairs off the rack and handed them to me.

"Here. These are all 32's, but in different designs. Why don't you go into the change room and try them on."

I followed the direction of his hand and took them into the change room. I stripped down to my briefs and slid on the first pair. They fitted beautifully and when I turned around and looked in the mirror, I could see how they accentuated my firm ass; I liked these. I tried on the second and third pairs, and as I was trying on the last pair, the salesman came into the change room.

"How's it going?" he asked, patting my ass. "These fit kinda tight."

I looked in the mirror and knew that before he had tapped my ass with his hand, I had started to get a hard-on which was evident in the mirror.

"I can see you like these," he said, smiling at me in the mirror, and focusing his eyes on my bulging crotch. "Now let's get you some attachments we can add to this outfit."

He disappeared for a moment and returned with a handful of other pieces of clothing and accoutrement, such as a studded collar, belts, waistcoat, leather jockstrap and a harness.

"Try these on and let's see what you look like."

The first item I picked up was the harness and didn't know how to put it on, so my salesman, who had remained in the change room, helped.

"What's this?" I asked, looking at the leather attachment which had a large metal ring attached to it.

He smiled and said, "It's a cock ring attached to the harness."

All I could say was "Oh!" rather stupidly.

"Come on, take off these jeans and let's get you dressed properly."

I was embarrassed to take off the jeans considering I knew that I had such a hard-on underneath, but with constant jibbing from the salesman, I did as I was told. The jeans came off.

"And the briefs," he instructed.

Down they came and there I stood with my massive erection for the salesman to see.

"You're quite a big boy, aren't you?"

I blushed and tried to cover up my erection, but without success.

"Slip your cock and balls through the ring," he said, trying to show me how, "if you can get that big thing through there."

We battled, because of my erection, but between the two of us we eventually managed to get everything through.

"How's that feel?"

"Tight and makes me even more horny," I replied, watching my cock throbbing in the mirror.

"That's what it's there for; now slip on these jocks," he said, handing me the leather jockstrap.

I slipped them on and tried desperately to fit my cock into them, but it remained peeping over the top of the waistband.

"Never mind about that, but I see you're leaking a bit," he said and wiped a finger across the tip of my cock, scooped up some of my pre-cum and licked it off his finger. "Hm! Tasty! Now put the jeans back on."

Again I did as I was told and I realized that my whole appearance was beginning to change. He stood back to admire his model, then picked up the collar.

"Let's put this on and see how you look."

The collar was placed around my neck and the studs shone in the change room light.

"I think that just about makes you complete. What do you think?"

I looked at myself in the mirror, turning in all directions to see front and back views.

"I like this, but I suppose I'll just have to get used to being a walking hard-on," I answered.

He laughed. "Well there's nothing wrong with that, and with what I've seen between your legs, you've got nothing to worry about, the guys will be falling all over you."

"Thanks for the compliment, but you don't think I'm overdoing it with all the leather?"

"Not at all. That's what you want isn't it?"

I nodded in agreement and so it was that I bought my first leather outfit.

"By the way, I'm Chad," I said extending a hand to shake his.

"Hi, I'm Josh."

"Well Josh, thanks for everything, but there's just one other thing I need to know – where am I going to wear these?"

He roared with laughter and said, "At the leather bars and clubs."

"But I've never been to one before."

"Listen Chad, there's a Mr. Leather competition being held at the Eagle Inn on Saturday, why don't you meet me there and I'll show you around."

I liked the idea and Josh's friendly nature.

"Thanks Josh, I'd really appreciate that. At least I won't feel so out."

"Trust me, you won't."

I eventually lost my erection, paid for my goods and headed home. I was happy with my purchases and happy that I had made friends with Josh.

Saturday arrived and a sense of excitement ran through me, knowing that I was going on an adventure that night. I wasn't sure exactly why I was doing this, but an innate sense told me that I had always wanted to do it. At seven that evening I showered and began to get dressed. Fortunately I managed to put on the harness and the cock ring before I gave myself a hard-on, but no sooner had I got it on, than my cock began a life of its own, rising and getting bigger each minute. My jocks and leather jeans were slipped on and I admired myself in the mirror. Even with only those items on I decided that I looked sexy – maybe I'd leave the dog collar behind tonight. I was now ready for action.

Josh and I had agreed to meet outside the Eagle Inn bar, but when I arrived I realized what Josh had meant – everyone was hanging around and everyone was in leather, so I didn't feel out of place. There were old guys and young guys, well-built ones and ordinary guys, some with dog collars and chains attached, being dragged by their partners and others in jockstraps and chaps, which I decided was incredibly sexy.

"Chad! Over here!" I heard Josh call.

I wandered over to where he was standing and admired his outfit. He was simply dressed in a pair of tight-fitting leather jeans and had on his head a black leather cap. His muscular chest was bare except for a beautiful tattoo which stretched across from his left bicep over his left shoulder onto his chest and over his left nipple. The design was almost floral with swirls and what looked like ornate leaves. My attention went to his chest and the intriguing design, then I noticed his ripe nipples – they were firm, large and extended a good half inch from his proud pecs. Although he was simply dressed, his height and majesty made him stand out in the crowd. A few of his friends came up and spoke to him and as soon as the doors opened, everyone flooded into the bar.

It was a fairly dark place with a heavy metallic décor theme. The stairs were metal, the bar counter metal and the bar stools were also metal but had black leather padding on them, and the limited lighting that there was, had metal light shades.

"Before things hot up here, let me show you around," said Josh taking my arm and leading me on a tour of the premises.

There were three floors to the bar; street level, where the main bar was, a basement area which had toilets and a couple of spaces where there were slings, and a small upper area, which had a maze with some glory holes. It wasn't necessary for Josh to explain each of these areas in detail as I was well aware of the various options on choice, but I found it interesting how he made each area sound sexy and elaborated on how they might be used. I took it to mean that he had much experience of using these various areas.

Josh and I made our way back to the ground floor to get some beers and to survey the scene. I stood looking at the guys who were arriving at the bar and saw how we all looked like clones: leather everywhere, but the strong, overwhelming aroma of leather was a turn on for me. I could feel myself getting worked up by the intense masculinity that was evident in the bar. Everywhere I looked I could see black and silver and men preening themselves. The number of men who were semi naked made it all the more exciting for me. Their muscles had been pumped and some had even gone to the trouble of smearing a thin layer of oil over their naked flesh, so that it glistened in the light and emphasized their muscles more. Maybe this was why Josh had arrived without anything covering his chest, except for a slightly oily sheen.

"Are you taking part in the competition, Josh?"

He nodded and smiled at me. "But I can see some stiff competition here tonight," he added.

I looked around and noticed about thirty other guys who might be taking part, but wasn't sure.

"What criteria do they look for in these competitions?" I asked, innocently.

"Oh, there're a few factors to be considered: it's not just the leather that you're wearing but how you look in the leather."

"Is that all?"

Josh laughed.

"No, there is something else that's taken into consideration."

"What's that?"

"You might find that part interesting," he replied, winking at me.

"So what is it?"

"Wait. You'll see later."

Music was blaring over some heavy speakers and the noise level both from people shouting to one another and the music created a frenetic scene. Suddenly, at 11.00pm, the music stopped and a voice was heard over a microphone telling all the potential contestants to meet below the small stage which had been erected near the dance floor. Josh and the others began moving there where their names were taken and each had a number written on their arm. Josh had a seven in red lipstick written on his right bicep. The contestants then lined up in numerical order and waited for the competition to begin. As each number was called, so that contestant mounted the stage, posed for the crowd and the walked up to a bar stool that had been placed on the stage, where the 'other' judging took place.

The first six guys made their way across the stage, some looking very inviting, I thought, and then it was Josh's turn.

Josh mounted the stage and immediately struck a pose with the spotlight glistening on his buffed body. As he stood there in the light, it was clear that he had no jockstrap or briefs under his tight jeans, as the complete outline of his huge cock lay down the left leg of his jeans, revealed to the world. He posed, just as a bodybuilder might, flexing his muscles and smiling to all, then he walked over to the bar stool. There was a hushed silence as he began to unzip his jeans. Josh pulled the front of his jeans open and inserted his hand. He pulled out his massive cock with its long shaft and bulging cut head and laid it on the leather barstool seat. The audience gasped. The judge took his ruler and measured.

"Eleven inches!" exclaimed the judge.

Immediately there were cheers, shouts, whistles and applause. A broad smile covered my face. I couldn't believe that he was SOOO big, but I was pretty proud of him. He stood there after the measuring had been completed allowing his cock to be admired by the crowd, then he slowly and seductively began to tuck it back into his leather jeans and adjusting its lie, then he zipped up again and left the stage. Everyone was crowding around Josh as he fought his way to where I was standing.

"Wow, you were great!" I said, excitedly when he reached me.

People were trying to speak to Josh and guys were touching him and patting him on his shoulder as though he had already won the competition. I didn't feel jealous with all the attention he was getting, but I could see that most of the guys coming up to him had one thing in mind; they wanted that cock! But then so did I!

The competition continued with some really hunky looking guys coming on stage, but when it came to cock size, Josh won hands down. After the last competitor had done his thing on the stage, the judges grouped together to decide on their results. The MC picked up the microphone to announce the results.

"Gentlemen, we have a tie for third place."

He gave the numbers of the contestants and both guys went up on stage to receive their prizes, which included leather goods, money and a sash. The second placed contestant was called and a young guy of about twenty-four with a really buffed chest encased in a harness, a studded collar around his neck and tight leather jeans made his way up on stage. I remember that his cock was a good length when he'd laid it on the bar stool and I remember thinking he might be nice to spend a night with.

"In first place and Mr. Leather 2010, number seven," shouted the MC.

Josh strode up to the stage while everyone cheered once more. He took the stage with an air of confidence and power and when he had his sash placed across his bare chest, as an encore, he slowly began to unzip his jeans. The crowd went wild with excitement at the prospect of seeing that massive weapon of his again, but at the last minute, he zipped up again – he sure knew how to tease!

It took him longer to reach me as more guys tried to hog his attention and get to touch him. Eventually when he reached me, I looked up at this giant of a man and asked, "May I give the winner a kiss?"

He didn't say a word, but grabbed me, hugged me to his muscular chest and our mouths met. I could feel the long shaft pressing against me and as we continued to kiss, there was a distinct changing in the hardness of his cock. I could feel his erection growing and jabbing into me, but I wasn't about to let the other guys get their hands on him.

Josh broke free and whispered in my ear, "Let's go downstairs where it might be a bit quieter." He took my hand and led me through the throngs to the stairs leading downstairs.

When we reached the cavernous basement, he took me to one of the areas where there was a sling.

"You know what would be the most valued prize for me tonight?" he asked, smiling at me.

I pretended I didn't know what he was getting at.

"I'd like your tight little ass," he continued.

It was my turn to smile. I stripped off my jeans and jockstrap and climbed into the sling. Josh raised my legs and rested them on the chains hanging from the ceiling and then began to work on my body. His mouth explored every inch of my body, bringing with it waves of ecstasy as his tongue touched different erogenous zones. My cock was dribbling pre-cum which he casually licked off and continued his journey over my body. His tongue found its way to my waiting ass, which he spread wider and attacked my pucker, lubricating it until his spit dribbled down my ass cheeks. He stood up and, holding his shaft firmly, aimed it at my entrance. Slowly he forced his way into my warm chute. I could feel his broad cock head spreading my opening and the feel of excitement hit me. I desperately wanted him in me, so I pushed to meet his thrust. Suddenly his shaft sank deeply into my opening. Both of us sighed as he sank deeper and deeper into me until his hips came to rest against my ass cheeks. We both smiled to each other as he allowed me the pleasure of feeling his cock slowly expand my ass chute.

Holding onto the chains of the sling, Josh began to slip in and out of my throbbing ass. He would allow his cock to exit completely, leaving me with an empty feeling, then he'd ram it back in. The sling was swinging with each thrust so it wasn't necessary for me to exert pressure to meet his thrusts. As he plowed into my tight ass, I noticed a few other leather guys standing watching Josh get off in my ass, but none ventured to join in. I think they knew that I was Josh's prize and not for anyone else's consumption, as it were.

Josh leant forward as he plowed into my ass and sucked on my throbbing cock. As he did this, I took hold of his ripe nipples that were ready for chewing on, and pinched them between my fingers. I know he liked the feeling because as I pinched them tightly, so he thrust harder into my ass.

Our breathing was becoming more intense and heavier and I knew that we were both nearing the moment we'd been waiting for.

"Josh, you're getting close. I'm gonna come," I gasped as he plunged into me once more.

"So am I," he grunted, holding onto my hips for support and speeding up his thrusts.

I felt his large cock head swell inside me and as I let fly with my first load of a number of shots of warm cum, so I felt the spasms as Josh shot his load into me. He continued plowing into my ass as he shot his load and with each shot, I felt the throb of his long cock, nudging my prostate as it did so. Again he leant forward, but this time in search of my mouth and our tongues met. As our climax began to subside and with our mouths still clamped firmly together, I could feel how his chest rubbed over my wet stomach and chest, massaging my warm cum over his own body. After a good few minutes, Josh slid his semi-hard cock from my ass, but remained clasped to me, kissing. I could feel the long shaft rest against my own subsiding cock and together they throbbed.

"Welcome to the leather world, Chad. You'll do well in this world, especially with me around to tame that fine ass of yours. I hope this is not going to be the last time I get access to that tight hole."

I liked his compliment and replied, "so long as you take care of me and teach me everything about the leather world, I'll be your slave."

He helped me from the sling and those who had been watching with envy, suddenly disappeared, but probably hoped for another day when perhaps I wouldn't be there and Josh might get hold of one of their asses to fuck with that massive cock of his.

CEDARWOOD

Cedarwood Forest, as described in the travel brochures, is regarded as a little piece of heaven. It's filled with tranquility, beauty and romance; if a forest can be romantic, and is a haven for people who want some time out in the country, wandering along shaded paths alongside meandering rivers and scattered lakes. It is the type of place that weekenders come to when avoiding the rush and crush of city life. Although it is a serene place, the only negative side to this forest is when someone comes face to face with a grizzly. Fortunately this is not often and in most cases the grizzly bears try to avoid confronting the humans.

Lance Butler was one of the most fortunate people who were able to spend most of his time in the forest; Lance was a forest warden. His job was to check out for forest fires and to guide people who wandered off the beaten track and naturally, to prevent any attacks by the odd grizzly who might wander along a path usually taken by humans.

Lance spent Monday to Friday in the forest in his compact, wooden chalet, and then over the weekends, he would go back to the city where he had an apartment, but to be honest, Lance enjoyed being in the forest more than being in the city.

Lance was a slim six-footer of about thirty years of age, who spent every day in the forest dressed in his traditional khaki-colored uniform, blending into the surroundings. Lance was more athletic looking than muscular, yet there was a sensual appeal to him. When confronting walkers in the forest he always had a gleaming smile for them and a twinkle in his eyes. His long, tanned, muscular legs always protruded from his short khaki shorts and this sight often brought admiring glances from the walkers. His dark hair, although not unnecessarily long, seemed to bounce like a softly billowing cloud as he walked along the paths in the forest, the dappled sunlight playing patterns over his face and arms. Often, when Lance knew that he was in an area seldom visited by humans, he would unbutton his khaki shirt or remove it completely and wander along the paths feeling the cooling shade on his buffed, yet hairless chest.

Lance had spent the last three years working in the forest as a warden / ranger and nothing untoward had ever happened to him or any of the people who had visited Cedarwood. However, one Friday during the summer months, he did come across an incident which had a great impact on his life.

Lance had set out from his log cabin around ten in the morning and headed towards the central part of the forest where he knew there was a fair-sized lake surrounded by evergreen trees. It was one of those places in the forest which might be considered to be a romantic area by some people, but to Lance, it was just another area that had to be inspected. It took him a good hour to reach the lake area and when he did, he was surprised to hear splashing.

The tranquil atmosphere was broken only by the splashing and the intense heat that the sun created, shining down onto the open water. Under the trees, Lance could feel the coolness of their protection, but when he ventured into the sunny area, the intensity of the heat was evident, so Lance chose to remain among the shelter of the trees.

The first thing that Lance saw as he neared the lake and the location of the splashing was a pile of clothing, scattered on the ground along the bank of the lake. The blue jeans contrasted with the blue of the overhead sky, the green shirt blended in with the undergrowth nearby and eth only object of clothing which was in sharp contrast to everything around the lake was a bright yellow jockstrap. Lance's eyes moved from one piece of clothing to the next until his eyes remained fixed on the yellow jockstrap. He wasn't sure why: maybe it was the color that attracted him so much, or it might have been his thoughts as to who would be wearing them.

Lance then turned his attention to the water and the splashing. Was someone merely enjoying themselves or were they in distress? He noticed a blond head submerge and then resurface. He could only see the back of the person's head, but he had already established that it was a man. The man in the water then began floating on his back, allowing the beaming sun to shine on his face. It was then that Lance saw that it was a young man, probably eighteen or nineteen; young and fearless. Lance could see that the young man was in no danger of drowning, but remained staring at him. Should he venture out and make contact with the man, he wondered? No. It was better to stay hidden among the trees.

After some time of floating on his back, the young man flipped over onto his stomach and dived under the water. Lance watched as the tanned back and untanned ass of the young man came out of the water and then disappeared under it again. He smiled ever so slightly to himself as he saw the young man's ass go under the clear water. Then the blond head surfaced again. The young man was obviously enjoying his freedom and seclusion and Lance was beginning to feel like an intruder to this solitude. Just then the young man began to swim towards the shore. Lance watched as the young man emerged from the water, droplets of cool moisture running down his lean, defined body. Lances eyes surveyed the young but handsome face, then moved down to the broad chest and tapered waist. He couldn't help, but his eyes didn't stop there, they ventured lower. The solid length of young manhood hung, swaying as he walked, long and proud. Lance's eyes remained fixed on the appendage as the young man walked to where his clothes lay. Without touching his clothes, the young man lowered himself onto a patch of sift, green grass and lay down on his back, letting the warmth of the sun dry him.

Lance had been attracted to the sight of the young man and had already felt the tingle in his groin as the young man strode to his clothes. As the young man lay drying in the sun, Lance felt his own appendage beginning to grow within the confines of his shorts. His hand slid slowly down to his engorged cock and adjusted its lie in his briefs. The young, fresh face and the taut, muscular body of the young man attracted his attention. He hovered for a moment and then plucked up courage to emerge from his secluded spot. He ambled casually towards the young man, hoping not to frighten him. As he neared the prostrate body, he noticed the early signs of the young man's erection. The long, thickening cock was beginning to enlarge in the sunshine, and so was Lance's within his briefs. When he was about three feet away from the young man, Lance stopped and admired the defined torso.

"Hi, there," said Lance, softly so as not to startle the young man. "Beautiful day, isn't it?"

Immediately the young man raised his shoulders and head from his prone position and tried to grab some clothes to hide his growing embarrassment.

"I'm sorry if I startled you, but it wasn't my intention. Please don't mind me, I was just admiring the serene view and was envious of you swimming in the cool water."

"Hi," replied the young man, throwing his yellow jockstrap over his crotch.

"Please don't mind me but I really don't think your jockstrap is going to do much good covering you there. I must say you have a beautiful body and should be proud to show it off. Do you mind if I sit next to you?"

"Um… no…I mean … not at all," stammered the young man.

Lance seated himself close to the young man where he would be able to look at the angelic face and taut body.

"Are you alone here?"

"Yes", stammered the young man. "In fact, I'm sorry to say, but I think I'm lost."

Lance looked somewhat startled to think that here was someone lost, yet thoroughly enjoying themselves as though they had no care in the world.

"By the way, I'm Lance," he said, extending a hand to the young man.

"Oh hi, I'm Brett," was the reply.

"When you say you're lost, are you being serious of just joking?"

"No, I really think I am lost. I've wandered about for a day and seem to be going nowhere, then I came upon this lake and its beauty just captured me so I decided to spend time here. And you?"

"Well, I suppose you might say it's your lucky day, if you are in fact lost, because I'm one of the forest wardens who patrol the area."

Brett smiled, grateful to know that he had met someone who knew their way around the forest.

"Would you mind if I took of my shirt?" enquired Lance, hoping that it would make Brett feel a little more comfortable being naked.

"If you want to."

Lance unbuttoned his shirt and peeled it off. He noticed how Brett's eyes followed the shape of his upper torso.

"You've also got a great looking body. It looks very athletic," said Brett, eyeing Lance's tight stomach.

"When did you come into the forest?" enquired Lance, trying to establish if Brett in fact was lost.

"I came in yesterday and when I thought it was time to head back, I couldn't remember in which direction to go…"

"… so where did you sleep?"

"I found some bushes and curled up among them, then this morning I tried to find my way out, but landed up here by the lake."

"I presume you're starving for something to eat?"

Brett laughed.

"You could say that."

Lance wiped a trickle of sweat off his chest.

"Phew! It's pretty hot here. I think I'm going to take a swim in the lake. Are you going to join me?"

Lance stood up and began to take off his shorts. When he was down to his briefs, he noticed he still had an erection and there was a wet patch in the front of his briefs. He hesitated, contemplating whether to take them off or not. He noticed Brett watching him and also noticed that Brett's hand had slid down to his partly covered crotch and had removed his yellow jockstrap, revealing his own hard-on. Seeing this, Lance made up his mind and taking the waistband of his briefs, pulled them down to his ankles and stepped out of them. Both men were now naked and both were fully aroused.

"Shall we go?" asked Lance, smiling at Brett.

"I'll race you," was the reply.

Both men raced to the water's edge and dived in. The coolness of the clear water hit them and they surfaced smiling at each other, like two school boys. Lance gazed into Brett's eyes and saw how the light blue shading of Brett's eyes seemed to melt into the color of the water. They were in water where they were unable to stand so there was much treading of water and occasionally, Lance's legs would touch Brett's and each time this happened, the two men smiled at each other.

"Wow, this is great," said Lance, diving under the water and heading in Brett's direction.

As he swam in the clear water, he could see Brett's hard-on still very much erect. As he neared his new young friend, he extended a hand and gently took hold of the solid flesh. Brett gasped and submerged under the water, seeking out Lance's cock. It didn't take Brett long to take a firm grip on Lance's throbbing cock and begin stroking it. Both men surfaced and giggled briefly until their mouths met and their arms encircled each other. Their legs were thrashing to try and stay above the surface of the cool water, until Lance suggested that they head to shallow water.

Both men swam closer to the shore until they could stand in the water. Brett circled Lance and as Lance was standing, so Brett swam up to him and wrapped his arms once more around Lance's waist, and then he ducked his head under the water and opened his mouth, taking in a mouthful of lake water and a good length of Lance's hard cock. Quickly Brett resurfaced, coughing and spluttering.

"I don't think you should try that until we're out of the water or you might drown in the process," said Lance, laughing at his friend's attempt.

Lance took Brett by the hand and led him from the water and took him back to where their clothes were lying. Both men lay back on the grass with Lance lying on an elbow admiring Brett. He gently placed a hand on Brett's chest and ran his fingers over the young man's chest, grazing each nipple and causing a tremble to run through Brett's body. Brett groaned ever so softly each time Lance's fingers ran over his nipples.

"Do you like that," whispered Lance.

"Hm!" groaned Brett, with his eyes closed.

Lance looked at the angelic face and moved his face closer until his lips touched Brett's lips gently and they kissed. Brett instinctively opened his mouth to allow Lance's tongue to venture in and explore. Lance's hand then slid over Brett's taut waist and reached the tip of his throbbing cock. Lance let his fingers graze over eth cut head of Brett's manhood, feeling the wetness from the water and the wetness from the drizzle of pre-cum that was leaking from the tip. Lance stopped kissing Brett and lowered his head until his mouth was positioned above the tip of Brett's cock. Slowly he opened his mouth and lowered his head, encompassing the full length of throbbing muscle.

"Aargh!" Groaned Brett as he felt the warmth encircling him.

Lance continued to rise and fall along the length of Brett's weapon, gradually bringing him closer to a climax.

"Be careful, Lance, you're getting me close," whispered Brett, giving gentle upward thrusts with his hips.

Lance released his mouth.

"Is that what you want, Brett?"

Brett, with his eyes still closed as if in dreamland, nodded, so Lance resumed his position.

It wasn't long before Brett's breathing became more urgent and louder and Lance could feel how stiff Brett's cock had become. Soon he felt the warmth of Brett's love juice enter his mouth and a loud sigh emanated from Brett.

After coming down off their high, both men lay in the sun, their arms touching and their breathing returning to normality.

"Shall we go for one more swim?" asked Lance.

Brett smiled, leaned across Lance's body and gently kissed him on the lips.

"Thank you Lance. That was absolutely wonderful."

"It was all my pleasure, Brett.

They rose and, hand in hand, they went back into the lake to cool off. Once they had enjoyed the pleasure of the water, they emerged and Lance suggested they head to his log cabin where they could have something to eat.

As the walked along the path, both men naked while their bodies dried, Lance couldn't resist admiring the naked, firm, but tight little ass of Brett as he walked in front of him.

"Are you in a hurry to get out of this forest?" asked Lance as they meandered along the paths.

Brett stopped and turned to his friend.

"Having met you, no; why what did you have in mind?"

"Well, I usually leave the forest on Fridays and head to the city, but I'm so happy being in your company and in this atmosphere, I was wondering if we couldn't spend a couple of nights together here in my cabin in the forest – if that's OK with you?

Brett smiled, wiggled his little ass at Lance and said, "I'd really like that."

PVC PRISONER

Chris opened his eyes and felt his head thumping from an over indulgence the night before. He had gone out to a bar, followed by a trip to a club and knew that he'd had quite a bit to drink, but didn't remember going home. His eyes began to become accustomed to the limited light that was shining and realized that his surroundings didn't look familiar. He tried to move but realized that he was unable to but couldn't fathom out why. Every time he moved his head to look around the room in which he found himself, his head ached from what felt like a thousand sledge hammers pounding at him. His body also felt very warm but constricted. Something tight-fitting was wrapped around his body but he couldn't make out what it was. Again he tried to raise his head and in doing so he could make out that instead of the clothes which he had worn when he had gone out, he was now wearing something that looked very dark in color.

A light was suddenly flicked on, blinding Chris and making him squint his eyes. He slowly reopened his eyes, allowing them to adjust to the new light, and saw that he was in what looked like a cellar as there was a flight of stone stairs which led up from him to a door near the ceiling. He looked down at his body and saw that he was tied to a narrow bench and the dark colored clothing that he was wearing looked like PVC and looked like it was a zipped waist coat with straps over his shoulders, but he could see that his lower torso was covered in a pair of shorts in the same fabric as the top and his legs were bare from the thigh down, so the jeans he had been wearing the night before had been removed and someone had put him in this outfit, but who?

He heard the door handle being turned and the door opening. Down the stairs came two men of differing ages; the taller of the two appeared to be in his early thirties, while the younger of the two was about mid-twenties. The older of the two was naked from the waist upwards and wore a pair of black leather chaps under which Chris could see a studded leather jockstrap, while the younger and shorter man wore a black rubber one-piece suit. Chris didn't recognize either of the men at first, until they explained the previous night to Chris.

"You had drinks with us at the club and when we invited you to come back to our place you agreed," said the older man, whose name turned out to be Vince. "We asked you if you wanted to have some fun with us and you agreed, but when we got home and came down here to the cellar, you were so drunk you were unable to do anything, so we left you down here to sleep it off," continued Vince.

"But why tie me up?" questioned Chris, wriggling and trying to free himself.

"So you wouldn't fall off the bench in the night," replied Dominic, the other young man.

"Well I'm awake now so could you untie me please?"

"Well we thought you might want to play with us," commented Vince, standing astride Chris's head on the bench.

Chris looked up and saw the large studded package protruding above him.

"I'm not into that sort of thing," answered Chris, turning his head away from the sight above him.

"What sort of thing?" enquired Vince, with an element of menace in his voice.

"You know what I mean," was Chris's reply.

"I don't know what he means, do you Dominic?"

Dominic merely shook his head and smiled down at Chris, still lying prostrate on the bench.

"Whips and chains and all that," said Chris, trying to demonstrate defiance.

"Nor are we into that are we Dom?"

"Certainly not, Vince. We don't like to hurt, we like to give pleasure."

Dominic positioned himself between Chris's spread legs and admired the encased crotch that looked most inviting. Dominic ran a hand over his own rubber encased cock and smiled at Chris as he did so.

"Wouldn't you like to feel how smooth and electrifying the feel of PVC is under the hand, Dom?"

"Sure would," was the reply.

"Then be my guest," said Vince, winking to his partner.

Dominic stretched out a hand and gently ran it over the outline of Chris's cock.

"Hm, the material feels so good and soft," said Dominic, continuing to caress Chris's cock. "I wonder if what's underneath is just as soft and what it tastes like."

"Try and see, you might like it," sniggered Vince.

Dominic knelt between Chris's legs and flicked his tongue as he approached the PVC covered bulge. His tongue ran slowly over the outline of Chris's length.

Vince watched Chris's reactions and smiled when he saw that the bulge appeared to be growing under the confines of the PVC.

"You like that, Chris?" asked Vince.

"No!" came the defiant reply, but still Dominic continued.

Eventually when Dominic rose to his feet, it was clear that both he and Chris had developed full erections. Although Chris had stated that he'd not enjoyed Dominic's actions, he felt within himself a sense of excitement as he felt Dominic's tongue glide over the smooth PVC material.

"If you did not like it, why did you consent to come back with us knowing what we had in mind?" queried Vince, stroking Chris's cheek with an index finger.

"I was drunk," came the disgruntled reply, "And besides, I'm not into guys; I get my kicks from women."

"From here, it doesn't look like that to me," replied Vince, pointing to Chris's ever increasing hard-on.

Vince, still standing astride Chris's head, began to lower his crotch over Chris's face until Chris could smell the distinctive, pleasing aroma of leather close to his nose. Chris closed his eyes, hoping it would all go away, but instead he felt the hard, cold touch of metal from Vince's jockstrap rub across his lips. His eyes shot open and he saw the glint of metal and the bulge that it hid. Vince ran his crotch across Chris's mouth hoping that Chris might open his mouth and begin to lick, but Chris turned his head away, trying to avoid contact. Vince again winked at Dominic who went back to working on Chris's PVC coated crotch.

At the crotch of Chris's PVC shorts and situated between Chris's legs was a zip which extended from midway at the back to the waistband in the front. Dominic slid his hand under Chris, took hold of the zip and slowly began to unzip the material until Chris's ass appeared and with it his balls. Dominic started to slurp on Chris's balls, taking each one gently into his warm mouth and running his tongue over each in turn. Chris couldn't help himself and began groaning with this pleasurable action, and as Dominic worked up Chris, so Vince continued to rub his hardening package across Chris's mouth until at last, Chris parted his lips and began licking over the metal studs. Chris wasn't sure whether it was the desire to gain access to Vince's cock, or whether it was the feel and smell of the clothing that they were wearing which was driving him on.

"You see, you do like it," chuckled Vince, as Chris's mouth explored ways of getting through the metal-studded jockstrap to what was hidden inside.

Chris tried to insert his tongue at the side of the jockstrap in an effort to reach Vince's lengthy cock. Vince leant forward a little enabling Chris to pop open one of the side poppers on the jockstrap, allowing it to be released and fall to the ground. Vince ran both hands over Chris's nipples under the PVC while Chris's mouth made desperate grasps to take hold of Vince's engorged uncut cock.

Dominic was about to unzip Chris's outfit completely when Vince shook his head.

"Don't unzip, Dom. Leave his cock encased and play only with his balls and ass."

Dominic obliged as he was advised, and Chris lay there with his balls protruding from his PVC suit while Dominic lathered then with caressing tongue licks.

Chris, by this stage, had engulfed Vince's swollen cock with his mouth and was slurping frantically, trying to get its full length as far down his throat as he could. Vince stood, eyes closed, enjoying the luxuriating feeling he was receiving.

"Aagh!" he groaned. "Not bad for a guy who says he's not into men!"

In Chris's mind, he was being completely aroused by not only Dominic's manipulation of his balls and that part of his ass which was observed through the unzipped opening, but also by the tightness of his own PVC covered torso and the deliciously aromatic smell of Vince's leather chaps, which were now very close to his face. Vince unzipped Chris's PVC top, revealing a young, muscular chest of well-defined proportions and continued to manipulate Chris's nipples, alternating between light touches with his finger tips to hard squeezes of each nipple, which caused Chris to rear up as far as he could, with each hard pinch.

At this stage, Vince was convinced in his mind that Chris was under their power and so he began to undo the ropes which had been tied around Chris the previous evening, in an effort to prevent him from falling from the bench. Chris was now unfettered and free to utilize his hands. Once he realized this, his hand went around Vince's legs, pulling him closer to Chris's mouth. Chris released Vince's cock and began to lick the leather chaps which encased Vince's strong legs. Not only did the leather aroma reach Chris's nostrils, but the smooth, leathery taste filled his mouth. To him it was like an erotic feeling. His cock throbbed under the PVC and began to leak pre-cum.

Now that Chris was free, Dominic lifted Chris's legs onto the bench and ran his tongue between Chris's legs, heading for that magical cave. His tongue reached the entrance and, with short, sharp flicks, began to make an entry. Chris moaned gently with each flick that lubricated the entrance to his magical cave.

Vince, having watched Dominic, moved from Chris's mouth and picked up a condom which he unrolled onto his erect cock and moved to behind Dominic.

"Take over, Dom. I want a taste of this sweet ass."

Dominic moved to the head of the bench where Vince had been and Chris began licking over the evident bulge under Dominic's rubber suit. Vince lifted Chris's legs into the air, held onto his hard shaft and aimed at the quivering, pink asshole. The head of his cock pushed gently at the entrance, and he watched as Chris's asshole immediately clamped shut. He licked a finger and slowly inserted it into the opening of Chris's asshole. The door to the cave flicked open allowing Vince's finger to enter, and immediately, the cave clamped shut around his finger. Inside, Vince wriggled his finger around Chris's innards, searching for the electrifying point, his prostate. He rubbed it and Chris let out a loud groan and Vince felt how Chris pushed his ass deeper onto his finger. All the while, Dominic's suit was glistening from the salivation which his crotch had received from Chris's mouth and tongue.

Vince replaced his finger with his now fully erect and hard cock. This time, there was no resistance from Chris. That magical cave opened wide and sucked in the weapon it so desperately wanted. Vince sank deeply into the cave and felt its comforting warmth.

Chris was holding onto Dominic's legs, pulling him closer all the time so that his tongue was moving between Dominic's crotch and his ass. Dominic's suit also had a zip to it, but much shorter than the one on Chris's outfit. Chris took hold of the zip and released Dominic's cock and balls which were greedily devoured by the waiting mouth. At last Dominic was now receiving a taste of pleasure from Chris, while Vince was pounding deeply into the tight, warm cavity.

"You like this?" grunted Vince in between thrusts.

A muffled sound emanated from Chris's preoccupied mouth, but Vince could deduce that Chris was in fact enjoying every bit of this experience.

Dominic was the first to reach his climax. He slipped his cock from Chris's mouth and fired his load over Chris's face, heaving chest and onto his PVC shorts. Chris continued to salivate on Dominic's balls as each load was fired. Vince watched this with excitement as he and Chris increased their thrusts until his body stiffened. He pulled out of Chris's warm ass, ripped off the condom and fired his warm cum over Chris's PVC covered crotch. Once he had depleted himself, he knelt between Chris's legs and licked Chris's balls, working his mouth up to where his warm cum lay on the swollen PVC covered bulge. He took hold of the zip on Chris's shorts with his teeth and slowly unzipped to reveal Chris's throbbing, wet cock. He licked it and tasted cum.

"Shit, the kid's come without us touching him," explained Vince, taking Chris's cock into his mouth and letting him have some pleasure. When he felt Chris's cock softening, Vince stood up and extended a hand to Chris in order to help him sit up. The three sat on the bench together, exhausted.

"Does this mean that you're still into women?" asked Vince.

Chris gave a sheepish grin without responding immediately. After a moment of thought, Chris responded.

"Let's just say it was interesting; interesting in the sense that if it weren't for the sensual feel of the suit I had on and the sexuality which you two gave off in your leather and rubber clothes, I don't know whether I would have enjoyed it as much."

"But does that mean you would do it again with a guy?" remarked Dominic.

"Certainly, if we did it like this. Who knows, I might even get my girlfriend interested in an outfit like this," said Chris pointing to his cum covered PVC shorts.

Dominic and Vince merely threw glances at each other at the thought!

PARALLEL WORLDS

Brad and David were twins, born to parents who were loving and kind and who often found it difficult to tell the difference between the two boys. Of course their mother, Margaret, insisted that she never had any problems in telling David from Brad, and although when one looked at them, one couldn't see any differing characteristics, their mother said that David, who was a few minutes older than Brad, seemed the happier of the two.

As the boys grew up they did the inevitable, they dressed alike, had similar interests and just seemed to be two rolled into one. They had both gone to the same school, played the same sports, did equally well academically and even chased after the same girl at one stage in their lives. They tended to be highly competitive, always trying to outdo the other, but as they grew up, it became apparent to those closely associated with them, that there were the beginnings of something different forming.

When they were of the age to go out and find work, this is where the first of differing views appeared. Brad went into the theatre as an actor and David became a teacher. Their parents seemed a little upset that Brad seemed to be 'wasting his intellect' in the theatre, but at no stage had they ever stood in the way of either boy's decision, so he was left to hit the bright lights. David settled down to a routine of 'entertaining' young children in another way, through the medium of education. Both boys were successful in their chosen careers and seemed extremely happy at what they were doing.

As the years progressed, they tended to part from each other, because of Brad's touring with shows, but they never parted company mentally. They often thought about each other and when the one suddenly had an ominous feeling about his brother, he was onto the telephone immediately to find out if his brother was all right.

When the boys turned twenty-one they celebrated their party together, with their parents and friends. The party was held at their parent's home over a weekend when Brad was not busy doing a show, so both boys were able to stay with their parents. Brad, however had brought a friend of his, who was in the same show, to spend the weekend of the party, and David, who had being dating a fellow teacher for a few months, brought her for the weekend.

The house was extremely spacious with a number of guest rooms, so there was no problem with accommodation. David was the first of the two boys to arrive for the weekend. He arrived in his sedan and unloaded the luggage on their arrival. His dad, Alan, was at the door to meet them.

"Hi, David, nice to see you again," said Alan opening the passenger's door.

"Hi, Dad," David replied, leaping out of the car and shaking his father's hand. "Meet my date, Cathy. She teaches with me."

David's father greeted Cathy and escorted them into the house.

"Has Brad arrived yet?" asked David as they entered the hall area of the house.

"Not yet, but he should be here very soon. He's also bringing a friend."

Just then David's mother came into the hallway and met them. She too was introduced to Cathy and seemed to be charmed by her elegance and presence. As they went up stairs to the bedrooms, David's father escorting Cathy, David's mother held on to David's arm and said, "she really looks like a nice young girl."

"She is Mum," replied David, squeezing Margaret's arm.

Cathy and David were shown their separate bedrooms where they proceeded to unpack and freshen up, while David's parents went back downstairs.

Later in the afternoon, Brad arrived with his friend, Rob. Naturally they were welcomed into the home by Brad's parents and they met Cathy and David. It had been decided that Brad and Rob would also have separate rooms, and they too unpacked and then went down stairs to meet the others for sundowners.

Brad and David spent some time with their mother discussing the plans for the party, while Rob and Cathy sat in the lounge with Alan enjoying a casual drink before dinner. Alan seemed to be taken by Cathy's charm and the thought had crossed his mind that she might indeed make a good wife for his son.

That evening at dinner, the six enjoyed not only the food but also the company. The conversations were intellectual and interesting and all seemed to get on. Occasionally, Brad would try to touch Rob's foot under the table as they spoke and often he was successful. When he did make contact, Rob would smile at Brad, knowingly. After enjoying a sumptuous meal, the six left the dining room for the lounge and coffee. David and Cathy sat together on a settee, while Brad sat on the carpeted floor at the feet of Rob's chair and Alan and Margaret were ensconced in two wingback chairs. While they enjoyed their after dinner coffee, they chatted about the party the following evening and among the things that were discussed was the possibility of being able to accommodate any of the guests who might over-indulge and need somewhere to spend the night. Margaret reassured the boys that they need not worry.

After they had checked all the plans for the following night's party, they decided to settle in for the night. Each made his or her way to their bedroom and undressed and readied themselves for sleep.

Brad stripped off and took a shower in his en-suite bathroom. The warm water trailed over the length of his body and he stood there luxuriating as the water caressed his torso. He eventually switched off the shower, took his towel and started to dry himself. As he walked from the bathroom into his bedroom, he was surprised to see Rob lying across his bed.

"What are you doing here? I didn't hear you come in!"

"I knocked on the door, didn't hear you so I popped my head in and heard the shower running so I thought I'd wait for you."

Brad threw himself onto the bed next to Rob.

"You know you look so sexy when you're all wet," said Rob, running a hand over Brad's smooth but wet body.

"Did anybody see you come in here?" asked Brad, a little cautiously.

"I don't think so," replied Rob with confidence.

"Well, are you going to lie there with your clothes on or not?"

"So do something about it," smiled Rob.

Brad pushed Rob flat on his back on the bed, unbuttoned his shirt then unzipped his jeans. Rob lifted his hips to allow Brad to pull his jeans down to his ankles. He lay there with only the bright whiteness of his Calvin Klein's showing. Brad stared down at this young muscular body with its taut abdomen and pumped pectorals. Brad's eyes moved from the upper body region down to the white briefs and noticed and swollen bulge.

Brad lowered his mouth to the bulge and ran his tongue over its length while Rob groaned gently with the pleasure that he received. Brad took hold of the waistband with his teeth and slowly pulled Rob's briefs down to his ankles, only to return and slide his wet, warm tongue and lips up the length of Rob's neatly clipped cock. When Brad reached the tip, he wrapped his mouth around Rob's cock head, and slowly sank down its full length until his chin came to rest on Rob's balls.

While Brad and Rob were enjoying the beauty of each other's body, David and Cathy lay in their separate beds in their separate rooms. Cathy's light was out all ready, but David lay in his room thinking about the party and his brother. As he lay in bed, his hand slid down to his crotch and encircled his balls, cupping them and squeezing them. This caused a reaction from his dick and as he did this, his thoughts were concentrated on his twin brother. He closed his eyes and in his mind he visualised Brad. How close were Brad and Rob he wondered? Were they lovers or merely good friends? When he thought of them as lovers he squeezed his balls and dick even harder. He imagined them in bed together with their arms encircling the other, making love. By now his dick was fully erect to its eight inches and he gently stroked its length, imaging how they might be making love and how he might be part of that action. After a while he reopened his eyes and wiped the pre-come from the tip of his dick. He rose from his bed, wrapped a towel around his waist, opened his bedroom door and quietly tiptoed down the corridor towards Brad's room. When he reached the door he wondered whether he should knock first, but on second thoughts, he gently turned the door handle and slowly opened the door. The lights were still on and Brad and Rob were wrapped in each other's arms on the bed. They didn't hear David enter nor did they hear him sidle into the room and close the door behind him. David dropped his towel to the floor and stood naked admiring his brother and Rob as their mouths seemed attached as their swollen cocks ground against each other's. David's hand went instinctively down to his own cock and he started to slide it up and down its length. As he did this, he slowly moved closer to the bed until he was alongside it. He ran a hand over Rob's silky smooth ass. Immediately Rob broke away from Brad's mouth and looked up to see David.

"Oh David!" gasped Rob, surprised.

Brad also looked up embarrassedly to see his brother. "What are you doing here?"

"I was lying in bed thinking of you, and I wondered about you and Rob, and something just made me come into the room."

"Does this sort of thing often happen?" asked Rob.

"I'm afraid that David and I are very in tune with one another," replied Brad.

"But what about Cathy?" Rob asked. "Where does she fit in?"

"I'm very fond of her, but there are times when I need something different," answered David moving onto the bed and lying on Rob and taking his cock into his mouth. Rob gasped when he felt the pressure that David exerted on his cock head. Rob seemed to be enjoying the company, but Brad was still a little bewildered. He broke away from the other two and looking at David in action, said, "David, how long has this being going on?"

David raised his head from Rob, and smiling at Brad, said, "Since school."

"But we were at the same school and I didn't know anything about this."

"Well I had to keep some things from you because I didn't know what you might think."

Rob spoke up. "So now you know about each other – let's get some action!"

David went back to working on Rob's cock, but this time Brad decided to attack his loving brother's dick. He slid between David's legs and kissed the tip of his eight-inch cut dick, running his tongue over the tip and digging his tongue into its piss slit. His brother's cock tasted good and as he engulfed it to its base, David let out a groan of pleasure. Brad loved the feeling of having possession of his brother. He worked his mouth up and down the full length of David's cock, lubricating it with his tongue and lips.

David flipped Rob onto his back and burrowed his face in Rob's bushy crotch, sucking on each ball and slowly working his way between Rob's legs until his tongue felt Rob's asshole. David's tongue shot into its opening and Rob gave a grunt of satisfaction. David raised his head.

"Baby brother, get me a condom and some lube."

Brad knew then and there what his brother's plan was, so he left the bed and opened a drawer, pulled out two condoms and some lube. Meanwhile David had gone back to working on Rob. Brad opened the foil of a condom and placing the opening of the condom on the tip of David's dick, he wrapped his mouth around it and began to slide the condom down the length of his brother's cock. David then put some lube onto a couple of his fingers and gently inserted two into the darkness of Rob's interior. Rob gasped and raised his hips as David did this. David slowly slid his fingers in and out of Rob's ass, spreading him and preparing him for the final assault. Brad scampered to Rob's face and placed his cock on Rob's lips. Rob immediately opened his mouth engulfing Brad's swollen cock down to its base. Brad started to face-fuck Rob while David pulled his fingers out of Rob's ass and placed the tip of his length at the opening and slowly pushed into Rob. Rob tensed for a moment, but as David's hard dick continued its journey into the unknown, Rob relaxed as he enjoyed the pleasure that he was receiving from David's dick rubbing up against his prostate.

While Brad was having his cock luxuriated by the hot mouth of Rob, he leant forward to kiss his brother, who was busy ploughing into Rob's ass. Their mouths became united and their tongues searched in each other's mouth while Rob stroked his own cock, lubricating it with some of his love juice, which was slowly leaking from the tip.

David removed his mouth from his brother's and whispered into his ear, "Join me in this pleasure."

"What do you have in mind?" asked Brad.

"Let's double fuck Rob."

"You mean at the same time?"

"Sure."

Brad pulled away from Rob's mouth and picked up the other condom, tore open the foil and began to unroll it along the length of his dick until it covered it from tip to base.

David held onto Rob and in one swift movement flipped him over so that David was now lying on his back on the bed while Rob was sitting astride David, impaled on his cock. David thrust his hips upward going deeper into Rob. Brad got off of the bed and moved to between David's open legs and watched his brother's huge dick sliding in and out of Rob. Brad greased up his cock and moved into position, aiming for Rob's ass hole. David pulled Rob's upper torso closer to himself, thus spreading his ass and opening it wider to be able to take Brad's cock as well as his own. Rob rose to the tip of David's cock and just before it was able to escape, Brad held both his and David's cocks together and slowly began the journey into Rob.

Rob groaned as the initial pain was felt, but Brad and David were patient and gentle, allowing Rob to lower himself onto both cocks. His sphincter expanded and both cock-heads disappeared together. He continued to lower himself slowly down the stems of these two stiff rods, as both brothers experienced the ultimate in joy. Their dicks were united as one and just as their minds seemed to be in tune, so their fucking action became one, both thrusting at the same time and having Rob push down to meet their thrusts. All three were crying out in an ecstasy of pleasure, as they knew that this couldn't go on for too long as they were all nearing their climax. Rob gave a sharp cry and immediately spewed forth his seed across David's chest. David felt its warmness and this was like an impetus to speed up. Brad realised what was happening so he too increased his action and both brothers exploded at the same time. Their gasps probably could have been heard miles away as they thrust deeper into Rob, their cocks rubbing against each other's. When they had nothing more left to give, Brad sagged onto the back of Rob, sweat pouring from both of them, as Rob fell onto David's chest and burrowed his face in David's neck. The three breathed heavily, but when they began to breathe normally, they detached from one another and lay together on the bed with contented smiles on their faces. After cleaning themselves, Rob and David returned to their bedrooms and all slept well.

The following morning, everyone in the house woke to a beautiful day and went down to breakfast. Cathy was the first down in the dining room, but soon Brad arrived.

"Happy birthday!" shouted Cathy and Brad's parents all at the same time.

"Gee, thanks," replied Brad, glowing.

Just then Rob and David appeared in the dining room. Again the group wished David a 'happy birthday' and there was much kissing and hand shaking. It was amazing how all three young men seemed to be glowing this morning.

"How did you sleep?" David asked Cathy.

"Like a log. I never heard a thing. Once my head hit the pillow, I was out like a light; and you?"

"I actually haven't had such a good night like that for a long time," replied David, smiling at Brad and Rob.

"And you, Rob?" asked Margaret.

"It was great, thanks Mrs Colley."

"I hope Brad didn't keep you up all night with his talking," she continued.

"He kept me up a bit, but it was great, thanks."

Both Brad and David shot him a glance, but he merely gave them both an angelic smile.

After breakfast, the boys helped to erect a marquee in the garden, which was going to be where the party was to be held. While they did the manual labour, the women organised the catering and floral decorations. By late in the afternoon, everything was complete and they all stood to admire their efforts.

"Mum, this looks fantastic," said Brad, putting an arm around his mother's shoulders.

"Thanks, everybody," said David, "This really is the greatest!"

Most of the guests were expected around 7.30p.m.and so after a final check to see that everything was in place, the family retired to their various rooms to have a quick sleep or just relax before the evening. Brad and Rob went to their separate rooms and had asked to be woken at 6 p.m. David and Cathy had retired to David's room and were sitting on the bed chatting to each other.

"I was hoping that you were going to come to my room last night," said Cathy in a rather coy manner, as she held David's hand.

"I was going to, honey, but when I got into the room, I felt so tired that I simply fell into bed," replied David, squeezing her hand and giving her an ingratiating smile.

"Well I hope I'm going to see you tonight?"

"Of course you are," laughed David, "at the party."

"I'm being serious," retorted Cathy, rather indignantly. "Unless of course you don't want to see me tonight?"

"Don't be so serious, Cathy. I'm only joking with you."

David felt a little awkward because he had truly enjoyed the previous night with Brad and Rob and hadn't in fact missed sleeping with Cathy, but he didn't have the heart to tell her.

Cathy leant closer to David and kissed him on the cheek.

"You smell so nice," she purred into his ear. "I could eat you up right here."

Her hands caressed his chest and he began to feel as though Cathy might not stop there, so he held her hands and prevented her from going any further.

"Let's save this for later, Cathy."

"You're such a spoil-sport," she replied, getting up from the bed and walking to the door. "I'll see you later at the party." She exited his room, leaving him wondering whether she was now upset or whether she had listened to him and was accepting his offer of something later. He sprawled out on the bed and almost immediately fell asleep.

The guests arrived and the marquee filled with merriment, laughter and music. Everyone was having a wonderful time and both Brad and David circulated amongst their friends, greeting everyone.

"By the way, David, what are you giving me for a birthday present?" asked Brad, putting an arm around David's neck as if to strangle him.

"Wait and see. I'm keeping it for later. And what have you got me?"

"Yours will be in your room later, as well," replied Brad.

"What do you mean it'll be in my room later?"

"It'll be put there later. That's all I'm telling you."

Cathy came up to the boys and linked her arm through David's. "What are you two discussing so earnestly?"

"I just asked David what he had got me for my birthday," replied Brad.

"Well what have you got for Brad?"

"That's a secret," retorted David, "but I'm giving it to him later."

"That's fine, but in the meantime, I need to dance," she said, and led David off to the dance floor, leaving Brad on his own.

"What are you doing here all on your own?" asked Rob as he sauntered up to where Brad was standing.

"Nothing much. David and I were just having a chat and Cathy came and took him off to dance."

"And what were you chatting about?"

"I simply asked him what he was giving me for my birthday."

"And what was his reply?"

"He just laughed and said I would get it later," Brad answered.

"That sounds a bit ominous, don't you think?"

"Oh come on, Rob, what devilish thing are you thinking of now?"

"I wasn't thinking anything devilish, but why would he give it to you later and not now?"

Brad thought for a while, and then smiled at Rob.

"Do you know what he's giving me?"

"Heavens, no! If I did, I wouldn't be asking you now."

"I suppose you're right. Oh well, we'll just have to have patience and wait for later."

Just then Margaret came out to see where Brad was.

"What are you two doing out here when all your guests are inside?"

"We were just getting some fresh air, Mum, but we're coming inside now."

At that, the two lads accompanied Margaret back into the thick of the party.

The party-goers enjoyed themselves all night until the early hours of the morning, when the last guest departed at around 2 a.m. As the last of the guests left, Alan and Margaret excused themselves and went off to bed.

"I think I'm also going to bed," said Cathy. "Are you coming too, David?"

"In a minute, dear. You go along and I'll join you later."

At that, Cathy said goodnight to the others and left. After she had gone, Brad turned to David and said, "By the way, you still haven't given me my birthday present yet."

"Neither have you," responded David. "However, yours is actually in your room."

"In my room!" replied Brad a little surprised. "I didn't see anything there."

"No, but if you'll give me a couple of minutes, I'll get it ready for you," continued David; and he raced up stairs to Brad's bedroom.

Brad and Rob were a little bewildered by David's actions, but they were content to wait and see what was in store. After about three or four minutes, Brad and Rob decided to go up to the room and see what David had prepared. As they entered the room, they noticed that the light in the room was dimmed and David was sitting in the corner.

"What are you sitting in the dark for?" asked Brad.

"Just get comfortable," replied David.

Both Brad and Rob sat down and waited for something to happen. Just then the en-suite bathroom door opened and from the light from the bathroom, Brad and Rob could see the muscular shape of a young man dressed in a tight white T-shirt and black leather pants. He moved into the center of the room and stood facing Brad. Slowly he began to swivel his leather-bound hips, thrusting his crotch forward every now and again. Every time he did this, all three of them could see the encased bulge growing with each thrust. He moved around the room like a dancer without music. His movement was smooth and erotic. His hands slid over every part of his body, hesitating every so often when he reached his nipples or his crotch. Brad noticed out of the corner of his eye, that David too was rubbing his hands over his own body and beginning to work on his crotch area. Suddenly, the leather-man took hold of his T-shirt and ripped it from his body, revealing a tightly muscled abdomen and chest, and two erect, hard nipples. Brad immediately felt a surge from between his legs and the start of a hard-on.

The leather-man continued his 'routine' around the room until he reached where Brad was sitting. He straddled Brad's legs and thrust his hips towards Brad. Brad couldn't resist the temptation to touch the leather-man and slowly slid a hand up the man's taut abdomen, to his nipples and grazed a hand over them. The leather-man continued to thrust his crotch towards Brad until Brad eventually placed his hands on the leather- encased bulge and squeezed its contents.

Brad slowly unzipped the man's jeans and opened the front of his leathers to reveal a white jockstrap. The man rose and Brad's mouth went down to the surface of the jockstrap and he gently kissed its contents. Rob and David, in the meantime, had also unzipped their jeans and were rubbing themselves. The leather-man lay on the floor at Brad's feet and encouraged him to remove his leathers. Brad obliged without a second invitation, pulling them from man's slim body and leaving only the white jockstrap. Brad then went down on his knees between the leather-man's legs and slowly licked his way up the muscular tree-trunk shaped legs until he reached the guy's crotch. He licked over the length of the man's bulge, smelling his manhood until he reached the tip of the jockstrap. When he had done so, Brad gripped it in his teeth and slowly pulled it down to reveal a beautiful, rock-hard cock that burst from the straining material. Once he had loosened it from its constraints, Brad began to luxuriate in the taste that filled his mouth as he worked over the man's length.

Rob and David had, by this time, stripped naked and had moved in on either side of the leather-man. Their hands were moving over his entire body, feeling its shapes and hardness. Rob then started to undo Brad's shirt and remove it from his body. Once he had done this, he began licking on Brad's nipples, getting them hard. Brad could feel his own cock straining to escape the constrictions of his jeans and he wanted to be free of these constraints. He continued to work the full length of the leather-man's engorged cock, sliding his mouth to its very base and holding his position there. David positioned himself at the leather-man's head and ran his swollen cock over the man's lips until the man opened his mouth to take the awaiting rod. David slowly immersed his cock into the depths of the man's throat, groaning as the tightness of the man's lips engulfed his cock.

Rob moved himself into a position next to Brad and joined him in licking the leather-man's cock and balls. Once Rob had joined him, Brad stood up and removed his jeans, allowing his swollen cock the liberty of freedom to sway in the air like a snake seeking something to attack. He returned to his former position and rejoined Rob to lather the muscle-bound man's cock with their lips and mouths.

"Why don't we all get on the bed?" suggested David, removing his saliva-coated cock from the man's throat and rising to his feet. The other three followed suit and the leather-man repositioned himself on the bed, lying on his back with his legs apart, waiting to be taken.

"I take it this is my present?" asked Brad, when he was close to David's ear.

"Sure is and I hope you like him because he's yours for the taking; and what have you got for me?"

"You've always wanted my ass, well tonight it's yours for the taking."

David smiled, not quite believing his brother.

The leather-man's legs lay dangling over the edge of the bed as Brad burrowed his face between them and sucked on the big man's balls, while Rob attacked the man's cock. Brad lifted the muscular legs into the air and aimed for the man's asshole with his tongue, preparing him for the eventual attack. While he was busy getting his 'present' ready for his own enjoyment, David had picked up some lube and come to behind Brad. He gently rubbed some of the lube over the opening crack of Brad's asshole and then slowly inserted a finger into his brother's warmth. Brad groaned with delight at the feeling and darted his tongue deeper into the leather-man's interior. Rob got a condom and unrolled it onto Brad's throbbing cock in readiness for the penetration.

As David's fingers sank deeper into Brad, so Brad pushed his ass back onto them. Brad lifted the leather-man's legs onto his shoulders for support and aimed his cock at the small pink hole that was waiting to be ravaged. The tip of Brad's cock touched the leather-man ass and almost as though there was suction there, Brad's cock disappeared into the unknown depths of the young man's interior. Both the leather-man and Brad gasped with delight at the same time, savouring the pleasure each was giving to the other. Brad felt the man's sphincter clamp tightly around the girth of his cock and hold him captive there. The feeling was intense and enjoyable. Rob had moved to the man's mouth and inserted his cock into the man's mouth, so the leather-man was now plugged at both ends.

David had watched his brother's entry and was being turned on watching his thrusts deep into the young man. Brad felt his brother's cock rub up and down the crack of his ass, teasing him before entry. He desperately wanted his brother inside of him. Brad pushed back in the hope that he would impale himself on his brother's cock, but David moved away slightly, again teasing his brother. Brad realised that his brother was doing this to drive him mad with desire. Again David moved closer to Brad and rubbed his cock against Brad's tight ass, and again Brad pushed back hard to try to capture David's cock, but as he did so, he slipped out of the leather-man's ass. The man gasped and as quickly as it happened, so Brad was back inside the warmth of the muscular tight ass. When David had thought that he had teased his brother long enough and knew that he had worked him up, he thrust forward sinking deeply into Brad so that he could feel his balls slap hard against Brad's buttocks. Brad pushed back to meet his brother's thrust and gripped tightly onto his brother's cock. The three young men were now attached to each other by means of deep lustful thrusts while Rob was being well-attended to by the luscious mouth of the leather man. Rob had also leant over the man's chest and was deep-throating the leather-man in a sixty-nine position.

Rob was the first to announce his intention to shoot his load, which the young man took down his throat without spilling a drop. When Rob had exhausted himself, he withdrew his cock from the man's mouth, but continued to slurp up the man's full length.

Suddenly the leather-man started thrusting harder onto Brad's engorged cock and Brad knew that he was close. The young man let out a cry and fired the first of many shots into Rob's throat, while his ass muscles clamped tightly around Brad's cock and his stomach muscles tightened as he shot his load.

At the same time, Brad couldn't hold on any longer and let out a gasp and started filling the condom with his love juice. David continued to pound his brother's ass as his brother fired load after load. He wanted to come with his brother and he knew he was about to do so. He held onto Brad's hips and thrust deeply, holding his position as he let fly. Brad could feel the warm shots being fired into his inside. After the first shot, David became frantic in his movement as he thrust again and again into his brother's ass, filling him with love.

After each one of the men had been satisfied, they collapsed onto the bed, lying next to one another, allowing their breathing to return to normal, but there was not too much sleep to be had during the remainder of the night as they made love many times over, and both David and Brad were very grateful to each other for the birthday gift.

The next morning, Cathy didn't have much to say to David, but soon after the party, David and Cathy broke up their relationship while David and Brad had developed a much closer relationship, both accepting their sexuality and Brad's partner, Rob.

THE VOLLEY BALL PLAYERS

I had sat on a bench, relaxing, watching a group of college students playing volleyball on the beach sand. I admired their athletic agility as well as their youthful zest and athletic bodies dressed only in shorts or Speedo swimming costumes, and could see their stomach, leg and arm muscles straining as they fought to keep the ball in play. These athletes were all lithe and they came in all shades, sizes and ages. As I watched them, I could also feel my heavy cock beginning to strain inside my running shorts. I imagined what it must be like to be on that piece of sand with those beautiful young men slapping each other on the back or hugging each other every time they won a point.

I noticed a blonde, six-footer with an amazing set of abs and a tight costume, so tight in fact, you could see that he was cut, who was constantly putting his arms around the shoulders of a darkly tanned youth who wore a tank-top and a tight pair of Lycra shorts. At one stage when the tanned youth, who might in fact have been of Brazilian extract, turned to face where I was sitting, my cock began to throb as I saw the enormous bulge inside the youth's shorts.

After watching the game for what seemed like half an hour, I heard the blonde say, "Hey guys, I've had enough – I need to take a piss." As he started walking away from the rest of the group on the sand, the tanned youth ran after him shouting, "Hey Pete, wait for me, I need one too." The two of them headed towards the nearby change rooms and I rose from the bench. The rest of the players who were left on the sand, all headed for the sea to swim and cool off, while I headed towards the same change rooms that the two guys were headed for.

When I entered it was very quiet, with only the smell of the sea abounding. On entering, there was a large open room with wooden benches around the walls and a set of lockers in the middle of the room. I walked quietly around the lockers but there was no-one in the room. Off this room was a door that led down a passage to the showers and toilets. I went quietly through the doorway, past the shower area and into the toilet area, but before I entered that area, I paused at the entrance because at the urinal stood Pete and the tanned youth. Both had their cocks in their hands and I could see that they were stroking themselves.

I heard Pete say, "I need that cock down my throat, José."

I could feel my own cock getting harder and thicker as I watched them. Unconsciously, my hand went down to my running shorts and I started rubbing myself. José turned to face Pete and for the first time I saw this gigantic weapon pointing straight towards Pete. As I saw his huge, uncut dick, I shivered with excitement. Pete knelt in front of José at the urinal, pulled his Lycra shorts right down to his knees, and began to lick the folds of José's foreskin.

As Pete's tongue entered the folds and licked over the piss slit, José gave a low moan. His dark eyes were on Pete who was about to take this meat down his throat. Pete licked the underneath of the stem and carried on down, wetting José's cock until he reached his balls. Slowly he took one ball into his warm mouth and gently rolled his tongue around it. Then he moved onto the other one; all the time José was groaning in satisfaction. Pete released that ball and then began to work his way up José's shaft with his tongue, licking and kissing. Although, at this stage, Pete was facing the entrance to the toilet area, his eyes were closed as he enjoyed this meal and didn't see me enter through the doorway. As I did so, his mouth engulfed José's dick and slowly his mouth began to swallow it whole, forcing the foreskin to roll back to reveal José's cock-head. I watched as he went slowly down the shaft and then pause, obviously to try to relax the back of his throat I thought, and once he had done that, he continued on down.

José let out a loud groan, "Oh fuck!" and began to fuck Pete's face. As he did so, Pete took his right hand from José's butt and started frantically stroking his own cock while I did likewise inside my shorts. Neither of them had seen or heard me yet, but I felt I had to make my presence known because I wanted to be part of this action.

I went quietly up behind José, whose head was thrown back in ecstasy, and put my arms around his chest and felt two hard nipples protruding from his tank-top. He turned his head in fright and I clamped onto his nipples with my thumb and forefingers. This obviously set him off because he started groaning louder and pumping harder into Pete's loving mouth. At that moment, Pete opened his eyes and saw me but it didn't stop him from continuing to take those ten-inches into the depths of his throat. While I rubbed José's nipples, my cock was rubbing against the crack of his ass, trying to get out of my running shorts.

José suddenly pulled his cock out of Pete's mouth and said, "Cool it guys before I blow my load."

With his hands on either side of Pete's head, he gently lifted him to his feet and began to kiss him, letting their tongues explore each other's mouth. For a moment I thought that they regarded me as an intruder, but as Pete freed his mouth from José's, he said, "Come with me. There's a room off the shower room", and proceeded to lead the way.

Pete took us into a small room, which had a table in the middle of it and a shelf on which some towels were piled. As I was the last into the room, I closed the door behind me and watched as Pete, with his back to me, pulled his Speedo down to his feet and then bent over to pick it up. As he did so, the cheeks of his ass parted and I saw this delicious pink manhole. José also saw it and gently rubbed a finger over and around it. Pete stayed bent over as José did this and quietly moaned with satisfaction. I pushed my running shorts down over my hips, down to my feet and stepped out of them. My cock was like a periscope looking for something to attack. I walked around to Pete's head and stood in front of him, my cock inches away from his face – how I wanted that mouth around it, especially after I'd seen the way he handled José. He opened his mouth and I felt his warm breath on my cock followed by the warmth of his mouth and tongue. This sent shivers through my body as he worked on my dick. In the meantime, José had got rid of his Lycra shorts and had his tongue up Pete's asshole. Every time José's Latino tongue pushed into that pink opening, Pete's sensations of pleasure were carried through his body to my dick. José then stood up, lubricated a finger in his mouth and slowly inserted his finger into Pete's hole. Pete was writhing in pleasure and was working even harder on my dick. When two fingers were inserted, Pete started pounding his own dick and mine slipped out of his mouth. I looked at it and admired how swollen the head was. Pete saw the pre-cum oozing from my cock and gently licked it off with his tongue and proceeded to swallow my erection once again.

José slowly withdrew his fingers, pulled a condom from his shorts, slid it down his long rod and aimed it at Pete's pink target. Pete felt this huge cock pressing at his entrance, stopped stroking his own cock and slowly pushed back onto José's pile-driver. Initially there was some resistance, but as Pete relaxed, he slid onto the massive pole with an "Aaagh!" José's face was a picture of total pleasure, having his ten-inches rammed into Pete's beautifully tight ass. They remained motionless for a while allowing Pete to get used to the size of José's cock and then José started slowly to pull the shaft out until the head was about to pop out and then slowly drive it all the way back in again. Every time he did this, Pete gasped with pleasure and sucked my dick. Watching José's huge pole drive into Pete's tight ass and feeling Pete's hungry mouth working on my cock was beginning to get me worked up. José's chest was heaving and I ran my hands over his chest and pinched his nipples. He let out a loud groan and started pumping Pete harder, and as he pounded Pete's ass, Pete's mouth moved faster and harder on my cock. I wasn't going to be able to last much longer. I suddenly felt a dizzy excitement.

"I'm coming," I gasped and my balls exploded, shooting my heavy load down Pete's throat. I groaned with delight and fucked Pete's face as José fucked his ass. He was breathing heavily as he sucked me dry and then I heard a muffled sound of ecstasy from Pete as he shot his load on the floor. He hadn't, in fact, touched his cock while José was ramming him because he was holding onto my hips. As Pete shot his load, so his ass muscles clenched tightly around José's cock causing José to gasp and speed up his fucking. With his cock tightly held in Pete's ass and me pinching his nipples, José cried out and sent his load flying into Pete. "Oh shit! Ohhh Fuck!" He pumped hard, slapping his balls against Pete's ass as he sent one load after another into Pete's inside.

Eventually his eruption subsided and he lay across Pete's back kissing his neck while I kissed José's. As Pete straightened himself up, all three of our faces were close to each other's and we just laughed. "I hope you didn't mind me joining in with you two guys," I said.

"Mind!" exclaimed the two of them in unison, "next time you're in the middle," said José.

As José's limp cock slid from Pete's ass, and he removed the condom, I noticed his cock still continued to throb and I thought to myself, "I can't wait. I need that cock now." I moved to José and grabbed his cock, squeezed it hard around its fatness and looked lustfully into his eyes. It throbbed in my hand and I could feel it beginning to grow again. I went down on him and wrapped my lips around his throbbing shaft. As I licked his shaft I could taste the salty-sweet cum that was left on his cock and as I sucked on his cock-head I drained what was still in his shaft. While I was busy licking his shaft, Pete came face-to-face with me on the other side of José's cock and also started licking up and down. Our tongues touched and as my tongue ventured into his mouth, I could taste the left over cum which I had earlier shot into his mouth and throat. Pete's mouth then went to José's balls and he burrowed his nose in José's crotch as he gently licked and rolled José's balls around his mouth. I busied myself trying to take José's long pole deep into my mouth and throat. I had never before taken anything as big as this down my throat, but I was determined not to let an opportunity like this go to waste. At one stage, I thought I would gag, but I relaxed my throat and slowly let it slide in. I've never felt such an exhilarating feeling before as José slowly started thrusting his pelvis forward and backwards. While he fucked my face, I thought of how Pete had taken José's cock down his throat and I convinced myself that they had done this before. While I was thinking of this, Pete's face re-appeared next to José's cock and as José's shaft withdrew from my mouth, so Pete's lips and tongue wrapped around the side of it and as José drove his shaft into my mouth, so Pete's mouth met mine.

I felt Pete's hand wrap around my stiff cock and start stroking it. I reciprocated while we both knelt on either side of José's cock as though we were worshipping this ten-inch idol. Throughout the whole time José had been groaning in blissful satisfaction until he eventually pulled away from us. He looked down at me and with a wry smile on his beautiful face, and holding his stiff shaft, he said, "Do you want this?" My lips were wet and saliva dribbled from my mouth.

"You bet," I said.

Pete got to his feet and walked to where the towels were. He grabbed a few and threw them onto the table in the center of the room. He then came back, took me by the hand and gently eased me onto the table so that my legs were hanging over the edge. He then walked around the table to behind me and, putting his large hands onto my shoulders, pulled me back into a lying position. I lay there looking up, face-to-face with his cock, which dangled seductively over my nose and mouth. All this time, José had silently watched, and when I was on my back with my legs over the edge of the table, he moved in between my thighs and lowered his mouth to lick and salivate around my balls.

A warm feeling tingled inside of me as José's warm tongue moved over my dick until his mouth engulfed it. It felt so warm and fulfilled inside his glorious mouth and I closed my eyes with a feeling of ecstasy running through my body. As I did so, I felt Pete's cock gently touch my lips. I automatically opened my mouth and proceeded to swallow this engorged pole. Pete's hands massaged my nipples and moved down over my taut stomach. I felt my legs being lifted as José's tongue moved between my legs towards my butt-hole and felt the tip of his tongue darting in and out. I could feel myself shuddering with pleasure as I was worked over at both ends of my body. I moved my head away from Pete's dick and told José that there were some condoms in the back pocket of my running shorts. While he crossed to where my shorts lay, Pete stretched across my body and took my throbbing cock in his mouth as I took his again. While we were in a sixty-nine position, I felt two wet fingers being inserted into my butt-hole one at a time. Just then I felt my legs being lifted into the air and Pete released his grip on my cock and raised himself from my body. I looked up and saw José standing between my legs. He moved in closer and I felt his huge cock rub against me. He then gently lowered my legs onto each of his shoulders allowing his hands to be free to guide his cock into my waiting hole. As he prepared to enter me, Pete's hands rubbed over my hardening nipples, which felt great. I relaxed and prepared for José's entry.

Slowly he began to push his barge-pole into me. There was an initial sharp pain as he entered me and I grimaced. He stopped where he was to allow me to get used to his huge size. Once he could feel me relax, he continued his journey. Oh it felt so good. I had never taken anyone so big before, and to feel his cock tightly squeezed into me, sent dizzying spells through my head and body. José began to get his rhythm going, but all the time being aware not to hurt me. At last I got used to his enormous size inside of me, and began to meet each of his thrusts. This turned him on and he started pumping faster and deeper.

While José had been entering me, Pete had stood and watched in awe while he rubbed my nipples between his thumbs and forefingers. I lay there on my back playing with my cock and balls, feeling ecstatic while José's cock pounded away at me.

Suddenly, Pete left us and walked over to where my shorts lay. "I hope you don't mind!" he said, taking a condom from the back pocket. Of course I didn't mind, but I wasn't quite sure what his plan was. He opened the packet and rolled the condom onto his erect cock. Once he had done this, he walked back to us and went and stood behind José. I suddenly realized what was going to happen – he was going to fuck José while José was fucking me. The thought sent a spasm of excitement through my body. José paused briefly to allow Pete to enter him. As José pushed onto Pete's cock, I thought he was going to slip out of me so I tensed my muscles and gripped onto his huge dick with my ass. When Pete started fucking José, it felt as if José's cock was going even deeper into me. Pete put his arms around José and held onto my legs that were still over José's shoulders. When he did this, it felt as if he was pulling me further onto José's dick. Every time José pummeled my ass, I could feel Pete beating José's. My hand feverishly worked on my own dick and I could feel myself getting closer to exploding.

"I'm not going to be able to hold on much longer," I groaned.

As I said that, José quickened his pace and the result was that his movement was getting Pete equally closer to shooting his load. I gasped and started shooting my hot cum all over my stomach. My ass muscles clamped tightly onto José's cock and I pushed myself onto his dick until the only thing that wasn't inside of me was his balls. He rubbed my cum over my stomach with his hands and pumped his cock into me at the same time. He was breathing heavily and I knew that he was going to come.

"Aaargh!" he shouted. "Oh yes! Oh yes!" and he pounded my ass.

I could feel his dick throbbing inside of me as his warm cum filled up the condom. As he came, so he started a chain reaction and Pete pumped his hot cum into José, grunting as he did so.

Once our bodies began to relax, Pete kissed the back of José's neck and slowly withdrew his cock from José. José began to pull out of me but I didn't want this to end. I held onto him for a moment hoping that he wouldn't withdraw his beautiful big dick. As he withdrew, my whole body relaxed and I closed my eyes – this had been fantastic. I felt someone kiss my limp, spent cock. I opened my eyes and saw it was José. He looked at me and said, "I like this, you little fucker."

Pete came round and kissed me on the lips. "Come, let's clean you up," he said.

We made our way to the showers and took turns in washing each other's body. Once we had dried ourselves and got dressed, we made our way out of the change rooms. As we came into the daylight, with Pete and José walking on either side of me, José said, "By the way, do you play volleyball?"

"No," I replied, "I've never learnt."

"Well, we'll be your teachers," said Pete with a glint in his eye. "We meet here on the beach every weekend, so if you'd like to play with us, just pitch up."

"Oh, I'll pitch up, even if it's not to play volleyball," I said laughing and putting my arms around my two newfound buddies.

ABOUT THE AUTHOR

LEW BULL recently had his fifth novel published, entitled *Shadows*. This novel adds to his collection of mystery stories titled, *Power Buddies; Wet, Wild & Willing; The Bonds of Friendship* and *Caribbean Cruising*. Added to these is his recently published anthology of exotic cocktail recipes accompanied by equally erotic stories entitled, *Cocktales*. His novel *Wet, Wild & Willing* was nominated for the 2008 National Leather Association (International) writing award. Other recent anthologies that contain his work include, *Cruise Lines; Taken By Force; Boys Will Be Boys; Don't Ask, Don't Tie Me Up - Military BDSM Fantasies; Service with a Smile; Pretty Boys & Roughnecks; Special Forces* and *Sex Time-Travel*. He lives in Johannesburg, South Africa and enjoys traveling as often as he can.

Bull

POWER BUDDIES

Power
Buddies

a novel by
LEW BULL

A BONER BOOK

Bull

Caribbean Cruising

Caribbean Cruising

a novel by
Lew Bull

A
Boner
Book

The Bonds of
Friendship

a novel by

Lew Bull

tales

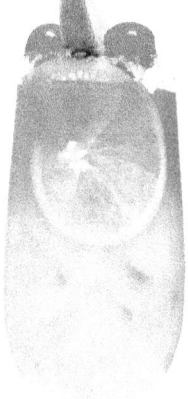

by

Lew Bull

Cocktales

www.ingramcontent.com/pod-product-compliance
Lightning Source LLC
Chambersburg PA
CBHW051658260626
47170CB00004B/1561